The Soldier's Lady

Books by Michael Phillips

Is Jesus Coming Back As Soon As We Think?
Destiny Junction • *Kings Crossroads*
Make Me Like Jesus • *God, A Good Father*
Jesus, An Obedient Son
Best Friends for Life (with Judy Phillips)
George MacDonald, Scotland's Beloved Storyteller
A Rift in Time • *Hidden in Time*
Legend of the Celtic Stone
Your Life in Christ (George MacDonald)

AMERICAN DREAMS

Dream of Freedom • *Dream of Life*

CAROLINA COUSINS

A Perilous Proposal • *The Soldier's Lady*

THE SECRET OF THE ROSE

The Eleventh Hour • *A Rose Remembered*
Escape to Freedom • *Dawn of Liberty*

THE SECRETS OF HEATHERSLEIGH HALL

Wild Grows the Heather in Devon
Wayward Winds
Heathersleigh Homecoming
A New Dawn Over Devon

SHENANDOAH SISTERS

Angels Watching Over Me
A Day to Pick Your Own Cotton
The Color of Your Skin Ain't the Color of Your Heart
Together Is All We Need

05C

The Soldier's Lady

A NOVEL

MICHAEL
PHILLIPS

BETHANY HOUSE PUBLISHERS
Minneapolis, Minnesota

The Soldier's Lady

Cover design by John Hamilton/The DesignWorks Group
Cover photography by Steve Gardner

Scripture quotations are from the King James Version of the Bible.

Published by Bethany House Publishers
11400 Hampshire Avenue South
Bloomington, Minnesota 55438

Bethany House Publishers is a division of
Baker Publishing Group, Grand Rapids, Michigan.

Printed in the United States of America

ISBN 0-7642-0042-9 (Paperback)
ISBN 0-7642-0145-X (Hardcover)
ISBN 0-7642-0177-8 (Large Print)

Library of Congress Cataloging-in-Publication Data

Phillips, Michael R., 1946-
The soldier's lady / by Michael Phillips.
p. cm. — (Carolina cousins ; bk. no. 2)
Summary: "The tragic romance of Emma and a wounded 'buffalo soldier.' When the two fall in love, it poses problems for William McSimmons' political career. Can their love keep them together?"—Provided by publisher.
ISBN 0-7642-0145-X (hardcover : alk. paper) —ISBN 0-7642-0042-9 (pbk.) —ISBN 0-7642-0177-8 (large-print pbk.) 1. Reconstruction (U.S. history, 1865–1877)—Fiction. 2. Plantation life—Fiction. 3. North Carolina—Fiction. I. Title II. Series: Phillips, Michael R. 1946- . Carolina cousins ; bk. 2.
PS3566.H492S66 2006
813'.54—dc22

2005032030

To our friends from many years ago of Campus Christian Fellowship (CCF) and InterVarsity at Humboldt State University. With you we learned, we studied, we questioned, we laughed, we struggled, we prayed . . . and we grew into faith. What can be a more powerful foundation for lasting affection than that! Judy and I still look back at those days and those friendships as among the richest in our lives, for which we are eternally grateful. We think of you often and miss you. The hearts of all those who were part of those special bonds will forever be united with us by ties of love. How dear you are in our memory!

Contents

PROLOGUE

As those of you who know something about me already know, I like to tell stories. When I was young, I used to make up stories to tell my little brother. We were slaves and life was hard, and stories helped the time pass easier.

As I got older, I realized that the best kind of stories weren't made-up "stories" at all. They were true stories. They were just what happened.

So that's how I first started telling about my life during and after the war, and about the people I grew to love through those times—Katie and her uncles, and Emma and Josepha, and Henry and Jeremiah. And I came to see that everybody's life is a story worth telling, because everybody's life is a "true story" just like Katie's and mine.

But it's sometimes hard to tell someone else's story. You have to try to think like they would think, and feel the kinds of things they feel. To tell someone else's story you have to "get inside" them, and that's a mighty hard thing to do. But then that's what makes another person's life worth telling—that inside part of them that's the real person God made.

If there'd never been a war and if slavery hadn't ended, maybe I'd have grown up to be one of those old white-haired slave women rocking in a chair with little black children all around, telling them all the old slave stories and singing them the old colored spirituals.

But the war did come, and slavery did end. I used to be a slave, then I was a free black girl. Change came to blacks like me all over the South. Change came to whites too. It was a time when this country was turned upside down in the way folks thought about the color of people's skin. So the stories I'm telling are the stories of black folks learning to be free and about white folks learning to live with free black folks, and about those times after the war when it was dangerous to be black, but also exciting. It was a time when things were changing so fast you could hardly keep up with them, in good ways and bad ways both.

I reckon I say that because there were good people and bad people, of both colors of skin. And some of the stories I have to tell are about both kinds of people.

What happened in those days involved danger and heartbreak because, though there are lots of happy memories, they were frightening times. But those of us who lived through them discovered how deep love can be. Because when it weathers change *and danger, love comes through stronger than ever.*

So I reckon you'd say those times taught us to endure heartache, but mostly they taught us to love.

River of Baptism, River of Death

1

As the sun slowly crept above the hazy horizon and then inched its way into the sky, it was clear enough to anybody who'd spent much time in North Carolina that this would be a hot and muggy day.

By ten in the morning it was ninety degrees. At noon it was over a hundred. Not a breath of wind came from anywhere. What work there was to be done around the plantation called Rosewood was finished by lunchtime, and no one felt inclined to go out in the hot sun after that if they didn't have to. The cotton and other crops would continue growing. The weeds in the vegetable garden would keep for another day. The animals would take care of themselves without any help until milking time came for the cows late in the afternoon. It was the kind of day that made the dogs too tired to do anything but lay sprawled out on the ground with their tongues hanging out. The chickens were too listless to make much racket. Only the cattle in the fields didn't seem to notice the heat. They just kept munching away.

"You want ter go dab dose feet er yers in da ribber, William?" said twenty-one-year-old Emma Tolan to her four-year-old son.

"Dat I do, Mama!" replied the boy eagerly. "Kin we go now?"

"We'll go right after lunch," answered Emma.

Forty minutes later, the tall slender black girl and chubby little boy of tan complexion walked away from the house hand in hand. They crossed two fields of green ripening stalks whose cotton the young mother would help pick later in the summer as she had for the past four years since coming to this place. Back then she had been a scatterbrained former slave with a half-white newborn son to take care of, fathered by her former master. She hadn't been much use to anyone all her life up until that moment, and she knew it. If ever anyone felt worthless as a person, it was she. Though she had been the oldest of the three girls thrown together by the war and left to figure out a way to survive alone, she had needed more taking care of than both the others combined.

On the memorable day when the white girl discovered Emma hiding in the Rosewood barn, she was babbling incoherently and frightened out of her wits, and her labor with little William's birth had already begun. But she had grown and changed in the four years since that day she had found her way here. The roots of that change had matured slowly and invisibly under the influence of her two friends and saviors, white Kathleen Clairborne, whose plantation it was, and black Mary Ann Daniels, whose home it became.

And new and even more far-reaching kinds of changes had begun to stir in Emma's heart a month or two ago, in the spring of 1869. These changes had been obvious to everyone at Rosewood—and what a strange assortment of people it was! Emma's countenance grew quieter. A look of peace and dawning self-assurance gradually came over her face. More often these days, rather than the most talkative, she was the quietest member of the Rosewood family around the kitchen table, sitting content to listen, watch, and observe.

Emma's soul had begun to come awake.

And that is about the best thing that can ever happen to anyone.

So as she and William made their way to the river on this hot June day, Emma was not thinking of swimming or playing in the water with her son to cool off from the heat. She was going to the river to remember.

She had been doing this so often these last several weeks, since that day she would never forget. Usually she came alone—to pray or sing quietly and let her heart absorb the memory of what she had felt as she had come up out of the water, face and hair dripping, face aglow with new life.

Praise Jesus! were her only words. She had not shouted them as in a camp meeting revival. Rising out of the river's waters, she had uttered them quietly, reverently, scarcely above a whisper. For the first time in the depths of her being she knew what those two eternal words meant. And her smiling heart had been quietly repeating them over and over since then . . . *Praise Jesus . . . Praise Jesus.*

Emma Tolan had begun to change before that day. But

her baptism sent that change so deep into her heart that she was still trying to grasp it. So she came here every few days—to sit as the river flowed slowly past her, to ponder what God had meant when He made her, and to reflect on what He might want to make of her now that she knew how much He loved her.

She could not know—how could she have known?—that she was being watched.

In this season of peace and happiness in her life, Emma was not thinking of the past, nor of the secrets she possessed, whose danger even she herself did not fully recognize. She was thinking of the wonderful now and the bright future.

But there was someone who *was* thinking of a dark past—of a time in her life she had finally almost forgotten. He had not forgotten. He had sent the watchers to watch, and to await an opportunity to bury the memory of that past forever, not in the triumphant waters of baptism, but in the dark waters of death.

Emma sat down at the river's edge and eased her bare brown feet into the shallow water as William ran straight into it.

"You be careful, William!" she said. "You stay near me, you hear. I don't want ter be havin' ter haul you outta dat water yonder cuz I can't swim so good."

Whether William was listening was doubtful. But he was in no danger yet, for the site where Emma had been baptized was far on the opposite bank, and the sandy bottom sloped away toward it gradually. He ran and splashed within four feet of the shore, to no more depth than halfway up his fat little calves, laughing and shrieking happily without a care in the world, until he was wet from head to foot. Emma watched with a smile on her face. It wasn't easy to pray with a rambunctious youngster making such a racket. But she was content to be there.

She had just begun to get sleepy under the blazing sun and had lain down on her back, when sudden footsteps sounded behind her from some unknown hiding place in the brush bordering the river. Startled but suspecting nothing amiss, Emma sat up and turned toward the sound. Three white men were running toward her, two bearing big brown burlap bags.

Before she could cry out, they were upon her. One of the men seized her and yanked her to her feet. It didn't take long for her to find her voice. She cried out in pain as the second man pulled her arms behind her. The third had kept going straight for William, threw the open end of one sack over his head, and scooped the boy out of the shallow water and off his feet.

"Mama!" William howled in fright. But the next instant he was bundled up so tightly and thrown over the man's shoulder that all he could make were muffled noises of terror.

Emma's pre-baptismal voice could now be heard a half-mile away, if not more. She screamed at the top of her lungs, struggling and kicking frantically to keep the second bag off her own head.

"You let him go . . . William . . . git yo han's off me . . . help—somebody . . . Miz Katie, help! Mayme!"

"Shut up, you fool!" yelled one of the men, trying desperately to calm her down. But even two of them were hardly a match for an enraged, frightened human mother-bear. She writhed and struggled and kicked with every ounce of survival instinct she possessed. As one tried to take hold of her shoulders and force her to be still, Emma's teeth clamped down onto his wrist like the vise of a steel trap.

He cried out in pain, swearing violently, glanced down to see blood flowing from his arm, then whacked Emma across the side of the head with the back of his hand. But it only made her scream the louder.

"Help!" she shrieked in a mad frenzy. "Git away from me . . . William, Mama's here . . . help! Miz Katie . . . dey's got William. Help!"

Two hands took hold of her head from behind, and the next instant Emma's voice was silenced by a handkerchief stuffed into her mouth. She felt herself lifted off the ground, kicking and wildly swinging her arms about and writhing to free herself. The three men now made clumsily for their waiting horses and then struggled to mount with their unwieldy human cargo.

The river was not so far from the house that Emma's screams were not plainly heard. The frantic cries quickly brought everyone running from several directions at once.

"Is that Emma?" called Katie in alarm, hurrying out onto the porch and glancing all about to see what was going on.

"She went to the river," said Mayme, running around from the side of the house.

"Where's Emma and William?" yelled Templeton Daniels, Katie's uncle and Mayme's father, as he ran toward them from the barn where he'd gone to prepare for milking.

"At the river," Mayme answered.

"William must have fallen in," he said. "Let's go!"

They all sprinted away from the house in the direction of the river.

Someone else had also heard Emma's cries for help. He had come to Rosewood as a stranger a few months earlier. At Emma's first scream he had burst out of the cabin where he had been bunking, a cabin that had been part of Rosewood's slave village before the war. He was now flying across the ground in the direction of the sounds.

He reached the river twenty or thirty seconds ahead of the others. He was just in time to see three horses disappearing around a bend of the river, two lumpy burlap bags slung over two of their saddles. A hasty look around what he knew to be Emma's favorite spot showed signs of a scuffle. Seconds later he was sprinting back for the house. He intercepted the others about a third of the way but did not slow.

"Somebody's taken Emma and William!" he yelled as he ran by. "They're on horseback!"

He reached the barn just as Templeton's brother, Ward, was returning from town. Though his horse was hot and tired, it was already saddled, and every second might be the difference between life and death. Ward Daniels' feet had no more hit the ground than he saw the figure dashing toward him, felt the reins grabbed from his hands, and in less than five seconds watched his horse disappearing at full gallop toward the river. He stared after it in bewilderment until his brother and two nieces ran back into the yard a minute later and explained what was happening.

The rider lashed and kicked at his mount, making an

angle he hoped would intercept the three horses he had seen earlier. He had no idea where they were going, unless it was toward Greens Ford, a narrow section of river which, in summer, was shallow enough to cross easily and cut a mile off the distance to town by avoiding the bridge downstream.

He reached Greens Ford and slowed. There was no sign of them.

Frantically he tried to still Ward's jittery horse enough to listen. A hint of dust still swirled in the air where the ground had been stirred up beyond the ford but on the same side of the river. He kicked the horse's sides and bolted toward it. If they had not crossed the ford, where were they going? Why were they following the river?

Suddenly a chill seized him as the image of the burlap sacks filled his mind. The rapids . . . and the treacherously deep pool bordered by a cliff on one side and high boulders on the other!

He lashed the horse to yet greater speed, then swung up the bank hoping to cut across another wide bend of the river toward the spot.

Three minutes later he dismounted and ran down a steep rocky slope so fast he barely managed to keep his feet beneath him.

He heard them now. They were at the place he feared!

He slowed enough to keep from sending the stones underfoot tumbling down the slope ahead of him, thinking desperately. What could he hope to do against three white men, probably with guns!

He began to slow and crept closer.

Suddenly a scream sounded.

"William . . . somebody help us!" shrieked a girl's voice.

He knew that voice! Whatever was to become of him, nothing would stop him now! He sprinted toward the sound.

"Dey's got William . . . help!" came another terrified scream.

"What the—" a man exclaimed. "How did she get that thing loose?"

"Just shut her up!" shouted another.

"It doesn't matter now. Let's do what we came to do!"

One more wild scream pierced the air, then a great splash. It was followed by another.

"That ought to take care of them . . . let's get out of here!"

Seconds later three horses galloped away as a frantic black man ran in desperation out onto an overhanging ledge of rock some twenty feet above a deep black pool of the river. It was easy enough to see two widening circles rippling across the surface of the water.

He ripped off his boots, stepped back, then took two running strides forward and flew into the air.

Buffalo Soldier

2

To tell you the whole story of what happened and why, I'll have to back up a bit.

It wasn't because of the stranger that such sudden and unexpected danger had come to Rosewood. It had started long before and would have come anyway. But the fact that he was there sure changed how it would turn out.

I remember that first day I saw him a few months back. After all that had happened around Rosewood, the plantation where I lived with my cousin Katie, the sight of one more new face shouldn't have surprised anyone. People had been coming and going around the place for years, ever since I'd first appeared at Katie's doorstep after my own family had been killed. Katie was white, I was half white and half black. Her uncle Templeton Daniels was my father. My mother, a slave, was no longer alive.

If Rosewood had become a refuge for strays and waifs and runaways, it hadn't been by intent. It just kind of happened that way. And so, on that day when Henry Patterson, our friend and Jeremiah's father, came riding up with the bedraggled-looking black man, like I say, it wasn't exactly a surprise.

But even beneath the dirt, the bloodstained jacket, and the look of obvious pain on his face from whatever injury he'd had, something about this particular stranger looked different. And when his gaze first caught my eyes, a tingle went through me and I knew instantly that a young man had come into our lives who just might change things in ways we could not foresee.

The stranger who'd come with Henry had ridden slowly into Greens Crossing a couple days before.

He was a Negro, tall, well built but thin, whether from natural build or lack of food it was hard to say. He appeared to be in his early or maybe middle twenties and looked weak and tired. Although the war had been over four years, he still wore the coat of the Union army. But it was so badly torn and so dirty, you could hardly tell it had actually once been blue. Some of the stains on it looked like dried blood.

To say that he looked weary as he rode would hardly be enough. The poor fellow looked as if he'd ridden a thousand miles without sleep or food and was about to fall out of the saddle onto the street. The horse was plodding along so slow he seemed as tired as his rider. It was clear it had been a long time since either of them had had anything to eat. Some of the bloodstains on his coat were darker, older stains, but others appeared more recent. From the look of his face and how he was slumped over as he rode, he might still have been nursing a wound somewhere in his chest or shoulder.

He was what folks called a "buffalo soldier." He was a black man who had fought for the North in the war.

If it was some kind of help he had come to town for, he couldn't have picked a worse place in town to go first. But how was he to know? So when he saw the sign that said General Store, he pulled his tired horse to the side of the street, leaned forward and half slid to the ground, then limped inside. Whatever was wrong with his chest, there was something wrong with one of his legs too.

Mrs. Hammond heard the bell and glanced toward the door. Now Mrs. Hammond was a lady who could be pretty irritating. She'd never had any use for the likes of blacks. And now that Negroes were free she could be ruder than ever.

Even if the color of the young man's skin hadn't been black, his appearance would have been enough to put her nose in the air. Her nose went even higher in the air when she smelled him.

She sniffed a few times, then looked him over as if he was a mangy dog that had wandered into her store.

"Morning, ma'am," said the stranger in a polite tone, though he spoke slowly and his voice was weak. It was the last thing Mrs. Hammond expected. "Might you point me in the direction of the livery?"

"It smells like you just came from there," she retorted.

"Sorry, ma'am," he replied. "I've been traveling awhile."

"It's down that way," said Mrs. Hammond, pointing vaguely toward the window and along the street.

"Much obliged, ma'am," he said, then turned and walked out, leaving Mrs. Hammond alone to mutter a few words under her breath about the deplorable state of the country since the war.

Leading his horse by the reins, he slowly walked up the street, attracting the notice of more and more sets of eyes from the shops and windows as he passed. Mrs. Hammond's were not the only mumbled comments of disgust at the sight. Blacks were not particularly welcome in the town of Greens Crossing, especially Yankee blacks. Resentment toward the Union blue, though his tattered coat could but faintly be recognized as a war soldier's coat, ran high among loyal Southerners. All blacks were getting those same kinds of rude looks from whites those days. It isn't that everybody was like Mrs. Hammond. But a lot of whites were.

The young man who had just arrived in Greens Crossing was certainly not much to look at. But unknown to the citizens—whose own respectability they prized above nearly everything—this stranger would cause more of a stir in the community, at least in the life of one of its leading citizens, than any of the string of strangers to arrive in their town over the past five years.

He did not himself yet know it. But his presence would bring mysteries to light that Mrs. Hammond herself could never have dreamed—secrets that would turn this community, and even the whole state, on its ear.

The young man limped toward the livery stable, pulling his horse along behind him. He found Henry Patterson inside, a black man like him who had been a freedman even before the war.

"I've got a horse that needs tending," he said.

"I kin take care ob dat," said Henry, glancing up. He looked the young man over. "'Peers ter me dat you needs some tendin' yo'self, son."

The stranger smiled.

"You're right," he said. "I ran into some trouble a while back. But I'll be fine, as long as I can keep my horse healthy. Do you own this livery?" he asked, glancing around.

"No, suh," laughed Henry. "It ain't quite come ter dat yet. Da Souf is changin', but not dat fast! Dey say us coloreds is gwine get ter vote one ob dese days, an' dat's somefin' I wants ter see wiff my own two eyes. But I's still jes' a workin' colored who gits my wages from a white man. But my boss is a fair man an' treats me kindly enuff."

"You think he'd mind if I bunk down in the back there for a night?" asked the stranger.

"Dat be right hard ter say, young feller," replied Henry. "I gots me a little place where I used ter sleep, though I gots anuder place me an' my boy calls home now—a place outside er town. So I don't reckon dere'd be no harm in you takin' what used ter be my bed er straw in da room out back fo a spell."

"I would be deeply indebted to you. All I need is a night or two of good sleep and I'll feel better and be on my way."

STRANGER AT ROSEWOOD

3

EARLY IN THE AFTERNOON OF HIS GUEST'S FIRST full day at the livery stable, Henry chanced upon him at the water pump behind the livery, jacket and ragged shirt on the ground beside him. It was the first time Henry had seen his guest bare skinned. He was trying to wash, though his right arm hung at his side. It was with effort that he attempted to operate the pump and splash water on his upper body at the same time.

"Whoa, son," said Henry, walking up behind him, "you din't tell me you wuz so bad beat up. Unless I's mistaken, dat shoulder er yers is needin' some doctorin'. It don't look none too good."

The young man turned and smiled a weary smile. "It's getting better," he said, "though not as rapidly as I might hope."

"You look like you got kicked by some wild horse. When it happen, son?"

"Several months back."

"No wunder you's walkin' 'bout like you's ready ter

drop. I tell you, you needs some doctorin' an' I'm gwine git you some." The instant he'd seen the man's bruises and wounds, Henry had known what he had to do.

"I've got no money for a doctor," said the young man. "I'll recover. It just takes time."

"Where I's gwine take you, you won't need no money," said Henry.

"Where's that? You got a black doctor around here who'll let me work for his services?"

"Better'n dat!" chuckled Henry. "I's gwine take you where you kin meet my boy. An' dere's a black lady who'll hab you eatin' right an' fixed up in no time. She ain't no doctor, but she's jes' 'bout da nex' bes' thing. By da look er dose stringy ribs, I'm thinkin' you cud use some er her vittles!"

"Where is this place? Is the lady your son's wife?"

Henry let out a roar of laughter.

"No, he ain't got no wife," he said. "It's a most unusha kind er place, dat's all I kin say. You's see fo yo'self soon enuff. We'll ride out dere dis evenin' when I's got my work done."

❧ ✵ ☙

Those of us who lived at the plantation called Rosewood—one of them was me, Mayme Daniels—were finishing our noon meal, drinking coffee and talking about plans for the rest of the day, when little William bounded in from the parlor, one of Katie's old McGuffey Readers *in his hand. He set the book on the kitchen table and tried to climb onto Jeremiah's lap.*

Jeremiah pulled him up onto one knee. "Hey, little man, you want ter ride a horse?" he asked. He bounced his knee up and down and William giggled. "When you get a mite bigger, I'll teach you ter ride da new horse Miss Katie gave me."

"I didn't give it to you Jeremiah, you earned it," Katie said. "You and Henry both. We can't have you working and living here at Rosewood and walking all those miles into town."

"Well, I'm much obliged. Dat young paint is still testin' me, but I've 'bout got him settled, I think."

"You sure have a way with horses, Jeremiah," I said. He looked across the table at me and we shared a smile.

Soon Katie and the others headed outside to their chores and Josepha disappeared into the pantry.

William handed Jeremiah the McGuffey Reader. *"Read to me, Jeremiah," he said.*

Jeremiah set William on the floor. "Time to head outside, little man."

I knew what Jeremiah was thinking.

"Jeremiah," I said, "if you'd ever like to learn to read, I could try to teach you."

Jeremiah thought for a moment, then shrugged. "I don't know . . . maybe."

"What about you, William?" I said, turning to the little boy. "Are you going to read someday—maybe even go to school?"

Jeremiah snorted. "No school round here wud take him."

"I read in the paper about a school for black girls

north of Charlotte," I said. "I'm sure there'll be a school for William someday . . . maybe even for you. If you don't want me to teach you, I'm sure Papa or Uncle Ward would. It's good to learn new things. Better yourself. . . ."

Jeremiah looked at me a little strangely. "You said I wuz good enuff fo you as I is."

"Of course you are, Jeremiah," I said. "I didn't mean—"

The door banged opened and an out-of-breath Emma stuck her head into the kitchen. "Jeremiah, dem cows are out again," she said. "Dat blamed fool horse er yers done chased 'em over da fence again."

"I'm comin'," said Jeremiah, rising.

Jeremiah strode quickly from the room on Emma's heels.

Several hours later, I was outside working in the garden when I heard horses approaching. I looked up and saw Henry coming toward the house with another horse alongside his.

As I walked toward them, Henry looked my way. "I brung us a man here what cud use some help an' some doctorin'," he said. "Wiff yo permission, I figgered Miz Katie and Mister Templeton an' y'all wudn't mind me an' Jeremiah keepin' him under our roof fo a spell.—Dis here's Mayme," he added to the man beside him.

"How do, Miss Mayme," he said with a pleasant but weary smile.

"I'll go get Katie and my papa," I said. "I'm sure it will be fine."

Before I could take more than a step or two, a shriek sounded and little William came bounding down the steps off the porch and ran straight toward the stranger as Henry got off his horse and then helped the stranger to the ground. As fond as William was of Henry and Jeremiah, seeing another black man was too great a temptation for his boyish energy and enthusiasm. He went straight for him, talking away like he'd known the man all his life. The stranger stooped down.

"Why, hey there, little fella," he said. "What's your name?"

"I's William, mister. You gwine stay wiff us?"

"I don't know about that, William," he chuckled, glancing up at Henry and me.

He slowly stood and looked at me again. "He yours?" he said.

"No," I answered. "He belongs to Emma. She's off chasing cows with Jeremiah, but she should be back soon."

"Jeremiah's my boy I told you about," said Henry.

By now Katie and Josepha were on their way outside and Henry explained everything to Katie. As I glanced toward the stranger again, it was obvious from looking at him and listening to him talk, even in his condition, that he was a gentleman. I'd never heard a black man who sounded so much like a Northerner.

Now the newcomer looked over at the white

man—my father—approaching. "Henry's brought us a man who needs some help, Uncle Templeton," said Katie. "He asked if they could put him up in their cabin with them."

"Of course. Welcome, son," my papa replied, extending his hand.

After the introductions were made, Katie glanced around. "Where are the others?" she asked.

"Emma and Jeremiah are bringing in the cows," I answered. "And Uncle Ward went over to Mr. Thurston's."

We were all standing there in sort of a circle. It became quiet as the young man looked around at us all one at a time. I couldn't tell what he was thinking.

"What you looking at so funny, mister?" said William.

I couldn't help it—I started laughing. Then Josepha started to chuckle, and pretty soon everybody was laughing.

"I think the man's wondering who all these people are," laughed my papa.

"And wondering whose house this is!" laughed the young man. "It looks to me like a mighty big and fancy house, and all I see is several blacks and what looks like a working man, meaning no offense to you, Mister . . . Daniels, was it?"

My papa laughed again. "Yes, Daniels, it is—and you're right, I don't look much like a Southern plantation gentleman!"

"It's not yours, is it, William?" said the man to William.

"No, it ain't my house. It's Katie's."

More laughter came from my papa at William's words.

"It's all of ours," said Katie. "We're a family here. And now that that's settled, why don't you come inside. We should see how badly you're hurt."

As Henry and Papa helped him toward the house, they sensed his hesitation.

"I know the war's over," he said, "but this is still the South not the North—whoever's house it is or isn't. I can't . . . go in there."

Henry laughed. "I tol' you dat dis was some kind ob unusha place. Why, son, dere ain't no colors in dis here place—jes' people dat care 'bout each other."

He glanced at the white man beside him, wondering if what he'd just heard was true.

"Henry's right, son," said Papa. "We may look a little mixed up, but we're a family like Katie said, and you're welcome wherever any of the rest of us are."

They continued on toward the house. The young man glanced over at me and smiled in appreciation. It was such a pleasant smile, even in the midst of his pain and the newness of being surrounded by folks he didn't know . . . it was almost like he already knew me, and knew that we were going to become much better acquainted soon.

Reunion
4

The black man who'd come with Henry was hurt worse than he realized. The wound on his right shoulder and chest and upper arm hadn't healed like it should and was pretty badly infected. By the time we got him inside and seated, Uncle Ward was back from Mr. Thurston's and everything had to be explained all over again.

When they got his shirt and jacket off, Josepha took one look at his shoulder and exclaimed, "Dis boy's hurt bad," she said. "We gots ter git him ter bed! But he needs him a bath first," she added, not one to keep from saying whatever she was thinking. "He don' smell too good."

A few glances and smiles went around the room.

"I think he needs something to eat too," I said.

"Ward and Henry and I will take him out to the washtub outside and take care of the bath," said my papa. "You ladies boil some water on the cook stove so we don't have to take time to build a fire."

"You scrub dat shoulder real good, Mister Templeton," said Josepha, "an' pour some whisky on dat wound."

"Kathleen, why don't you fetch us some clothes of your daddy's or brother's," added Uncle Ward.

"I'll go down to the cabin," I said, "and make a bed—where do you want to put him, Henry?"

"I reckon on da couch dere in da corner ob da big room. I reckon dere'll be room fo us all."

Within the hour, the poor man must have thought he had walked into a tornado of activity! Here he was being waited on hand and foot by two white men, a black man, a black lady, a white girl called Katie, who everyone acted like owned the place just like William had said, and another black girl—me. Henry had said a mouthful when he called Rosewood "a most unusha place!"

By suppertime, every inch of his body was clean and he was wearing fresh new clothes, with Josepha fussing over the bandages and poultices she was trying to apply amidst the comings and goings of everyone in the house. Everyone had been so busy over him that it wasn't till Josepha had the supper on the table that we all looked around and realized that dusk was falling and we still hadn't seen anything of Emma and Jeremiah.

We sat down and my papa prayed and we started to eat. We had just gotten started when the door opened and Jeremiah and Emma walked in. They were laughing and talking and still sweating like they'd been halfway across the county. Their faces *were aglow like they'd had the time of their lives.*

"Where have you two been!" exclaimed Papa.

"Dose blamed cows ran us halfway ter Oakwood!" laughed Jeremiah. "Didn't dey, Emma?"

"Dey's 'bout da dumbest creatures under da sun, dat's fo sure!" laughed Emma.

"Finally we had ter git clean on da udder side ob dem," Jeremiah went on, "an' dat took some runnin', an' den we made a racket ter git dem turned aroun', but den—"

Suddenly Jeremiah stopped. He had just pulled out a chair to sit down. All of a sudden he realized there was an extra person at the table. His eyes shot wide open.

I glanced over at the stranger out of the corner of my eye. His face had almost the same expression as he stared back and forth between Jeremiah and Emma. I wondered which one of them had gotten his attention like that. Then his eyes came to rest on Jeremiah as the two young men stared at each other in shock.

"Why dat's . . . dat really be," Jeremiah said, trying to find his voice. "Dat really be you, Micah Duff!"

Hearing his name and the familiar voice, a huge smile spread over the newcomer's face.

"It's me, all right, but I don't believe my eyes! Is that you . . . Jake!" he said.

"Whatchu doin' here, Duff!"

"I met this man in town and—of course . . . Patterson!" he exclaimed, now looking back and forth between Henry and Jeremiah. "I didn't put the two

names together before now. I can't believe it!"

"You two knows each other?" said Henry in surprise.

Already Jeremiah had taken three great strides around the table as the stranger stood up. And now the two embraced in true affection. Tears flowed from both sets of eyes. But Jeremiah felt Micah wince and then first realized his weakened condition. Suddenly their former standing with one another was reversed. It was Jeremiah who was strong and Micah who needed care.

They both stepped back, eyes glistening as they continued to behold each other with shakes of their heads and smiles of wonder.

"Dis is Private Duff, Papa!" said Jeremiah. "He's da man I tol' you 'bout who saved my life—twice!—an' wuz such a good frien' ter me when I wuz wiff da soldiers."

"Well, effen dat don't beat all!"

"How you come ter be here, Duff?" asked Jeremiah again.

"A long story, Jake. I guess it goes to show what the Good Book says, that sometimes the Lord is guiding your steps when you least know it. I hadn't a notion you were anywhere within a hundred miles."

"Maybe now we kin return his kindness ter you," said Henry. "He's in need ob some help dat maybe we kin gib him."

Jeremiah sat down, his shock and excitement not enough to disturb his appetite, and within moments he and the man called Micah Duff were talking *away furiously, both catching up on the years since they had seen each other and reminiscing about all they had been through together during the war. All the rest of us listened in amazement.*

"You've grown and changed, Jake," Mr. Duff was saying. "From a distance I don't know if I would have recognized you."

"I's five years older, Duff," laughed Jeremiah. "I wuz jes' a kid back den, an' a pretty mixed-up one a lot er da time, which I reckon you recall well enuff."

"Everybody's got to grow up in their own way, Jake. But it's more than that too. I can tell."

"I reckon you's right. I suppose I've changed more on da inside den da outside."

"That's good, Jake. That's the best kind of growth."

"I had a friend who tol' me some things I didn't like hearin' too much," said Jeremiah with a curious smile. "But his words got down in dere an' did dere work in my heart, an' I finally started gettin' my grain growin' a little straighter den it wuz before.—Ain't dat right, Papa?" he added, glancing toward Henry.

"I reckon so. We both done a heap a growin', ain't we, son?"

"Well, I am happy to hear it," said Duff.

He smiled at Emma, seated across from him. But Emma kept her eyes on her plate. All through the meal, Emma had been uncommonly quiet, though William had inherited enough of her talkativeness to make up for it! She kept hanging back as if having a stranger around made her feel uncomfortable. It reminded me of how she'd been at first when Aleta had been with us.

I reckon I was a little quiet too. I couldn't help stealing a glance now and then at the stranger who had come so suddenly to Rosewood but who wasn't a stranger anymore. I felt a feeling of thankful admiration to finally see the man who had saved Jeremiah's life.

"You remember dem Dawsons?" asked Jeremiah. "Dat place we stayed when I got laid up?"

"How could I forget that place!" laughed Micah Duff. "We were lucky to get out of there alive."

"Everybody didn't git out ob dere alive," said Jeremiah in a serious tone.

"What do you mean, Jake?"

"I went back later, but I wuzn't in time ter save dat fool Mister Dawson's life. His anger got hisse'f killed."

"Why did you go back?"

"Kind ob like you comin' here. I jes' wound up dere wiffout plannin' it."

"What happened? You get into a fight with Dawson?"

"No, not me," answered Jeremiah, shaking his head. "But dose two ladies—dat fool girl an' her mama—dey wuz in a heap er trouble. A couple bad niggers had come an' dey killed Dawson an' would likely hab killed dem too ef I hadn't come along when I did. I heard dem screamin' an' I crept up an' managed ter git da women away from dem. But I wuz too late fo Dawson."

Jeremiah went on to explain what had happened. The story sobered us all. But just as quickly Jeremiah and Micah Duff continued on, each telling the other what they'd done and where they'd been after parting, and Jeremiah telling about coming here and finding Henry.

"Well, we sure appreciate what you did for Jeremiah, son," said my papa after they were pretty much caught up, though Micah Duff still hadn't told us much about the incident that had got him hurt like he was.

"Everybody's got something to give everyone he meets," he said. "We can all learn and grow from everyone else. Jake and I just happened to be together at a time when maybe he needed to hear some of what I had to say. I'm just glad we were there for each other. And now here you all are at a time when I suppose I need more help than I realized."

We were all done eating now and it got quiet. Again Micah Duff glanced around the table at us all one at a time. He came to Emma and paused. Gradually the most peculiar expression came over his face. She giggled and looked away. Then he kept looking around at the rest of us.

"But I'm still more than a little confused about how you all fit together," Micah Duff said. "You're calling him Papa," he said, now looking over at me again, "but you're black and he's white." Then he glanced back toward Emma. "And where do you fit into it, Emma—are you two sisters?"

She was still looking away and shook her head

without saying anything.

"Yeah, we're a mighty strange bunch!" said my papa. "It all started with Katie and Mayme—they're cousins, you see. Katie's mama—she was my sister. So that's why I'm Katie's uncle. Katie's mama and daddy had a black lady . . ."

He paused and looked away for a second or two. Finally he took a breath and continued.

"They had a lovely young black lady," he said in a soft voice. "She wasn't really a slave but a maid to Katie's mama—and when I came for a visit, I suppose you would say I fell in love with her. Mayme is our daughter."

He looked at me and smiled a little sadly.

"My mama's dead now," I said, "but Papa and I have each other, don't we, Papa?"

He nodded.

"So you both grew up here?" asked Mr. Duff to Katie and me.

"No, my mama was sold to another plantation not far from here," I said. "That's where I knew Emma and Josepha—we were all slaves there."

"So . . . where do you fit in?" he asked, turning to Uncle Ward.

"I sometimes wonder if I do!" laughed Uncle Ward. "I can understand your confusion. I had a pretty hard time figuring it out too when I first came. Let me see if I can explain it. I'm his brother," he said, nodding to my papa, "which makes me Katie's uncle . . . and I'm Mayme's uncle too," he added, nodding toward me. "And . . . actually I think I'm

also the one who owns this place . . . leastways that's what they tell me!"

When supper was finally over, Henry and Jeremiah took Micah down to his bed at their place. He drifted off to sleep and slept like a rock. He woke up the next day refreshed but weak and could hardly get out of bed. Josepha declared that if he hadn't come when he had, he wouldn't have lived another week. I don't know if that's true or not, because Josepha sometimes exaggerated. But that's what she said.

He remained in bed for several days, Josepha tending him like a ministering but fussy angel. By then little William, who had been fascinated with the strange newcomer from the moment he had seen him, was one of his most devoted attendants, dogging Josepha's steps and babbling constantly to Micah as he stood for hours beside his bedside and came and went from the cabin to the house fifty times a day with all the energy of a four-year-old.

Emma, meanwhile, though she listened to many of the conversations between her son and Rosewood's newest boarder from the landing outside the cabin, remained shyly hesitant to go in.

New Friends
5

After two or three days, on a day when Henry and Jeremiah had gone into town early, I hadn't heard anything from Micah Duff all morning. By then he had been getting up and around again and seemed to be feeling a lot better. Not seeing anything of him by late morning, I began to get concerned.

"Have you seen Micah this morning?" I asked Josepha, who was kneading great lumps of bread dough in the kitchen.

"I ain't seen hide er hair ob dat boy. I been so busy wiff dis bread I din't have time ter go check on him."

"I'll go if you like," Katie offered quickly. I hadn't even heard her come downstairs and into the kitchen. She was wearing one of her better dresses, and her hair was all combed into a pretty little topknot.

Josepha looked over at Katie and eyed her up and down. "Mercy, mercy, mercy," she humphed, punching the bread dough with each word.

"He's bound to be hungry," I said. "There's plenty left from breakfast, isn't there?"

"Too much," Josepha said. "Can't stand to see nuthin' go ter waste. Henry and Jeremiah lef' wiff only a few corncakes."

"I'll fix up a tray for him and take it down," I said.

"I can," said Katie again.

Just then our neighbor Mr. Thurston rode into the yard, and Katie had to go out and see what he wanted.

I walked down to Henry and Jeremiah's cabin carrying a tray of corncakes, eggs, bacon, and a small pot of coffee. From the house as I glanced back, I saw Emma in the window watching me. I smiled and waved, but she shrank away inside, which was a mite peculiar I thought. She'd been acting a little funny for several days. I wondered if she was feeling all right, or was coming down with something.

I knocked on the door and heard a voice call out from inside. I opened the door and went in. Micah Duff was still lying in the bed Henry had made for him on the couch across the room.

"Hi," I said. "I was worried about you so I brought you some breakfast. You feeling okay?"

"Yeah, just lazy, I suppose. It feels good to lie here. I've been sleeping on the ground so long this feels like a white man's hotel to me."

I set the tray down on the table. Micah tried to sit up halfway but stayed stretched out on the couch.

"Josepha said I ought to check your bandages. Do you mind?"

"No . . . that's fine."

I walked over to the couch. He unbuttoned his shirt. I felt a little funny getting so close to him and felt my neck getting warm. But he sat still like a gentleman and waited. I pulled his shirt gently down from his shoulder so I could see the white cloths Josepha had wrapped around his chest and shoulder. There was no blood or anything leaking from them, so I pulled his shirt back up, then smiled and stepped back.

"It looks fine," I said. "You like a cup of coffee?" I asked.

"Sure—that sounds good."

I poured a cup and took it to him.

"Thanks. That smells good and strong."

"Don't I remember Jeremiah saying that you were the coffee maker for your army unit?"

"Jeremiah?" he repeated in a questioning tone.

"Yes . . . Jake, I mean," I added. "Wasn't that what you called him?"

"Oh . . . right. I forgot. Jeremiah . . . hmm—that will take some getting used to!"

He sipped at the cup. "Yeah, I used to make the coffee," he said. "But that was a while ago."

He glanced toward me. "You want to sit down?" he asked.

I pulled a chair out from the table and sat down as Micah took another drink of coffee.

"Where are you from?" I asked.

"Illinois," he answered.

"I didn't think you sounded like a Southern colored."

"Neither do you."

"I was a slave until the war," I said. "But being around Katie and learning to read—I suppose I tried to improve how I talked too. Katie's taught me a lot of things."

"How did you and she come to be here? You're cousins, right . . . isn't that it?"

"That's right."

Briefly I told him how our families had been killed and how I'd come to Rosewood and then about my papa—Katie's uncle Templeton—and how I'd found out about him and my mama.

"So you're all family here?"

"I suppose in a way—though not Henry and Jeremiah and Emma—well, Henry and Jeremiah are, of course, but not Emma or Josepha."

"Still, family or not, this is a pretty remarkable place."

"I reckon it is, all right. It feels like we're all family. Katie's the remarkable one. She's the reason we're all here."

I glanced over at Micah and saw him smile. "I've never met a white woman like her, that's for sure," he said.

"Where's your family?" I asked.

Micah didn't answer immediately. His smile faded and a sad look came over his face.

"I don't suppose you'd say I've got any family," he

said. "That's why I joined up when the war broke out, and why I've been more or less drifting ever since. Not that I haven't been trying to find work, but things seem more difficult for a black man now than they ever were before."

"I'm sorry," I said. "It sounds like things have been hard for you."

"Yeah . . . they have. But that's part of life. I'm not complaining. God has been good to me. And now suddenly here I am with a roof over my head and new friends taking good care of me. Who could have it better than that!"

"Speaking of all that, this breakfast of yours is getting cold!"

"I'm ready for it now. I just needed that coffee first. But if you don't mind, could you help me up?"

I went over to the couch. He reached up his free hand, and I took it and pulled gently. With a wince or two, he got himself up to a sitting position, then slowly stood.

"Thanks," he said. "I didn't realize how bad this shoulder of mine was. But it's on the mend now."

He walked over to the table and sat down.

"You'll join me, won't you?"

"I've already eaten," I said.

"Then just keep me company. Where are the others?"

"Henry and Jeremiah went into town," I said, getting Micah a plate and a fork and spoon. "They left early this morning."

"That's right. He mentioned they had to pick up

some seed or something," Micah said, dishing out some eggs and a couple of corncakes. "This looks like a feast!"

❧ ✲ ☙

Jeremiah had gone into town early with Henry and had just returned with a wagonload of supplies. He pulled the wagon to a stop in front of the barn. He jumped down and headed toward the cabin he and Henry shared to see how Micah Duff was feeling.

As he approached, however, he slowed his step. He heard unexpected voices coming from inside—Micah's voice mingled in laughter with another voice, a girl's voice talking and laughing along with his.

It was Mayme's voice.

Jeremiah hesitated and stopped. He listened just long enough to hear them go on with their conversation, both talking freely and obviously enjoying themselves. Then he turned and walked back up toward the house. What he was feeling he couldn't exactly tell, but strange sensations were swimming through his brain.

Why shouldn't they be visiting and enjoying each other? They were two of the best friends he had ever had in the world. Why did the sound of their voices and their laughter make him feel funny?

He walked into the kitchen. Emma was at the counter shaping Josepha's bread dough into loaves.

"Hi, Emma," he said, sitting down at the table.

"You jes' git back from town, Jeremiah?" she asked.

"Yeah, a couple minutes ago."

"You seen Mayme out dere?"

"Uh . . . no."

"She went ter take dat Micah Duff some breakfas', but dat wuz an hour ago an' I ain't seen her since."

Jeremiah sat without replying. Slowly he got up.

"Well, I reckon I ought ter git dat wagon unloaded."

"You need some help, Jeremiah? I's jes' 'bout done wiff dis bread."

"Uh, yeah . . . sure, Emma—thanks. Won't be quite da adventure we had wiff dose cows, but I'd sure appreciate da help."

"I's be out ter join you in a jiffy."

AMBITIONS

6

SOME FOUR MILES FROM GREENS CROSSING, IN THE house of a wealthy plantation notable for the absence of any black person anywhere on it, a man of approximately thirty-two years sat in the leather chair of his upstairs office. He was thinking about the excursion he had planned for the following day.

He was not the master of the place but rather the owner's son. He had spent his whole life here, and hadn't minded it. And while he had a certain grudging respect for his father, whose name he shared, the fact was, his father was only fifty-three and was still strong as an ox. His mother had died years before, but his father would be master of the plantation for years to come. His own wife was mistress of the place, but he would just be his father's son until he had grey hair of his own. If he didn't make something of his life soon, it would be too late.

He had realized for some time that there was no future around here sufficient to satisfy his ambitions. He was meant for bigger things.

He hoped tomorrow's trip to the state capital would set him on the path to a future with more promise than merely growing wheat and cotton for his father.

What this man could possibly have to do with the plantation called Rosewood and its assortment of blacks and whites may have been a mystery to some. But the fact was, there were more connections between the two plantations and its people than most people in the community had any idea.

Why I would want to tell about this man, and even how I could, is a mite hard to explain. All I can say is that it wasn't easy to find out some of the things that happened. I had to ask a lot of people a lot of questions, and some of what I found out I didn't find out until a long time later.

But concerning the why *I need to tell about this man is because my own story is interwoven with his in so many ways I could not possibly explain them all.*

In fact, I grew up on the very plantation where he now sat thinking. Back when I was young, there were dozens of black slaves all about the place, including me and my family, and a house mammy called Josepha and a dim-witted black house girl a year older than me called Emma. Back then we were all slaves and this man's father was the man we called Massa. And the Massa's sons were mean and ornery and I'd felt the sting of their whips on my bare back more times than I can remember and have still got the scars to prove it.

So when I say that this man's story and my own were all tied up together, you can see what I mean. He was the kind of man a former slave never forgets.

And he had a secret he didn't want anyone to find out about. There were only a handful of people who knew his secret.

I was one of them.

When William McSimmons, Jr. walked into the Raleigh office of North Carolina congressman Robinson Galbreath, a brief thrill surged through him. This might be *his* office two years from now! He did his best, however, to hide his lustful glances at the well-appointed décor and what it represented. He needed this man's help. It would not be wise to appear too eager.

He greeted the congressman with a shake of the hand and took the chair that was offered him. The congressman glanced over the letter that had been lying on his desk when his guest arrived and which had prompted the meeting.

"Your father says you are planning a congressional run for my seat," said Galbreath. "And that you want my support."

"He told me you were plainspoken," smiled the younger McSimmons.

"You can't succeed in politics any other way," replied the congressman without returning the smile. He had seen no humor in it. "Try to hide something from the public and they will always find you out in the end."

"I couldn't agree more, sir," said McSimmons. "To answer your question—yes, I am considering a run and would be most grateful for your support. When word reached us of your retirement after this term, I began to consider the possibility. My father thought I should talk to you."

"Your father and I are old friends. I owe him a great deal. So for his sake I will give the matter due consideration. What makes you feel you are the man to represent the people of North Carolina in Washington?"

"I would hope, sir, that my age and vision for the future of the South could be seen as representing, as it were, the *New South*. My contacts with certain men of influence with capital to invest in our region will make for new opportunities for our people which I believe will enhance North Carolina's growth."

"Carpetbaggers, you mean?"

"I would prefer to think of them as men, like myself, looking realistically toward the future now that the war is behind us."

"And there's nothing in your resume, no past indiscretions, no skeletons in any closets, that could come back to bite you? I don't want my name mixed up in anything—"

"I assure you, sir," said McSimmons, "there is nothing I would not be willing to have completely known. I am happily married to a dear woman and my life is an open book."

"And your wife," said the congressman. "What does she think?"

"She is very supportive. She would be willing to relocate to Washington."

McSimmons did not add that the congressional seat had originally been his wife's idea, and that she was a more opportunistic social climber than he. She had, in fact, been urging him to run *against* Galbreath before the announcement of his retirement.

The two men continued to chat informally for another five or ten minutes. Neither particularly liked the other. But in politics that hardly mattered.

When William McSimmons boarded the train two hours later to return to Charlotte and then to Oakwood, it was with a smile of satisfaction. He had done well, he thought, to endear himself to the old man. With Galbreath's endorsement, his own election would be in the bag.

It was time to make plans for a formal announcement, probably sometime this spring. His wife would want to make an event of it. And why not? The more publicity involved, and the more influential people they could invite, the better.

In the meantime, he would make himself more visible and respectable in the community. He was not thinking about his secret right then. But it wouldn't be long before he would start thinking about it.

And wondering what to do about it.

A Mighty Fine-Looking Man

7

Micah Duff gradually gained his strength and before long was out of his bed and back on his feet. With the ploughing and planting already under way, there was plenty to be done, and Micah and Jeremiah were better friends than ever—more like brothers than anything. They were almost inseparable.

Spring advanced and again the shoots of cotton and wheat and other crops began to color the landscape with carpets of green. The earth warmed and rich smells rose from it, and life at Rosewood seemed a good thing to us all. There had been no more incidents with the men dressed in white robes, and we hoped maybe people were at last getting used to how things were at Rosewood. Having Micah with us added new interest and excitement and zest to our lives.

It wasn't every day we had a newspaper around the house, but whenever Uncle Ward or my papa went into town, they usually bought one from Mrs. Hammond, which might have been every couple of weeks.

I heard some muttering one day as I walked toward the kitchen from the parlor and came in to see Josepha sitting at the table humphing to herself over the paper they'd brought home yesterday. Then she went back to reading and seemed engrossed in it for another minute.

"I didn't know you could read so well, Josepha," I said. "I've never seen you with a newspaper before."

"I kin read well enuff, Mayme chil'. Dere wuz a time in my life when I had as much learnin' as any white lady. It's jes' dat I don't git much occasion ter use all dat no more."

"It sounds like you were reading something that upset you."

"I jes' oughta keep my big mouf shut," she said. "It's jes' dat when a man goes struttin' 'bout like he's somebody important when I used ter take him on my own knee fo his mama before he got old enuff ter take the whip in his own hand, well, den I ain't got no use fo a man like dat."

"Who are you talking about?"

"Jes' dat blamed McSimmons boy here," she said, pointing to the paper. "It says he's fixin' ter run fo Congress or somethin'. Dat boy ain't fit ter lick his daddy's boots. Now he's settin' hisse'f up as a big important man, when he ain't—"

Josepha stopped whatever she had been about to say. Emma had walked in a few seconds behind me *and now stood listening. She always got both quiet and afraid when the subject of William McSimmons came up. I could never tell what she was thinking, fondness for her son's father, or fear of him.*

At almost the same time the men all came in together, talking and chatting. Micah Duff was doing his best to help with some of the chores around the place, though his shoulder was still a little weak. That would have put an end to anything more being said about William McSimmons, except that my papa saw the newspaper lying on the table where Josepha had been reading.

"What do you think about that," he said, kind of to everyone at the same time, "our neighbor McSimmons running for Congress!"

I don't think he realized anyone had read the paper. I doubt he thought Josepha could read at all, because it seemed like he was about to go on and tell us about it. But before he could say a word, Josepha answered his question in no uncertain terms.

"I kin tell you what I think of it," she mumbled, "an' dat ain't much!"

Uncle Ward laughed. "Why's that, Josepha?" he said. "You got something against the man?"

"I got more den jes' somethin' against him, an' dat's da truf."

"Josepha used to work for McSimmons," said my papa, "didn't I tell you that, Ward?"

"I used ter be dere slave's mo' like it," said Josepha. "I ain't sayin' ol' Master McSimmons wuzn't kind enuff, an' his poor wife, God bless her—but the

young one an' his wife—dey wuz bad'ns. Dat's why I lef'."

I saw Micah Duff listening to everything, and Emma was quieter than usual. She glanced toward him once then looked away almost shyly. Getting used to new people around always was a little hard for Emma, and I could imagine it was the same with Micah Duff. She had probably never known a black man that acted so much like a white, so knowledgeable and refined. Neither had I!

I saw him glance with a look of question toward Emma. "We were all from the McSimmons plantation," I explained to him, "—Emma an' Josepha an' me. My family were field slaves, and when they were all killed at the end of the war I escaped and wandered here. Josepha and Emma were house slaves, so they weren't hurt. Then Emma came to Rosewood, and then Josepha a year or two later."

Uncle Ward and Papa started talking about it again.

"This guy McSimmons, has he got what it takes for Congress?" asked Uncle Ward.

"Hardly. That man's an evil snake," answered my papa. "He's got money, though—both his father's and his wife's. Word is his wife's family's dripping with it."

A few seconds later Emma left the kitchen. After a minute I got up and followed her. She was standing at the back window of the sitting room looking out over the back porch toward the fields and trees in the distance. I put my hand on her shoulder. I was pretty sure she was feeling all her old fears again about William McSimmons.

"We won't let anything happen to you," I said.

Emma turned and cast me the most forlorn look. "You's always been so good ter me," she said softly. "I don't know why, but you has."

"We love you and William," I said. "You'll be safe here."

"You won't tell dat Mister Duff 'bout me an' him, will you, Mayme?"

"Not if you don't want me to, Emma. I'm sorry if I said too much in there."

"Dat all right. You didn't say nuthin'. But I jes' don't want him ter know I's such a fool as ter git inter dat kin' er trouble."

"You're not a fool, Emma. You're a fine young mother. Sometimes things happen that we wish hadn't. But I won't say anything."

She smiled and hugged me so tight I could hardly breathe.

"Thank you, Mayme," she said. "You's da bes' friend a girl cud hab." She paused. "Cud you make sure William's all right fo a short spell? I jes' want ter be alone . . . jes' fo a minute or two."

"Of course, Emma."

She smiled again, then went out the front door and slowly down the porch and across the grass. I'd hardly ever seen Emma cry, but I think that's why she wanted to be alone.

She was quiet for several days after that.

Henry and Jeremiah left for town again early one morning where both had full days to put in at the livery stable and Mr. Watson's mill.

The morning had hardly begun and Micah Duff had only been out of bed long enough to drink one cup of the strong coffee Henry had left for him when he heard a commotion outside. He pulled on his boots, then picked up his cup again and wandered outside.

There was Templeton Daniels getting down off a wagon loaded with boards and tools.

"What's going on?" asked Micah, walking toward him. "It looks like you're getting ready to build a house!"

"It's not quite that ambitious," laughed Templeton. "We just thought we would fix up one of the other cabins down here—this one next to Henry's."

"Let me finish getting dressed and grab something to eat and I'll give you a hand. What's the occasion—are you planning to hire more hands for the summer?"

"You never know when someone else might show up around this place," answered Templeton. "People seem to come all the time out of nowhere."

"People like me!" laughed Micah Duff.

"To answer your question," Templeton went on, "no, we've got no plans to hire anyone. We're not necessarily expecting anyone either. Ward and I thought we ought to fix the place up for someone who's already come."

"Oh . . . who's that?" asked Micah Duff.

"You."

"Me!"

"We thought it might be getting a little crowded in there for the three of you," he said with a nod toward Henry and Jeremiah's house. "Now that you're mending up so nice, I thought you'd like your own quarters."

"I appreciate that," said Duff, "but it's really time that I thought about moving on."

"Moving on . . . to where?"

"I don't know—wherever I was going before I rode into town."

"But that was no place, I thought."

"I suppose you're right at that," laughed Micah.

"So why not stay a spell?"

"I can't presume on your hospitality forever. And I'm afraid I can't pay you. I'm flat broke."

"Who said anything about hospitality?" returned Templeton. "I was planning to put you to work."

"Ah, I see . . . well, that might change things, all right."

It was quiet a minute. When Templeton spoke again, his voice was more serious. "What is your long-range goal, son?" he asked. "Where *were* you headed anyway when you rode into town? Knowing you—because you're a pretty smart young man—I doubt it was *completely* aimless."

Micah thought a minute. "Honestly I didn't really have a destination in mind," he said. "I'd been going from place to place looking for work, but these are hard times for a black man."

"Yep, I understand that. Well then, saying you had the money, what would you do? Would you keep wandering around North Carolina?"

Micah thought awhile again. "I suppose I'd like to go

out west someday," he said after a moment, "and get a little spread of land. I've only been as far as Missouri, but I'd like to get to Oregon someday. I suppose if I have a dream in life, that's it."

"Seems to me you've done a lot of wandering without getting too far," said Templeton. "Maybe you ought to work awhile and save up enough money to follow that dream."

"That sounds good, all right, but sometimes it's not so easy. A man's got to have a job. And getting a piece of land ain't easy when you're a black man."

"True enough. But you can't just be aimless either, or the things you hope for will never happen. Take it from a man who never knew what he wanted till it bit him in the face, and who wasted too many years accomplishing nothing. If Oregon's your dream, son, then figure out a way to get there, and don't wait till you're too old to enjoy it."

"What was it that bit you in the face, as you say," asked Micah. "What was it that made you see what you really wanted out of life?"

Templeton nodded slowly with a curious, sad smile on his face. "That young lady up there at the house named Mayme—that's who it was," he said. "She and the memory of her mother, I should say. Once I found out she was my daughter, everything changed for me—though it took me a while to realize it. Having somebody to love—that makes all the difference."

"Yeah, I can see why—she's really something," said Micah. "She's got . . . I don't know, an energy and enthusiasm for life that's special, all right. I can see why she would change things for you. She is quite a young lady."

Templeton looked at Micah with an expression of question. But he did not pursue what more the young man might mean.

"She's made my life more than I ever thought it would be, I'll say that," he said after a couple of seconds. "But you go on and get dressed, son, and finish your breakfast and then come help me with this lumber. Ward'll be down to help us directly. We thought we'd patch the roof first, then replace a few floorboards. We'll have this place livable in a day or two!"

*

From an upstairs window in the house, Emma and Katie and I happened to be watching as my papa and Micah Duff walked up to the barn for some things an hour or so later, talking and laughing like old friends.

Actually Katie had been standing at the window first. I saw her and walked up behind her. We stood a minute just looking at the two of them as they disappeared into the barn.

"What are you thinking?" I asked.

Katie looked over at me and smiled. It was a quiet and peaceful smile.

"I guess I was thinking . . . I don't know—just how wonderful it is what God has done here. Isn't it, Mayme?" she added, glancing over at me. "How could we have ever known, that first day when we saw each other downstairs in the kitchen . . . that was such an awful day. I didn't know how I would

keep living at all . . . yet now, look—there are two wonderful men out there—did you see them just now, laughing and talking. We didn't even know them then . . . well, I knew Uncle Templeton, but you didn't, even though he was your father. And now here they are part of our lives, just like everyone else. It's really wonderful how good God has been to us. I am so thankful that we have a family again . . . and for you especially, Mayme."

Emma walked in before I had a chance to reply. She came over and joined us at the window. A minute later Papa and Micah walked out of the barn again, each holding the ends of two long planks. Their voices carried up to where we stood watching, though we couldn't make out their words.

"I wonder what they're talking about," said Katie. "They act like they've known each other for years."

"I have a feeling Micah Duff is that way with anyone," I said. "Remember how Jeremiah talked about him, like Micah was always able to tell what he was thinking."

"And he's so good-looking," said Katie.

I glanced over at Katie. She saw that I was surprised by what she'd said.

"What?" she laughed with a questioning tone. "He is . . . don't you think?"

"But he's black," I said. "Do you really think he's good-looking?"

"Why, you mean because I'm white? You thought Rob Paxton was good-looking, didn't you?"

"Yes, but that's different."

"No it's not," said Katie, "I think Micah Duff is about as handsome as anyone I've seen, don't you, Mayme?"

"Well . . ." I said, looking down again to Papa and Micah Duff now walking back toward the cabins. Even though their backs were turned, I remembered his face well enough. And Katie was right. "Yes," I said, giggling a little, "he is a mighty fine-looking man, all right."

"What do you think, Emma?" asked Katie.

"I reckon you's right dere," nodded Emma. "I jes' hadn't thought ob it afore."

"You hadn't noticed him!" said Katie. "How could you not have noticed?"

Now Katie started giggling even more.

"What are you thinking?" I laughed.

"I was just thinking . . . oh, wouldn't it be the most . . ."

Now she broke out laughing like she couldn't stop.

"What is so funny!" I said.

"I was just thinking what the people in town—and especially Mrs. Hammond!—what would they say if I was to marry a black man?"

I stopped laughing and looked at Katie in shock.

"Katie Clairborne," I said, "you're not really thinking . . . I mean—what are *you thinking!"*

"Nothing . . . I'm not thinking anything—only . . ."

She stopped and glanced away. I couldn't believe it—Katie's face was red. I don't ever think I'd seen her embarrassed like that before.

"But . . . but could you really marry a black man, Katie?" I said after a minute. "You're not really thinking that . . . are you?"

"You could marry a white man, couldn't you, Mayme?"

"Well, maybe, but that's different—I'm half white."

"I don't think it's different at all," said Katie. "Of course anyone who did would get plenty of grief from whites and blacks both. But, yes—I could marry a black man, if he was the right man—if he was sensitive and kind and I could talk to him . . . and if I was in love with him. Why shouldn't I? Love's the main thing, isn't it, not the color of someone's skin."

We stood staring out the window another minute or two until the two men had disappeared from our sight.

When Jeremiah returned from town after work late that afternoon, even before he could see the buildings of Rosewood, he heard the sounds of Micah and Mr. Templeton where they were talking and laughing as they sat on the roof of the cabin pounding nails into the new boards and shingles they had put in place. At the first sound of their voices Jeremiah guided his horse forward to join them.

Then a great laugh from Templeton Daniels sounded. Jeremiah hesitated. Mayme's father had never laughed with him like that. Suddenly Jeremiah felt strange, isolated and distant, like an outsider, and not a part of the conversation and camaraderie the two men were obviously enjoying with each other.

Why did their laughter and conversation make him feel this way? Was he jealous that Micah could laugh and talk with Mayme's father like an equal, man to man . . . was he jealous that Micah could speak like a white man . . . that he was intelligent and could read books?

Such thoughts did not exactly form themselves in Jeremiah's brain. But he felt them in his heart. They were unsettling and confusing. Slowly he turned the reins away and took a more roundabout route to the barn. Earlier in the day he'd seen Deke Steeves in town. He always knew, when he ran into guys like him and Weed Jenkins and Jesse Earl that they looked down on him like he was trash. All whites looked down on people of colored skin as inferior, except for unusual whites like Katie and Mr. Templeton and Mr. Ward. But there weren't many like them, that was for sure.

But Jeremiah knew he wasn't really inferior in any way to a rough like Deke Steeves. Inside he felt every bit Steeves' equal.

But the feeling that had just surged through him was something he had never felt before. Suddenly he felt inferior . . . to another *black* man, even a black man he considered a friend.

Templeton had always treated him well enough. But Jeremiah knew he was beholden to Templeton Daniels. They could never really be *friends*. But it was different with Micah. He and Templeton were behaving like they *were* friends. And for some reason he couldn't explain . . . it hurt to know that he could never be like that. He could never really be on the same level as Micah.

And . . . what about Mayme? Jeremiah thought.

After meeting Micah, how could she not see the same thing that was suddenly so obvious to him—that he could never measure up to a man like Micah Duff? The fact was, Micah would be so much better for Mayme. She had to notice it too.

Alongside Micah Duff, what did he have to offer her? Not much.

❋

"I've got an announcement to make!" said my papa at supper that evening. "I've talked Micah into staying with us for a spell as our newest hired hand!"

"Well, dat be right fine, Mister Templeton," said Josepha. "I had da feelin' dat boy was gettin' da itch ter be pullin' up stakes agin and he ain't ready effen you ax me."

"It's one more mouth to feed, Josepha," said Uncle Ward.

"You let me take care of feedin' da moufs aroun' here, Mister Ward, an' you jes' make sure we got enuff food."

"It's wonderful!" said Katie, smiling warmly at Micah. "We're very happy that you're going to stay."

Seeing the smile on Katie's face reminded me of what she'd said earlier when we had been looking at Micah from upstairs.

Just how fond of him was she!

❋

Reading, Writing, and Ranching

8

Most of the Rosewood family began to gather in the large kitchen for lunch. Josepha had rung the bell outside and was setting plates and serving bowls on the table as everyone wandered in. The newspaper she had been looking at a few days before lay open on the table and Mayme, who had been helping Josepha with preparations for lunch, sat down and began to read one of the stories aloud.

" *'It is with great,'* " she read, then slowly tried to make out the next word, " *'an . . . tic . . . uh . . . pa . . . shun . . .'* "

"*Anticipation,*" sounded a voice behind her. Micah Duff had just walked in with Jeremiah and Ward. "Keep going—you're doing fine," he added.

Mayme smiled and bent down to the paper again.

" *'It is with great anticipation that workers for the Union Pacific,'* " she went on slowly.

As she read Micah slowly walked to the table and stood beside her.

" '*. . . and Central Pacific Railroads continue . . . uh . . . feverishly to lay down their tracks, ap . . . approach . . .*' "

"*Approaching,*" said Micah, looking down over Mayme's shoulder, his head close to hers as she read.

"Some of the words are long!" laughed Mayme.

"That's all right. You read very well. Go on."

"I'll try. '*. . . Approaching one another closer and closer every day, each racing to cover more ground than the other. They will almost surely meet . . . sometime next month in early May in the . . . vicinity of Pro . . . pro . . . mon*'—I'm sorry, I don't know that word," said Mayme.

"It's the name of a town in Utah," said Micah. "Promontory Point—that's where they expect the tracks to meet."

"That's what it says next, isn't it?" said Mayme. " '*. . . Then at last will the two coasts of the great American . . . continent be joined by . . .*'—you finish it, would you please?"

" '*. . . the great iron bands of railroad,*' " Micah went on, " '*and the dream of seeing California and the mighty Pacific Ocean will be only as far away as a ride of several days in a comfortable coach behind a great steam locomotive.*' "

Mayme looked up at Micah, still standing close, and smiled. "Thank you—that was fun. Katie's the one who mostly taught me to read, didn't you, Katie?"

"All you needed was a little help," said Katie, walking over to join them. "And then you were smart enough to pick most of it up on your own."

By now Josepha was hustling everyone to the table.

Emma scooted William's chair closer to the table, his little hands and sleeves still wet from a washing at the pump. Jeremiah came in and quietly sat down next to him, and Ward and Templeton soon followed.

"How did you learn to read so well, Micah?" asked Katie as they took chairs beside each other.

"I taught myself too," replied Micah. "I asked lots of questions, I listened to what I was told and I worked at it and got some simple books when I had the chance. I *wanted* to read, so I worked hard to learn. Then there was a fellow I told Jake about called Hawk, who helped me just like you helped Mayme. Everybody's got to have somebody, don't they, to help them through the rough spots."

Everyone looked around the table at one another. They all knew just what he meant. They'd all been doing that for each other for several years.

"Anyway," Micah went on, "Hawk helped me figure out a lot of things about life besides reading. But by the way," he added, turning to Katie, "what should a man like me call you? I've heard *Miss Katie* and *Miss Kathleen*, and I think even *Miss Clairborne*, and just *Kathleen*. I still haven't quite figured out how everything around this place works, so I don't want to misspeak."

Katie laughed with delight. "We're *all* trying to figure out how this place operates, aren't we, Uncle Templeton!"

"That we are, Kathleen!" he said, joining her in laughter.

"Well, Mr. Duff," said Katie, "my uncles call me Kathleen, Josepha and Henry usually call me Miss Kathleen, and people who don't know me very well call me Miss Clairborne. Mayme and Emma used to call me Miss Katie out of respect. But I prefer that my best friends just call me Katie. After all, that's my name."

"So what should I call you?"

"Call me Katie."

"Then you have to stop the *Mister* Duff and call me Micah."

"All right . . . *Micah,*" said Katie with a smile and a slight reddening of her cheeks.

By now lunch was in full swing and Micah brought the conversation back around to the subject of the newspaper article about what was called the transcontinental railroad.

"Just think what it would be like to go west," he said excitedly. "All the way to California!"

"It ain't all it's cracked up to be," said Ward Daniels with a cynical expression.

"How do you mean?"

"It's not the land of milk and honey people make it out to be. California's just like any other place."

"Is there really gold, Mr. Daniels?" asked Micah.

"Sure. And there was lots of it at first," Ward replied, "though it's mostly all been found by now. But all it did was make men into greedy animals. There's a lot of things that money can't buy."

"Your gold saved Rosewood, Uncle Ward," said Katie.

"I suppose you're right," nodded Ward, "and I'm thankful for that. But gold can't buy family, can it, Templeton?"

"Nope, it sure can't."

"So you were in the gold rush, Mr. Daniels?" asked Micah.

"The tail end of it, I reckon you'd say."

"That sounds like a story I want to hear!"

"Good luck," laughed Ward's brother. "He won't even talk to me about it.—Tell them," added Templeton to Micah, "what you told me about going west."

Micah glanced at him, thought a second or two, then nodded.

"I'd like to go west," he said, "that's my dream anyway . . . have a place of my own, raise cattle, maybe horses," said Micah, more thoughtfully now. "It'll probably never happen, but I think about it."

"Why couldn't it happen, Micah?" said Mayme excitedly to Micah where he sat between her and Katie. "You're well now and the war's over and now there's a train that goes all the way there."

"Not quite yet!" laughed Micah. "Next month!"

"All right," she said. "We don't want you to leave, anyway. But I bet you *will* go to California someday! You might be one of California's first black ranchers!—Are there coloreds in California, Uncle Ward?" she asked.

"Not too many. Lots of Mexicans and Chinese. Not many Negroes."

"I wonder if coloreds like us will ever be able to go places like that and see faraway places of the world," said Mayme.

"You just said that you thought I could," said Micah.

"I meant you, not me."

"Why not you too? What do you say, Mayme—you and me, we'll make a trip to California and show them what blacks are like!"

Mayme laughed. "I doubt that is something I will be doing anytime soon! I'm not like you, Micah. You've already seen lots of the world. You're an adventurer."

Micah roared with laughter. "I rode into Greens Crossing, by Josepha's account, more than half dead," he said. "And you call me an *adventurer*!"

"Well, you're still an adventurer compared to me."

"I don't know, Mayme. You've got a lot of the adventurous spirit in you too. Unless I miss my guess, so do you, Katie," he added, turning to Katie. "I've got the feeling the world's just begun to hear about you two!"

"We might say the same about you, Mr. Duff," said Katie.

"*Micah*, remember?"

"Oh . . . sorry. In the South we are always taught to call people *mister*. But you know what I mean . . . *Micah*—maybe the world's just begun to hear about you. I still agree with Mayme that you're the bold and daring one."

Micah laughed again. "All right, then, we'll set the world on its ear together someday—all three of us—you and Mayme and I. We'll set *California* on its ear, how's that!"

Templeton laughed. "Listen to these young folk, Ward!" he said. "Were we that way when we were young—with all kinds of dreams?"

"I think we were, Templeton," replied Ward, "but ours were more *schemes* than dreams."

"Yeah, I see what you mean. These three are adventurers. We were just drifters."

"That's all I've been for several years," said Micah, a little more soberly.

"All that's changed now, son," said Templeton. "Meeting these two girls does that to folks. Run into

Mayme and Katie and things change in a hurry!''

''I can see that!'' laughed Micah. ''I'm feeling the change already.''

When lunch was over, though the others were still talking away about the railroad and the west, Jeremiah got up and left the kitchen. He hadn't said anything for a while, for most of lunch, in fact.

He walked outside around the barn until he was out of sight from the house. Emma too had been mostly quiet during the conversation. She now slipped out of the house, leaving William splashing in the dishwater beside Josepha. She had seen Jeremiah go, more than half suspected the cause, and now followed him. Emma found him sitting on a pile of boards behind the barn, staring down at the ground. She walked over and sat down.

''Everythin' all right wiff you, Jeremiah?'' she said.

He glanced toward her and forced a smile, though it didn't seem like a very happy one.

He said nothing for several minutes. The two continued to sit side by side.

''You ever wish you cud read, Emma?'' said Jeremiah at length. ''I mean read real good, so's you cud read a newspaper like dey wuz doin', or even a book?''

''Not till I got ter Rosewood,'' answered Emma. ''Dat's when everythin' changed fo me.''

''Yeah, maybe me too.''

''I never thought much 'bout nuthin' afore dat,'' Emma went on. ''I figgered readin' an' such-like wuzn't somethin' coloreds wuz supposed ter do. But Josepha kin read real good, an' now Miz Katie's taught Mayme ter read, though

I think Mayme cud already read a little. She has her mama's Bible, you know. You know how ter read at all, Jeremiah?"

"A little, I reckon, but not much," he replied. "Micah tried ter teach me some during da war. But I wuz a mighty stubborn cuss back den. I kin write my name."

"Dat Mister Duff, he's a nice man, all right, ain't he? Katie says he's good-lookin'."

The words stung Jeremiah's ears. He was afraid Katie wasn't the only one who might think so. "Yeah, I reckon dat's so," he said. "He's good-lookin', all right. But maybe he's *too* nice."

"Whatchu mean, Jeremiah?"

"Nuthin'."

"You must er meant somethin'. Dat what you come out here thinkin' 'bout, how he's bein' maybe a little too nice . . . ter Mayme?"

Jeremiah glanced over at Emma. How could she have known exactly what was on his mind? "I don't know," he said, ". . . I guess I's jes' wonderin' ef he an' Mayme . . . aw, never mind. I don't want ter say nuthin' more 'bout it."

"Yeah, I noticed it too," said Emma. "It ain't dat hard ter see dat dey's . . . well, you know what I mean, cuz you seen it too. But it's gwine be all right, Jeremiah. I's sure it ain't nuthin'."

"How can it be nuthin' when dey's lookin' at each other dat way? An' how's I ever gwine . . ."

He stopped and looked away.

"What, Jeremiah?"

"I don't know . . . I's jes' wonderin' . . . I reckon from

da very beginnin' I wondered ef I wuz good enuff fo her."

"Good enuff fo Mayme, you mean?"

"Yeah."

"Course you are, Jeremiah—you's 'bout da nicest young man I's eber known."

"Aw, I don't know, now wiff Micah here . . . I don't know. How kin a boy like me dat ain't got nuthin' and can't do nuthin' an' can't even read—how kin I not worry 'bout what's gwine happen?"

"Mayme likes you real good, Jeremiah."

"But sometimes you can't help wonderin' . . ."

Again Jeremiah did not finish what he had been about to say.

"Wonderin' what?"

"I don't know . . . it's jes' dat—well, you an' me, Emma, we's both jes' two coloreds dat were slaves an' dat ain't got no learnin'."

"Mayme wuz a slave."

"Yeah, but Mayme an' Micah—dey's different . . . dey's got learnin' an' dey knows things. Don't you see what I's talkin' 'bout. Didn't you hear dem talkin' 'bout the three of dem together doin' things an' habing adventures? We's different, Emma. You an' me's different den all dey wuz talkin' 'bout."

"I reckon dat's so—you an' me's a lot alike, ain't we, Jeremiah?"

"Seems like it, Emma."

"An' my William likes you real good, Jeremiah."

Jeremiah turned and smiled. "He's a good little rascal, Emma," he said. "I like him too. If I eber hab a son er my own, I hope he's as good a boy as William. You's been a good mother ter him, Emma."

"Dat's right kind er you ter say, Jeremiah."

It was quiet for two or three minutes as both pondered their future in ways neither could quite yet put into words.

"What you think 'bout all dey wuz talkin' 'bout," said Jeremiah after a while, "'bout goin' west an' all dat?"

"I don't know, Jeremiah," said Emma. "I reckon it soun' mighty fine fo folks like dem, fo Mister Duff an' Mayme, an' Miz Katie. Dey's da kin' er folks dat kin do things like dat. But I's jes' a dummy . . . I cudn't neber do nuthin' like dat."

"You ain't no dummy, Emma."

"You knows what I means . . . I mean compared wiff Mayme an' Mister Duff. Dey's smarter den most blacks—leastways, smarter den me. And you heard what Mister Templeton called dem—advenshurers. I ain't none er dat. I's jes' a poor, dumb nigger girl wiff a baby ter take care ob. Not dat habin' an advenshure wudn't be right nice, but dat's fer folks like Mayme, Mister Duff, an' Miz Katie. You want ter see da Wes', Jeremiah?"

"I don't know, not so much. I reckon I's as happy here as anywhere."

"Sounds like Mayme sure wud like ter see it."

Jeremiah said nothing. He was afraid Emma was right.

Emma stood up. "I gots ter be gettin' back. Dat boy er mine's gwine be raisin' Cain wonderin' where I's got ter."

Jeremiah stood with her and slowly they walked back to the house together.

Lunch gradually broke up and people wandered away from the table. I had been so absorbed in the discussion with Micah and Katie about California and the West that I hadn't noticed Jeremiah leave the house. When I first noticed it, I realized that Emma was gone too. I was puzzled at first, wondering if they'd left together. But then, Micah and Katie and I started talking again.

As we all wandered away from the table I walked out onto the back porch.

I saw Emma and Jeremiah walking toward the house from the barn. They were talking quietly together.

All of a sudden I became aware all over again how pretty Emma was. How could any young man not notice it? I was so plain-looking alongside Emma. It had hardly ever bothered me before. But all of a sudden it did. It stung me to realize it, after all Jeremiah and I had been through together and what we had meant to each other such a short time ago. But I couldn't help thinking how good he and Emma looked together, and how content Emma seemed to be with him.

I tried to shake off what I was thinking. I went quickly back inside to help Josepha with the dishes before they saw me.

Cows and Confusion

9

I walked out through the fields one afternoon to bring the cows in for milking. About halfway there I heard footsteps behind me. I turned and there was Micah running to join me.

"Where are you off to?" he asked.

"To get the cows," I said. "It's nearly milking time."

"Mind if I tag along?"

"Of course not. It will save me having to run after any bothersome ones."

"By making me run after them instead?" laughed Micah.

"If you're feeling well enough to run across the field just now, you can chase down a cow!"

"Thanks a lot!" he laughed.

We fell into step together.

"Where are they?" he asked.

"In the field yonder—just past those trees," I said. "We move them from field to field as the grass

grows. As they eat one field down, we move them to the next."

"It sounds like a lot of work."

"Keeping milk cows is never-ending work, in more ways than milking them twice a day. But we could all live off the milk from them, so how can we complain? It's how we feed ourselves."

"Do you sell any of the milk?"

"We thought about it, but lately so many people are angry at us and especially at my papa and Uncle Ward for what we're doing here, that we don't think many would buy from us."

"Angry . . . why?"

"Because of blacks and whites together," I said. "They think we—I mean me and Josepha and Henry and Jeremiah and Emma—us coloreds—they think we're uppity and don't know our place. But I think they hate Uncle Ward and Papa even more for treating us like equals."

"It is the most remarkable place I've ever seen," said Micah.

"I suppose I'm used to it by now," I said. "We all treat each other normal, like people ought to be treated. But maybe it is unusual—like you say."

"Believe me, it is. I doubt there's another plantation like this in the whole country."

"I am very glad you found your way here," I said.

"I hardly found my way," laughed Micah. "I believe I was led here. But either way—I am more grateful than I can say—both to God for guiding

my steps, and to you all for opening yourselves to me the way you have. I feel like I've known you all for years."

"Are you—" I began, "I mean . . . you mentioned God leading you here. I just wondered . . ." I hesitated.

"What?" he asked.

"I'm not sure how to say it," I said, smiling a little awkwardly.

"Am I a Christian, you mean? Is that what you wanted to ask?"

"I guess that's something like it," I said.

"Yes, I am," Micah answered. "I try—though not as successfully as I would like—to order my ways by what I think God would have me do, and to follow the example of Jesus Christ as much as I can."

"Jeremiah told me a little about some of the things you and he talked about. I hope you don't mind."

"Of course not," smiled Micah. "My life is an open book. If anyone finds anything useful from it, they are welcome to it. I have nothing to hide."

"That's probably as unusual a thing as you say Rosewood is."

Micah laughed. "I'm sure you're right. Nevertheless, it is how I try to live. How else can people really know one another and love one another than by being open and honest and transparent?"

I'd never heard a man talk like Micah Duff! To imagine that a black man who wasn't much older than me could know so much and speak with such confidence and wisdom . . . I found myself almost in awe of him!

We were walking close together now and had entered a small grove of trees between the fields. It was quiet and peaceful and we were in no hurry. It felt good to talk and share with someone who seemed to understand everything, and even seemed to know what I was thinking as I tried to say it.

"Katie and I, after we got together here," I said, "we were so young and alone and afraid, and we knew we were in a desperate situation. We tried to talk to God and do what He wanted us to. But we really didn't know what to do. I had a Bible of my mama's, but neither of us learned too much about living with God from our parents. We believed in God, but we didn't know how to live like Christians. We tried, and Katie and I talked about it a lot. But I've still got so many questions."

Micah laughed. "That's good," he said. "Asking questions is how we learn more about God. What kinds of questions?"

"I don't know—like what Christians are supposed to feel like and maybe questions about God too, and what He's like. It is confusing sometimes. A lot of what you read in the Bible doesn't seem to make much sense."

Micah laughed again. "You like to say what you mean!"

"Why shouldn't I? It doesn't make sense not to."

"I agree. But most people don't. They try to hide

the things that don't make sense to them. But the Bible has things in it that confuse everyone. Why not admit that being a Christian is confusing at times? At least that's the way I see it."

"What confuses you about being a Christian, Micah?" I asked.

He thought a minute.

"That's a perceptive question, Mayme," he said. "Hmm . . . I think I would say that life's hard, that things get spread around so unevenly, even randomly. Why is life hard for some and others seem to have it easy? That's a hard question. But a Christian just has to take life as it comes and then live in those circumstances as God would have him, whether they are easy circumstances or hard ones."

"Do you think God tries to make circumstances easier for Christian people?"

"That's another really good question," said Micah. "If He did, that would sure be a reason to be a Christian—knowing God would be making life easier for us. I've thought about that a lot."

"And . . ." I said.

"I don't think God does try to improve our circumstances."

"Why not?"

"Because outward circumstances are not of primary interest to Him."

"What is, then?"

"The inner condition of our hearts. He cares what kind of people we become on the inside. I don't

think He is too concerned about what kinds of events or situations are used to make us into people that are His children. Maybe even the hard circumstances work better for that. Maybe as God looks at it, the whole thing is upside down from how we are looking at it. Maybe hard times are actually better for us, and that's why God doesn't always make the lives of Christians smooth and easy."

"I've never thought about that before," I said.

"It's a little different way of looking at the Christian life, all right. But it's helped me to keep the hardships of my own life in perspective."

I wanted to ask more, but somehow the time didn't feel right. And the fact that we had almost reached the cows put an end to the discussion.

I opened the gate to the field and walked around one side to get behind them. The cows gradually headed through the gate and back toward the barn. Micah and I followed, walking slowly behind them.

"It seems to me that God must have answered most of the questions you said you had earlier," said Micah.

"Why do you say that?" I asked.

"Because God's life is obvious in you," Micah replied. "I sensed immediately that you were God's daughter."

"Thank you," I said. "That's nice of you to say."

"I mean it. You are an extraordinary young lady, Mayme. It's good to talk to someone . . . do you know what I'm trying to say? . . . who understands, both

what it means to be black, but the greater issue of what's involved in being a Christian. Thank you, Mayme. There are not many people I've been able to talk to like this."

As we emerged from the road through the trees, with the barn in sight in the distance, one of the cows got stubborn about going back. Suddenly she bolted into the adjoining field of growing corn and lumbered clumsily across it, then stopped and began munching away on the small green stalks.

"Hey, watch that one!" shouted Micah.

"I've got her!" I yelled. I tore after her, trying to swing wide and get behind her, but she saw me and ran off again in another direction. Micah saw my dilemma and ran to try to cut the ornery thing off while the other cows continued to meander toward the house and barn.

But as awkward as cows look when they're running, they can still run faster than people! It took us both five or ten minutes running back and forth and dashing to cut off one line of escape or another to get the stupid thing back with the herd.

Just as we had nearly joined the others as they moved methodically along, the rebellious cow tried once more to make a brief dash for it. Afraid that the whole thing was about to start all over again—and I was tired!—I sprinted as hard as I could after it.

As I did I slipped as I ran through a patch of mud.

"Oh no!" I cried as I sprawled onto my face.

Micah came running just as the cow thought better of another flight and came back and fell in line behind the rest.

"I'm all right!" I said. "I just lost my balance."

He reached down and helped me to my feet.

"You're a mess!" he laughed.

"What do you expect?" I laughed playfully. "I've been chasing cows. And at least I won't be tracking in cow manure on my shoes."

Micah glanced down at his boots.

"Ugh!" he exclaimed.

"Now who's the mess!" I said. "Come on!"

I broke into a run as Micah hurried to join me and we raced back to the cows. By the time we neared the barn, we were walking together again, though still laughing and teasing each other about our respective messes. A playful spirit seemed to get into us both.

Papa walked up as we herded the cows toward the barn. He looked at us up and down, head to foot, then shook his head with a smile.

"You ready for some help with the milking?" he asked me. "Or were you planning to teach Micah here the fine art of pulling milk out of a cow's udder?"

"This refined Northern boy!" I said, nodding toward Micah with pretended seriousness. "I don't think he could!"

"Now I ask you, Mr. Daniels," said Micah, "is this fair? She has been giving me a hard time ever since . . . well, I admit I stepped where I shouldn't

have. But I did help bring these ladies in from the pasture. For all she knows, I am as experienced at milking cows as she. But she gives me no chance. She ridicules me and rejects my humblest and sincerest efforts to be helpful!"

"Yeah, you're right," smiled Papa. "She's an ornery one, all right. I'd stay clear of her if I were you!"

"Perhaps I should do exactly that," said Micah. He turned and began to walk away as if I had hurt his feelings.

"So, Mr. Micah Duff," I called after him, "how many cows have you milked?"

"For your information, young lady," he called back, "I have never milked a cow in my life."

"I thought so!"

"But if you can do it, I can do it!"

"Ha!" I laughed. "It's not so easy."

"Well, I'd stay for a lesson, but I told Mr. Daniels I'd help him shoe the new horses. At least someone around here appreciates my skills. . . ." He threw his hands in the air and again walked off. "Rejection . . . rejection! Wherever I go it's the same!" he said as he went. "Women playing with men's feelings like they were toys."

I kept laughing as Papa and I got the cows inside and into their stalls. I stood up after tying the last cow to her rail and turned. There was Papa staring at me.

"What are you grinning about?" he asked.

"I'm not grinning about anything," I said.

"Sure you are. There's a smile on your face a mile wide."

"Then . . . I don't know, maybe it's just—I don't know. I'll quit smiling then. Let's get this milking done."

He still kept staring at me and a curious expression came over his face.

"You're not sweet on him, are you, Mayme?"

"What . . . on who?"

"Who do you think—Micah Duff!"

I was glad it was dark in the barn because I could feel my face burning bright red.

"Of course not," I said, ". . . why would you think that?"

"You sure could fool me!" chuckled Papa.

"But I think Katie might be," I added.

"Whatever you say's fine by me," Papa said. "But I've never seen a look like that on your face before. If it means what I think it means, you'd better tell Jeremiah before it goes too far . . . although, I don't know, he and Emma would probably do fine with each other too."

"Papa, what are you saying!"

"Nothing, only that things are getting a little too mixed up around here for me to keep track of."

❧ ✵ ❧

Though no one had seen them, two others had been watching Mayme and Micah coming toward the barn behind the dozen cows. They had also heard their playful banter and had drawn a similar conclusion about its meaning as had Templeton Daniels.

From her upstairs window, Emma had been watching ever since they had run after the stray cow. For reasons she did not fully understand herself, she continued to stand at the window as they drew nearer and nearer, until at last she could hear their voices as they laughed and chided each other.

Katie was right. Micah Duff was just about as good-looking a man as she'd ever seen. If only William could have a daddy like him or Jeremiah someday.

But seeing the two having such fun together confused Emma's mind and heart. Finally she turned away from the window, wondering where Jeremiah was.

Where Jeremiah was as the herd of cows and their two herdsmen made their way toward him was, in fact, inside the barn.

He had been cleaning out the last of the previous night's straw and muck in preparation for the evening milking when the unmistakable sound of Mayme's high-pitched laughter carried over the fields toward him. A pang shot through him as he suspected its cause. He crept to the door and looked out from the shadows. There were Micah and Mayme a hundred yards away. He shrunk back a few steps and watched their approach.

Then he remembered the stalls. He needed to get them finished!

Quickly he turned back inside, grabbed the pitchfork again, and hastily completed the last of the stalls and spread them with fresh straw. He had just finished when he heard Mayme's father outside. Every word between the three of them about Micah's competence at milking reached his ears.

With the first clopping of hooves on the hard brick floor toward the stalls, Jeremiah suddenly realized he did not want to be seen. He didn't want to embarrass Mayme—or himself. But it was too late to get out. He glanced about, then hurried to the depths of the barn and slunk down in the darkness behind several bales of hay.

The voices he heard following the cows in, though he could not see their faces, were ones he knew intimately—

". . . *not sweet on him, are you Mayme?*" came Templeton's voice through the darkness.

It was all Jeremiah needed to hear. No amount of protestation on Mayme's part could dislodge the searing words from his brain.

". . . *better tell Jeremiah . . .*"

". . . *he and Emma'd probably do fine with each other too.*"

The words reverberated in Jeremiah's brain and he could not stop them. But he could not get up and leave until the milking was done.

For another forty minutes Jeremiah lay crouched on the floor and listened to Mayme and Templeton as they talked about Micah Duff and what an extraordinary man he was.

When they finally left, it required some stealth for Jeremiah to get out of the barn and clean himself up without being seen so that the aroma of the stalls would not betray where he had been for the past hour.

He was late for supper and had difficulty explaining his strange disappearance for the latter part of the afternoon.

He said little throughout the rest of the evening, as did Emma. The conversation between Micah Duff, Mayme, and Katie, however, flowed well enough without them.

A Trip
10

Ever since Uncle Ward had come to Rosewood with the deed to the property Katie's mama had signed over to him, he'd been a little uncomfortable knowing that he was the owner of Rosewood when he really considered that it ought to belong to Katie.

And besides that, he didn't want to run the risk of Rosewood being in jeopardy if something should happen to him. I know he and my papa talked a lot about it, and with Katie some too. Uncle Ward wanted to make some changes to the deed so that Katie and Papa—and even me—were part owners too. Uncle Ward had planned to go see the local lawyer, Mr. Sneed, about it some time back. But since none of us, especially Katie, trusted the man, Uncle Ward had put it off until now.

He announced one day that he was going into Charlotte to see a lawyer there and he wanted Katie and me and Papa to go with him. Besides changing the deed to the property so that his wasn't the only *name on it, Uncle Ward said he was going to make a will too. He wanted to make sure nothing like what happened with Katie's uncle Burchard could ever happen again. He didn't trust the local lawyer to do that either. There was a lot of bad feeling about the two Daniels brothers and their "plantation full of niggers," as the locals called Rosewood.*

Speaking for myself, I was just glad to be getting away from Micah and Jeremiah for a while!

Katie looked over at me as we left, and bounded down the road away from Rosewood behind our uncle and my papa, and smiled. She took my hand and gave it a squeeze. I think she had been feeling the awkwardness too.

What she was feeling toward Micah Duff, I didn't know. As close as Katie and I were, I wasn't ready to ask her quite yet.

❧ ✵ ❧

As Jeremiah watched the carriage bound for Charlotte disappear from sight, he too felt a strange sense of relief. Maybe now he could get his brain clear. He had thought everything with Mayme was all settled . . . until Micah had appeared. Now he wasn't sure what was going on!

Jeremiah walked into the barn to unfasten the cows from their stalls and get them outside to pasture and on with their day's business.

❧ ✵ ❧

As we went, Katie and I didn't talk too much at first. Maybe we were both absorbed with our own thoughts. I know I was! As much as I loved everyone we were leaving behind, I'd been too unsettled for the last couple of days from the things Papa had said to me to be able to think straight.

After Papa's words inside the barn, suddenly I felt shy and awkward around Micah Duff. We'd had such a good talk and such fun together. But all of a sudden I started walking around like a silent scarecrow. I know he saw the difference because he looked at me funny a time or two.

What if Papa was right? If he had noticed me behaving peculiar, had everyone else noticed too? What did Jeremiah think? Though he'd seemed to be happy whenever he was with Emma . . . maybe he hadn't noticed anything at all!

Oh, it was all so confusing! Life had been simpler when there hadn't been any young men around. And when we were younger and weren't thinking about them. But I was nineteen now and would turn twenty in August and I couldn't help it, I was thinking about them now!

So like I'd said, bouncing away from Rosewood in our nice traveling carriage, Papa and Uncle Ward in the front and me and Katie on the padded leather seat behind them, was a relief. It was just the four of us, without all the complications of everyone else. I feel a little bad for saying that, but it's what I was thinking.

The trip to Charlotte wasn't like the trips we took

with everybody every year to celebrate the end of the harvest. This was what I guess you'd call a business trip, though Katie and I had been looking forward to it almost more than we wanted to let on to the others. It didn't take long before we were talking excitedly about all we wanted to do and see and about getting to stay in a hotel room together—alone, just the two of us—and go shopping and eat in restaurants. We were excited anticipating what a good time we were going to have.

⁂

Meanwhile, in the kitchen in the lull following the hubbub of breakfast and the departure of the four, Micah sat at the table lingering over his last cup of coffee as Emma cleared up around him. Josepha had disappeared to the chicken coop.

"So what do you think, Emma?" said Micah, taking a sip from his cup, "—here we are—you and me, a couple of blacks, sitting like this in a white man's plantation house, another couple of blacks outside . . . and not a white person anywhere to be seen. It's just like Henry said when he first told me about Rosewood—a kind of *unusual* place! It's pretty remarkable for Ward and Templeton to trust all the rest of you like they do."

"I neber thought 'bout it like dat, Mister Duff—you reckon dey really do, like you say, *trust* us?"

"It appears so to me, Emma. There's nobody here but us Negroes. I would say that's a pretty high level of trust!"

"Dat's good, ain't it, Mister Duff?"

"It's always good when people trust each other, Emma. At least I think so."

"What ef people's bad, Mister Duff? Dere's bad folks dat'll take advantage ob a person's trust."

"Well, that's true," nodded Micah. "I suppose that's the chance you take when you trust people. But I think I'd still rather be a trusting person than a suspicious one. It takes more character to trust than it does to be suspicious."

"*Character*—whatchu mean by dat?"

"Inner strength, or maybe maturity," said Micah. He paused and thought for a few seconds. "Being a good person," he added, "strong, selfless—those are qualities of character, Emma."

"You mean like Miz Katie and Mayme."

He looked at her deeply, then slowly smiled. "Yes." He nodded. "Mayme and Katie are certainly young women of character. But they aren't the only ones."

"I know—you's be meanin' Mister Templeton," said Emma. "He's a right fine man."

"Yes, he is," smiled Micah. For now he kept what else he was thinking to himself.

"How you git ter be so much like a white man, Mister Duff?" asked Emma.

Micah threw his head back and roared with laughter. "How do you mean, Emma?" he said, still chuckling.

"You talks so good, an' you's smart an' always sayin' dose important kind er things."

Again Micah laughed. "Why can't a black man be just as intelligent as a white man?"

"I don' know," said Emma. "I jes' neber met one dat wuz."

"Well, I don't know if I am or not, Emma," laughed Micah. "All I try to be is myself and be the best myself I can be."

Already, with the others gone from Rosewood less than an hour, Emma had begun to feel more relaxed around Micah Duff. Without realizing it, she found herself gradually opening up and talking more freely.

"But saying important kinds of things like you said, that's not necessarily all there is to life, Emma. And besides, a person's character is formed by what a person *does* and what a person *is*, more than by what he says. You know how to do a lot of things, Emma. You're always helping someone with something. That's character too, Emma."

"You really think so?"

"Of course—it's a spirit of helpfulness."

"Mayme taught me ter do things," said Emma. "I reckon I learned ter try ter help folks from watchin' her. She taught me and Miz Katie everything. Back when I wuz a slave I wuzn't good fer nuthin' but runnin' errands. They'd always tell me to go fetch a rug or mop or go git somebody. All I eber did wuz help pretty white girls fix dere hair. But Mayme, she knows how ter do everythin'."

"But it's also who you *are*," said Micah, "that makes you a person of worth."

"I ain't worth nuthin'," said Emma. "But Mayme, dat's her, all right. She kin do things like you say, but she's a fine person too—she's about da finest person in da worl'."

Micah nodded. He did not like to leave the discussion at that, but perhaps Emma wasn't quite ready to look at herself differently. He knew such things took time.

"Well, Jake's likely got those cows out to pasture by now," he said, rising, "I suppose I better get out there and help him with that fence we are going to put in."

* * *

As we bounded along the road south between Greens Crossing and Charlotte, Katie and I found ourselves talking about Micah Duff, though I was still too embarrassed to tell her what Papa had said that day. But Katie was going on and on about him like she'd never met anyone so wonderful in her life. And I suppose she hadn't . . . and neither had I, come to think of it.

Before she'd only said how good-looking he was, and I hadn't really taken her too seriously—I mean in thinking that she might actually be interested in him . . . for herself, I mean. But now with the way she was carrying on about him, I began to wonder if she was more interested than I had realized.

It didn't occur to me that the two men in front were probably hearing every word we said. All of a sudden, Uncle Ward turned around.

"Say, Kathleen," he said, "that Micah Duff is quite a young man. He seems fond of you too."

Katie's face turned red as a beet. That's when I knew that his words must have hit pretty close to home.

"He's . . . oh, he's nice to everyone, Uncle Ward," Katie stammered.

"Yeah, maybe . . . but you never know—you're a

pretty fine-looking young lady."

Papa turned around and glanced at us, then threw me a little wink and got that twinkle in his eye that meant he was having fun with somebody.

What was he thinking, I wondered!

After that Katie didn't mention Micah Duff once more the whole way.

Complications in Charlotte and Elsewhere

11

JEREMIAH AND MICAH WERE BOTH BARE-CHESTED and dripping with sweat from the hot sun that same afternoon as they dug holes and set the fence posts for a new section of fence across one of the grazing pastures. It was one of their first chances to work alone together for a full day since Micah had arrived. He had asked about Jeremiah's years since they had parted long ago, and how he had come to find Henry. Most of the past two hours Micah had spent listening to Jeremiah's story.

"Everything you are telling me is truly remarkable, Jake," he said. "The Lord was guiding your steps here just as surely as He was mine."

"I reckon dat's so," nodded Jeremiah. "But as good as it's been wiff my daddy, an' as appreciative as I am fo his kindness toward me, I still habn't been altogether at ease in my mind all dis time on account er runnin' out on you like I done."

"That was a long time ago, Jake—think nothing of it."

"But I regret it, Duff. You wuz good ter me when I needed help, an' I been wantin' ter ax yo forgiveness eber since—so now I'm axin' for it. I's sorry, Duff."

"Thank you, Jake," said Micah, looking deep into Jeremiah's eyes. "As far as forgiving you is concerned, I did that the day you left. I never thought ill of you then, and I think all the more of you now to see how you've grown into such a fine young man."

"Thank you, Duff."

As Jeremiah and Micah were working a half mile away from the house, Josepha returned from her chores outside. She found Emma in the kitchen. Emma had been thinking about her conversation earlier in the morning with Micah Duff. A smile had unconsciously come to her lips. Josepha saw it as she entered and half suspected the cause. A scowl spread over her face in response to Emma's smile.

"Whatchu lookin' at me like dat fo, Josepha?" said Emma. "You lookin' daggers at me!"

"You jes' watch yo'self, girl," said Josepha.

"Whatchu mean by dat?"

"Jes' dat dere's two fetchin' young men out dere dat's bof got eyes fo you."

"Whatchu talkin' bout! Ain't nobody got eyes fer me!"

"All I's sayin' is don't you git yo'self in ober dat fool head ob yers agin. Don't you go back ter da way you used ter be."

"I ain't neber goin' back ter dose days, Josepha. You oughter know dat. I's different now."

"I hope dat's so, girl. But folks don't change as much as dey think dey do."

"Well, I done learned my lesson."

"Dat's all well an' good, and women says dat all da time," persisted Josepha. "But den a man comes along an' dey forgets agin, lose dere heads and gits foolish all ober agin. Women are da biggest fools in da worl' sometimes, how dey lose dere heads ober some men dat ain't got but one thing on dere mind."

"Oh, but Jeremiah and Micah—dey ain't like dat!"

"Eben men like Jeremiah and Micah got eyes in dere heads."

"Not for no dummy like me with a pickaninny on her hip. Besides, dey bof got eyes fo Mayme."

Josepha grunted and muttered something about the "blind foolishness of young folks" that Emma couldn't quite make out.

Leaving his shovel standing in the hole he'd just dug, Jeremiah straightened, pushing his hand into the small of his back to work out the knots from being bent over for so long.

"I reckon dat's 'bout enough fo today," he said.

Beside him, Micah also straightened. "Amen," he agreed. Micah stood tall, leaning on the handle of his shovel and staring off in the direction of the river. "Say, how's the fishing in that river?"

Jeremiah followed his gaze. "Dere's a couple deep pools where dere's always some catfish," he replied.

"Let's go get some!"

"Well, it's late enough in da day, I reckon. The sun ain't so hot now. Might be we cud catch a few."

"Is there enough time before supper?"

"Always enough time fer fishin'!" Jeremiah grinned. "I'll go fetch two poles."

Micah took Jeremiah's shovel and hoisted both over his shoulder.

"How 'bout you dig some worms out ob da garden?" Jeremiah said.

"Great—more digging." Micah smiled, but set off quickly on his task.

A short time later, the two young men walked across the field toward the river, their damp work shirts tied around their waists. Sweat still gleamed from their bare arms and chests and mud still clung to their boots and pant legs. A bucket swung from one of Jeremiah's hands and two cane poles were slung over his shoulder. Micah carried an old baking-powder can full of dirt and worms.

As they approached the bank, Jeremiah untied his shirt and tossed it across the bent trunk of a tree. The tree's exposed roots grasped the bank while its misshapen trunk curved sharply and reached out across the river, a few feet above its slow current. It was Jeremiah's favorite spot to fish. Dipping the bucket full of water, Jeremiah said, "Mayme and me came—"

Abruptly he stopped.

Micah looked at him closely. "You two sweet on each other, Jake?"

Jeremiah stared out at the sun, where it hung lazy over the treetops in the western sky. Then he shrugged. "We came here to talk, dat's all."

He handed Micah a pole and a new subject. "We

should hab brought William wiff us," he said. "Dat boy loves ter fish."

"Good idea. Next time we will."

Micah held out the baking-powder can. Jeremiah wiggled his fingers inside and came out with a nice fat worm. He laced it on his hook. "Now, let's git down ter business."

Soon both men were standing at the river's edge, baited lines in the water.

"Now, what you wants to do," Jeremiah said, "is give da line plenty er slack. Let da worm go deep."

Jeremiah watched as Micah did as he suggested.

"I hardly ever went fishin' till I come here. Slaves don' git much time fer fishin'."

Micah nodded, eyes on his line. "I tried fishing in the Chicago River once with nothing but some twine and a twisted-up hatpin I'd found."

"Any luck?"

"I snagged an old hat." Micah shrugged. "Guess I had the right hook for it. Kept my little head warm all winter."

Jeremiah grinned. "Dat's better den we's doing right now."

They stood for several minutes without speaking, the silence broken only by the occasional birdcall.

"William is some boy," Micah said after a time. "Imagine what life will be like for him. He won't grow up on the street like I did, nor as a slave as you did."

"Dat's right."

"No one will ever take a whip to him or take him from his mama."

Jeremiah nodded. "He kin fish and play instead of workin' sunup to sundown. When I wuz his age I was already workin' fo da master. Not in da fields, but around da place, stacking wood and slopping pigs."

"William can be anything he wants. Do things you and I never dreamed of. Maybe even go to college. He could even be a doctor or lawyer someday."

"You really think dat cud happen, Duff?"

"I don't see why not. Everything is changing for blacks."

Jeremiah thought back to his recent near-hanging at the hands of an angry lynch mob. "Not everything," he said.

Suddenly, Micah's line went taut. "I've got something!" he said. After about a minute he hauled in a green, whiskered, nine-inch catfish.

"Beginner's luck," laughed Jeremiah.

Micah extracted the hook from the cat's lip and dumped the slippery creature into the bucket.

"Didn't even get my worm," he said, then cast his line back into the river.

Several minutes later Micah's line went taut again.

"Oh, man, got me a big one this time!" he shouted, excited as a boy. "But I think he's wrapped my line around one of those branches."

Jeremiah looked up, and Micah nodded toward the bent tree. Struggling to keep the slack out of his line, Micah stepped up onto the trunk and walked a few feet out over the water, trying to get closer to the place where his line was snagged.

"I'll get you yet. Don't you think I won't," Micah cheerfully called down toward the water. "Micah Duff always lands his catch."

Micah jerked the pole, then leaned forward to angle the

line away from the submerged branches. Suddenly he lost his balance and fell headlong into the river.

Jeremiah couldn't help bursting into laughter as Micah hit the water—pole, pants, boots and all.

Duff came up sputtering. "Guess that's what I get for bragging," he shouted, trying to catch his breath.

"Cudn't happen to a nicer feller, I'd say," Jeremiah said, still chuckling. He stepped out onto the tree with practiced ease and grinned down at Micah.

"Think it's funny, do you, Jake?"

"Dat I do."

"You're just mad cause I caught all the fish and you got skunked."

"Looks to me like dat last fish caught *you*. Hook, line, and sinker."

"Yeah?" Micah reached low and splashed a full arm-load of water up at Jeremiah, drenching his pants legs. "How about that?"

"Feels good. I's still hot from digging."

"Then this ought to feel even better." Micah jumped up and pulled Jeremiah off the tree, sending him sprawling into the river.

It was Jeremiah's turn to come up sputtering. He lunged for Micah and dunked him under the water.

"Yer right, dat do feel good," he said when Micah resurfaced. "I don't know why we didn't just jump in the water in da first place."

❦ ✲ ❦

We'd left Rosewood as early as we could that day, but even traveling at a pretty good clip we didn't get to Charlotte till two or three that afternoon. Uncle Ward had made an appointment with a lawyer for late that afternoon. He wanted to get the business out of the way first before we went to the hotel we'd stayed at before and then spend the next couple of days having fun.

I don't know what I'd figured, that he'd go into the man's office alone, or maybe with my papa. But he wanted all four of us to go up in the building to see the lawyer with him, even me.

It was a fancy office, the finest I'd ever been in, with dark wood walls and paintings and leather chairs. It even smelled expensive!

We all sat down. The man looked at me a time or two with an unpleasant expression, like he didn't like the idea of a black person being in his office.

"Like I told you in my letter, Mr. Snyder," Uncle Ward began, "we're all kin here and we own a plantation north of here that's sitting on about seventy or eighty acres. My name's on the deed, but I want to get it changed so that all our names are on it together, or make a will or something so that if something happens to me, the property will go to my brother here, and the girls."

"The . . . girls?" Mr. Snyder repeated, glaring at me. "Surely you don't mean her too." He nodded his head in my direction.

"I do mean her, Mr. Snyder. She happens to be my niece."

"And my daughter," added my papa with a little annoyance in his voice.

"I see," said the lawyer. "And just what is it you want me to do—I could draw up a new deed, and a will—whatever it is you want."

"Maybe both, then," said Uncle Ward. "Can you make a new deed with all our names on it?"

"That can be done. In what shares of ownership?"

"Hmm . . . yeah, now that I think on it—equal shares might not be altogether right, would it?"

"I would think not. Surely a black girl—"

"That's not what I meant," interrupted Uncle Ward. "The place belongs more to Katie than to any of the rest of us."

"Uncle Ward, I don't want to own more—" began Katie.

"Can you make the share of ownership anything?" Uncle Ward asked the lawyer.

"I suppose so," replied the lawyer.

"Then it ought to be mostly yours, Kathleen, and Templeton's."

"But, Uncle Ward," said Katie, "Mama gave the deed to you. And your money saved Rosewood. I won't let you make me more owner than you. If you are determined to put all our names on the deed, then that ought to be enough."

Uncle Ward thought a minute, and slowly nodded.

"Maybe you're right, Kathleen," he said. "Four equal shares—that may be the best way."

"But surely," began the lawyer again, "you don't

mean to suggest that a colored girl—"

"Look, Mr. Snyder, I thought we had all that settled—she is not a colored girl, she is a girl, a young woman, and my niece. She is as much a part of this family as the rest of us."

"But, Mr. Ward," I now said a little timidly, "the man is right—I don't deserve—"

"Mayme," interrupted my papa, "you let Ward and me decide what's fair here. You two girls worked to keep Rosewood going when he and I were off gallivanting around the country. You and Kathleen deserve as much as either of us. Isn't that right, Ward?"

"That's right."

Katie and I looked at each other, but neither of us spoke again.

When we left the man's office half an hour later, Mr. Snyder had instructions to draw up a new deed to Rosewood in four equal shares, and single wills for my papa and Uncle Ward to leave their portions to Katie and me when they died.

And that's how I got to be a one-fourth owner of a big plantation in Shenandoah County. I still can hardly believe it.

Our business completed, we left for the hotel.

❧ ✵ ❧

The following morning was ironing day. Emma and Josepha stoked up the kitchen stove good and hot with wood right after breakfast and got their two irons heating and kettles of water boiling for steam. Henry went into the livery for the day, but Jeremiah didn't have to work at Mr. Watson's. He and Micah left for the pasture with a wagon of supplies to finish digging the fence holes and setting the posts in place.

By midmorning the kitchen itself was a steam-filled oven from the heat of the stove and steam and irons . . . and it was going to be a hot day outside too. Emma and Josepha were both dripping with sweat.

"Lan' sakes, I gots ter git a breath of air!" exclaimed Josepha, setting the iron in her hand back on the stove. She folded the trousers she had finished and placed them on the pile. "We gots ter open some doors and windows and git some air in dis place! Whew!"

She walked out just as Jeremiah bounded up the stairs of the porch.

"It's parful hot in dere, Jeremiah," said Josepha.

"I kin see dat," he grinned. "You look like you been standin' under a water pump."

"What I looks like's none er yo neber mind!"

"Den I's jes' pop in an' git somefin' fer me and Micah ter eat."

"You jes' had breakfast! Whatchu be needin' wiff mo food so soon?"

"We's growin' boys, Josepha. We gots ter eat."

"You grow much more, son, and you'll be a blamed giant!"

Jeremiah laughed and continued inside.

"Howdy, Emma!" he said.

"Now you finish dem dresses like Mayme and me

taught you," Josepha called back to Emma through the open door.

"Yes'm . . . hi, Jeremiah."

"Anythin' ter eat aroun' here?"

"Help yourself—dere's always milk an' cheese and bread an' you kin look in da pantry ef you want."

"Mayme taught you to iron?" said Jeremiah as he got out a loaf of bread and sat down to slice it.

"Dat she did."

"I thought you wuz a house slave, not her."

"I wuz, but I wuzn't too smart," said Emma. "Reckon Mayme taught herself here at Rosewood. Mayme had ter teach me everythin' after I come here. She even taught me ter be a mama."

"You's a good mama, Emma. I doubt she had to teach you dat."

"Well, I don't know, I wuz a ninny when I come here—jes' a babblin' ninny."

"I doubt it wuz as bad as all dat!" laughed Jeremiah.

"Oh, wuzn't it! You din't know me den!"

"Well, it don't matter. You ain't one now."

"You really think so?" asked Emma.

"Of course, Emma. Besides it don't matter none, anyway. Sometimes we gotta learn from folks dat's smarter'n us. Maybe dey're better'n us, but den maybe dey got sent ter us ter help us git better ourselves, who can say? Look at me—I wuz a mess too. I reckon I learned as much from Micah as you done from Mayme. He taught me a lot 'bout life too afore I got here, though I wuz too stupid ter know it at da time."

He paused and glanced over at Emma where she stood

at the stove, switching irons in her hands.

"You want ter go out an' sit on da porch an' hab a glass er tea, Emma?" he asked.

"Dat sounds right fine, Jeremiah. But Josepha'll git after me fo not finishin' dis dress er Miz Katie's."

"You let me take care er Josepha!" laughed Jeremiah. "Katie won't be needin' dat dress fo days. An' it's hot an' steamy an' ef Josepha needs some fresh air, why not you? Come on out ter da porch wiff me, Emma. You pour us some tea an' I'll go fetch us a couple chunks er ice from da icehouse."

When Josepha walked back toward the house ten minutes later from the direction of the outhouse, she heard laughter and conversation coming from the porch. As she came around the side of the house, there sat Jeremiah and Emma on the porch bench together, each holding a cold glass of tea.

"What you two doin' dere?" she said.

"Jes' havin' some tea an' talk, Josepha," answered Jeremiah.

"I thought I tol' you ter finish up dem dresses," she said to Emma.

"An' I tol' her Katie's not gwine be needin' dat dress anytime soon an' ter come out an' hab some tea wiff me," said Jeremiah.

"Well, dat ain't none er yo concern dat I can see, Jeremiah," retorted Josepha. "I told her ter do it, an' dat's dat. Come on inside, Emma."

"Now jes' you wait a minute, Josepha," said Jeremiah. "Ain't nobody round here nobody's slave no more. Or ain't you heard dat? Who put you over Emma dat you kin boss her aroun' like dat? How old are you, Emma?" he said, turning to Emma.

"I ain't sure exactly—I think somethin' like twenty-one."

"Dere, you hear dat, Josepha—Emma's a growed-up lady an' she don't need no bossin' from nobody, 'less it's Katie herself or Mister Templeton or Mister Ward, cause we's *all* working for dem. But she don't need no bossin' from you, an' dat's da truf."

"Humph!" mumbled Josepha, too surprised at Jeremiah's words to say a word.

"So she jes' gwine sit here with me a spell longer," Jeremiah went on, "an' ef you don't like it, den maybe Emma an' me'll jes' go fer a walk down by da ribber an' you kin finish dat ironin' yo'self!"

With a look of speechless shock on her face, Josepha continued inside, muttering to herself what was best no one else heard.

Emma looked over at Jeremiah and slowly a smile spread across her face. She leaned toward him. "Dat wuz brave, Jeremiah!" she whispered. "I'd neber dare talk ter her like dat!"

"Aw, Josepha don't scare me wiff all dat talk like she does."

Emma started giggling as she remembered the look on Josepha's face. "I don't think *anybody's* eber talked to her like dat, except maybe Mistress McSimmons."

"Well, I reckon I'd better git back ter Micah," said Jeremiah, gulping down what was left in his glass. He stood. "Thanks fo da tea, Emma."

"Don't forgit da bread an' milk you wuz takin'."

"Oh . . . yeah, thanks."

Jeremiah hurried back inside, grabbing up the parcel of food, dashed over and gave Josepha a quick kiss on the cheek before she could object, then darted from the house.

"Bye, Emma," he called after him.

Emma sat for a minute more on the porch, slowly sipping her glass of tea, thinking about how good it felt to have a man stand up for her. Slowly she rose and went back into the kitchen where Josepha was waiting for her in silence.

Late in the afternoon Emma heard a shriek and knew instantly that it had come from William. In terror she ran from the house, frantically looking every which way to see where the sound had come from.

Another wild yell sounded. It had come from behind the barn! Her heart leapt into her throat as she thought of the woodpile out there. What if a rat or a snake had come out from hiding and bit him!

She tore from the house and rounded the corner of the barn just as a third shriek burst from her son's lips.

Emma stopped at the sound and stood gaping at the sight in front of her.

There was Micah jogging around in a wide circle, William on his shoulders laughing with delight.

"Look, Mama!" he called to Emma. "I's got me a horsey!"

Micah glanced toward her and smiled broadly. As Emma's fear subsided she could not help breaking into laughter herself to see William having such fun.

"He's gettin' too big fo me ter gib him rides like dat!" she said.

"He'll be on a real horse before long," rejoined Micah, cantering over to where Emma stood beaming.

"This is quite a boy you've got, Emma," he said as he slowed. "You ought to be real proud."

"I reckon I is at dat."

"You've done a good job with him."

"I jes' want him ter hab da best life he deserves."

"You deserve a good life too, Emma."

"Me, I ain't nuthin'. I want him ter hab better'n me."

"Well, you both deserve a good life."

"Whatever I got, I owe to Miz Katie and Mayme."

"Hey, horsey, gid-up . . . gid-up!" called William, growing impatient with their talk.

Micah laughed and began running again across the ground.

Emma stood watching and William continued to call out to her, enjoying his ride ten times more with his mama now watching his daring adventure.

The unexpected sound of a carriage driving up behind them interrupted the ride and laughter. They ran around, William still on Micah's shoulders, to the front of the barn to see Ward, Templeton, Katie, and Mayme approaching.

❧ ✵ ☙

"Whatchu doin' home so soon?" said Emma, running up to greet us. "You jes' left yesterday!"

We climbed down from the wagon, weary after the long two days riding to Charlotte and back.

Josepha came out of the house, dish towel in hand with a look of bewilderment on her face just like Emma's and Micah's. The only one who didn't seem to see anything unusual in our early return was William.

As Micah set him down on the ground he ran over to give Katie and me hugs as if we'd been gone a week.

"Let's just say things didn't go as we'd planned," said my papa, pulling down the carpetbags. "Things have changed since we were all there."

"What happened?" asked Micah.

"The hotel where we usually stay has changed their policy," said my papa irritably. "They wouldn't let Kathleen and Mayme share a room. Made me so mad I almost lost my temper."

"Why didn't you go someplace else?"

"We did, but it was the same story everywhere—either no blacks at all, or separate accommodation for blacks. We searched the whole town but could find no place to stay. Reconstruction they call it . . . the New South."

"What did you do?" asked Micah.

"It was getting late and we were angry and tired and frustrated and finally just decided to come home. We drove an hour out of the city under the moon, then slept alongside the road—nearly froze to death since we didn't think to take blankets, then got up at sunrise and came the rest of the way."

"But it wasn't a total loss," said Katie. "Look at this book we bought in a bookshop in the city." She

held up a book by some fellows called the Brothers Grimm. "I can't wait to read it."

Emma followed Katie and me inside while Micah helped Papa with our bags, and Uncle Ward tended to the horse and carriage.

Master and Mistress

12

William McSimmons had not been sitting around doing nothing in the matter of trying to find out what had happened to the result of his dalliance five years earlier with one of his father's house slaves.

That the lame-brained girl had run off and disappeared and not been seen or heard from again gave him hope at first that perhaps she was dead and the child with her. Or, if not dead, so far away that he needn't worry about her popping up again at an inconvenient time.

But in his heart of hearts, he couldn't help but worry. He had a bad feeling. What he felt came from no guilty conscience. How much of a conscience he had at all in the matter was doubtful. The fool girl had been colored. What did it matter what happened to *her*? He was just afraid of getting found out. If his secret was discovered, it would doom any chance he had for a political future. North Carolina voters were not quite ready to elect a man with an illegitimate black child on his resume.

"Have you thought any more about when you will

make your formal announcement and first speech?" Mistress McSimmons asked.

"I'm thinking early summer," her husband replied. "There's no hurry. Everyone already knows. I thought we would wait until the weather is pleasant. It will give you the opportunity to play the hostess with a real nice Carolina garden party—just like before the war."

"Then we should begin planning it," she said. "What about that brat of yours that's wandering around God knows where? Have you cleared that up yet?"

McSimmons turned a dark look on his wife.

"You don't really think it's going to turn up now, after all this time?"

"I want to take no chances."

"If someone had any intention of trying—"

"Look, William," she interrupted, "I will not be made a fool of in public. I told you before and I will tell you again—do something about it so that we do not have to spend our lives wondering. I will not put on a lavish lawn party with every influential politician and plantation owner for miles, and their wives, only to have some colored wench sneak in and walk up to you, hold out a child in a blanket, and say, 'Here, this colored baby is yours!'"

"Don't be ridiculous, Charlotte. If the child's even still alive, it wouldn't be a baby by this time."

"All the more reason. I tell you, William, I will not be humiliated. I refuse to be haunted by your, shall we say, *indiscretion* for the rest of my life. You figure out a way to deal with it once and for all, or you can count me out of your political ambitions. When I go to Washington it will not be to have myself talked about in connection with such sordid matters. I will not be made a spectacle of."

William McSimmons walked into Sheriff Jenkins' office in Oakwood. He made sure the door closed behind him, then sat down.

"Bill," said the sheriff.

"Sam," nodded McSimmons. "What can you tell me about those two Northerners I've been hearing about—the ones causing all the trouble."

"You mean the ones with the coloreds?"

"That's them."

"The Daniels brothers," nodded the sheriff. "They're no carpetbaggers, that's for sure, but even worse if you ask me. I've had words with them a time or two."

"They dangerous?"

"Naw—couple of sissies who seem to think niggers oughta be treated like everyone else. If you got trouble with them, why don't you come out one night with me and the boys? We can take care of things. We been there a time or two already."

"I can't afford to get involved in any of that," said McSimmons. "I've got to be respectable, you know, if I'm going to get to Washington. My wife's putting me in three-piece suits—"

"I can see that!" laughed Jenkins.

"That's not the worst of it!" rejoined McSimmons. "She's got me going to social functions, kissing babies, letting old women fawn over me—it's dreadful. But I suppose such is the life of the politician, and Charlotte's been hankering to be a politician's wife ever since she met me."

"No more whipping the darkies out behind the barn, eh?"

"I'm afraid all that fun is gone," answered McSimmons with a sigh. "Respectability is all I have to look forward to—the boredom of respectability."

"Then what's going on between you and the Daniels brothers?" asked Jenkins.

"Nothing much . . . a personal matter. Is it true what they say about the darkies at the place?"

"It's true—more niggers than whites—girls, kids, an old sow who used to be one of your slaves, even old Henry Patterson's taken up with them."

"Kids too, huh?"

"That's what I hear."

"Black or white?"

"Don't know. I've never actually laid eyes on any myself—it was night when I paid them a visit."

"I get your meaning, Sam," grinned McSimmons. "You know . . . it would really help me out to know more of what's going on there."

The sheriff's eyebrows rose, but he quickly masked his speculation. "If I hear anything, I'll let you know."

The would-be politician rose. "Thanks, Sam," he said. "And, uh . . . this little conversation will stay just between the two of us, won't it?"

"I've already forgotten you were here at all," replied the sheriff.

Sometimes It Hurts to Be Black

13

After Jeremiah and Henry had come to live in the cabin at Rosewood, and all that Jeremiah and I had been through together and the promises we'd made to each other, I felt a little funny about going down to his and Henry's cabin alone. Somehow it didn't really seem right, things being the way they were between us and all.

So for some time Emma had been in the habit of cleaning up their place once a week and gathering up the laundry and tidying the place up. At first, after Micah Duff came, she seemed a little reluctant but she kept going down and cleaning up as usual.

That was what she was doing late one morning the day after our return from the city. Lunch was ready and the men were all back from town and chores.

"Where's Emma an' William?" asked Josepha as she set a beef roast on the table.

"She's down at the cabins, remember, Josepha?" I said.

"Somebody go fetch her," said Josepha. "She must not hab heard da bell, an' dis meat'll git cold effen we wait too long."

"I'll go," said Jeremiah. He was through the door before I had a chance to ask if he wanted me to go with him.

It was five or six minutes later when Jeremiah and Emma came walking back to the house together. But the sound I heard was little William's voice, not theirs. He was giggling and laughing so hard you could hear him from a hundred yards away.

I looked out one of the kitchen windows. There were Emma and Jeremiah walking back from the cabins, talking freely and with smiles on their faces. William was between them and they each had hold of one of his hands. They were swinging him back and forth in the air and he was laughing with glee.

Suddenly a voice sounded beside me.

"That little boy needs somebody like Jeremiah," it said.

It was Micah. I hadn't heard him walk up beside me.

"He's a good little boy," he added, "but he needs a father."

"Uh . . . yes, he loves black men, that's for sure. He lit up the day you got here."

"Yeah," smiled Micah, "I remember. But you can tell he's especially close to Jeremiah."

I didn't say anything more. What was there to

say? Micah was right. Emma, William, and Jeremiah did look awfully good together.

When lunch was over I wandered away from the house. A lot of mixed-up feelings were stirring around inside me. I walked toward the woods. I didn't realize that someone was watching me go.

It was about thirty minutes later when I heard footsteps. I expected to see Katie. No one else knew about this place. I wiped at my eyes and turned around. The smile I'd tried to force onto my face for Katie disappeared.

There stood Micah Duff.

"I, uh . . . I'm sorry," he said. "I followed you. I could tell at lunch that something was wrong. I've seen it all day. If you would rather be alone, just tell me and I'll go . . . but I thought maybe you would like to talk."

I tried to work the smile back onto my face and tell him it was all right if he stayed and to ask him if he wanted to sit down. But trying to smile just made my eyes fill up. And as for saying anything, my voice came out in a croak, and I started crying again.

Micah walked over and sat down beside me. He put his hand on my arm.

"Do you want to tell me about it?" he said softly.

"I don't know," I said, half sobbing. "I'm sorry . . . I don't usually cry . . . I don't ever cry . . . but it's just—"

I started in again. This was mortifying, to bawl like a baby in front of a man I'd only known a few weeks!

"Just what, Mayme?" said Micah. His voice was so tender and compassionate that just the sound of it calmed me down a little.

I tried to breathe in and out a time or two. But my breaths came in jerks.

"I suppose I can tell you," I said after a minute. "You would . . . probably understand . . . but I can't even tell Katie. . . . That's the worst of it, not being able to tell her . . . she and I tell each other everything, but . . . she just couldn't understand this."

"Did something happen on the trip to Charlotte?" he asked.

"Yes," I whimpered.

"Was it about the hotel?"

"Yes!" I answered, starting to cry again. "It was so awful . . . I spoiled it for them . . . but there was nothing I could do—all those people looking at them and then glancing over at me and then their faces getting such looks of disgust on them, like I was . . . like I was I don't know what! Oh, Micah—it was so humiliating. But I felt so bad for Katie and Papa and Uncle Ward. They had wanted to have a good time in the city, but they couldn't with me along. I've never felt so low, so dirty, so worthless in my life. Living at Rosewood . . . I'd forgotten how mean people can be . . . but . . ."

I turned away sobbing.

"You don't really think you spoiled it for them, Mayme . . . do you?" asked Micah.

"I don't know . . . it seemed like it. They were so disappointed."

"Don't you think they were disappointed for how you were being treated more than for themselves?"

"I'm sure you're right. Actually, after the third or fourth hotel turned us away, Papa started to get really angry at the way people were treating me."

"Have you talked to him about it?"

"No—I've been too embarrassed . . . and afraid I'd start crying," I added, looking up at Micah with a faint smile. "I didn't want anyone to see me cry. I hadn't counted on being followed!"

Micah smiled. "Sorry. I didn't know."

"I'm the strong one around here," I said. "If they saw me crying, they would think . . . well, I don't know what they would think! But yes, you're right, they were more embarrassed for me, and I suppose I was more embarrassed for them. It was so awful. Poor Katie—she felt so bad for me."

We sat for a few minutes in silence, just watching the little brook go by in front of us. I took two or three deep breaths and gradually felt myself coming back to my normal self.

"Do you know those kinds of looks white people give you?" I asked after a while. "Do you get them too?"

"All the time," replied Micah.

"Even in the North?"

"Not so much. But after the war it's been worse."

"What do you do?" I asked.

"Ignore them. What else can you do?"

"But how can you—it makes you feel so worthless to have people look at you with disgust like that."

"You have to ignore it and just be who you are."

"But how can you feel good about yourself when your skin is brown, when the whole world is looking at you in the same way they would look at a dog?"

"The whole world isn't looking at you that way," said Micah, "only ignorant, foolish people. What should you care what they think?"

"But it still sometimes hurts to be black."

"Yeah, maybe," Micah nodded. "I know the feeling, but a long time ago I had to decide what it meant to be me, *just me, not white, black, not what anyone else says or thinks I should be . . . but just me. Who I thought I was, who I really was, who God wanted me to be—that was all that mattered. Once I came to terms and made my peace with that, then I was able to live with myself no matter what anyone thought."*

"But doing that's not so easy."

"No, not easy at all," nodded Micah. "But if you're black, or brown like you say, or different in any way, you've got no choice. You've got to ignore the looks and just be who you are. Otherwise you'll get angry and bitter yourself and then you're no better than they are. An angry black person is just as bad as an arrogant white person. I wouldn't want to be either."

❦

Sam Jenkins had been giving a lot of thought to the

conversation in his office three days earlier with William McSimmons.

Something peculiar was going on. What . . . he couldn't be sure.

But he had the feeling McSimmons had more on his mind than what he'd said. And it wouldn't do anyone in this town any harm to be on William McSimmons' good side if he got lucky and made it to Congress.

He didn't know what kind of men Congress wanted. Sam Jenkins could think of a dozen men within ten miles that had twice the intelligence and three times the horse sense of William McSimmons, including the boy's father.

Old man McSimmons was a straight-talking, hard-working, good, fair man. His son was a hothead and an idiot. But he had married an heiress and social climber who had dressed him up in a three-piece suit and shoved him into politics. Maybe that was the kind of man they wanted in Washington. It didn't matter anyway. Nothing Washington did made any difference in a little place like Oakwood.

The "New South" the papers were calling it. Probably William McSimmons would fit in with the carpetbaggers and everybody else swarming into the region. Maybe William McSimmons would wear that suit long enough for his wife to turn him into a respectable Southern gentleman. Jenkins doubted it, but you could never tell.

In the meantime, it wouldn't hurt to be on the man's good side . . . just in case. That's what he wanted to talk to his son about.

"Weed," said the sheriff when he and his son were alone, "I got something I want you to do. Might be some money in it. I can't tell yet. We'll have to see what turns up first."

Storm and Stories, Laughter and Tears

14

Sometimes the rain could come on without warning. The storm that broke on us in May of 1869 reminded me of the time the flood had surrounded us and turned Rosewood into an island.

Katie, my papa, and Uncle Ward had all gone into town for some business at the bank that had something to do with the changes and the lawyer in Charlotte. They wanted me to go too, but after what had happened in the city, I was still a little shy about going into town. I'd had enough looks from Mrs. Hammond and Mr. Taylor at the bank, I didn't want anyone looking at me funny right now. So I stayed home.

All of us but Josepha and William were out at the pasture where Jeremiah and Micah were putting in the new fence. Henry hadn't gone into town that day, so he was helping them string wire along the new posts and pull it tight. Emma and I had just tagged along for fun. Even hard work is fun when you're working with people you love and you're all working together. We were trying to help but I don't think we did much. Pulling fence wire taut takes more strength than we girls had. But we were pretending to help anyway!

The rain hit so hard and so suddenly, we just stood there for a second or two staring up at it. Then we grabbed the tools and bolted for the nearest cover we could find. That happened to be Henry and Jeremiah's cabin. We crowded through the door, soaking wet in the less than a minute it had taken us to get there, laughing and all talking at once.

Henry went to his stove to stoke it up and add a few more chunks of wood. Within minutes we were standing around it, beginning to warm up. The rain was pounding on the roof so loud we almost had to shout at each other to be heard.

We didn't know it but Josepha had gone to the window of the big house when the torrent broke and saw us running for cover. A few minutes later the cabin door opened and Josepha trudged in, bundled up from head to foot and struggling to carry William, who was wrapped in a blanket and asleep in her arms.

We all looked at her, wondering why she'd gone outside in the middle of the torrent.

"What you doin' here, Josepha!" I laughed.

"Lan' sakes, I ain't neber heard it rain like dis!" she said. "I didn't want to be alone up dere wiff all dis goin' on."

"William's still sleepin'?" asked Emma.

"Dis boy kin sleep through anything. Probably nap right through da second coming."

Emma took the limp bundle from the older woman's arms and laid William on Jeremiah's bed.

The rest of us continued to stand around the warm stove. It seemed like the rain was all anyone could talk about.

"It flooded here—what was that, Emma, four years ago," I said. "You remember that?"

"I remember," nodded Emma. "Dat wuz mighty fearsome!"

"It didn't pour down like this," I went on to Micah, "but it just kept raining and raining and never stopped. The stream and the river finally met and destroyed the crops and surrounded the house. We were scared it was going to keep right on coming until the house itself floated away! You remember that, Henry, when you came rowing over the water to us."

Henry chuckled to himself.

"Dat I do," he said. "Dat wuz some flood, all right! Dat wuz afore I knew altogether what wuz goin' on wiff you ladies . . . you an' dat dere scheme er yers."

Emma and I laughed to hear him say it like that.

"What scheme is this?" asked Micah, glancing back and forth between Emma and me with a smile of question.

"We called it Katie's scheme," I answered. "We were trying to keep anyone from finding out there were three girls all alone at Rosewood."

"Why?"

"We din't want ter git caught," said Emma, "ain't dat right, Mayme? We wuz feared er gittin' caught by Katie's kin er maybe bad folks dat'd do bad things ter three girls all alone like we wuz, ain't dat right, Mayme?"

The look of puzzlement on Micah's face didn't go away. I went on to explain the circumstances of how we had come to be there and why we tried to make the plantation seem like there were grown-ups still taking care of everything.

"But then Henry found us out," I said. "And then my papa—though I didn't know he was yet—and then pretty soon Uncle Ward came, and after that everyone knew!"

"But dat scheme er Miz Katie's—it wuz fun while it lasted, weren't it, Mayme?" said Emma with a big smile of pride.

"It had its fun times and its scary times, Emma, I'll say that!" I laughed.

We were still pretty wet, but it wasn't an especially cold day. The fire was burning good and warming us up, and we all gradually sat down on a couple of chairs and the couch that had been Micah's bed after he came. As I'd told Micah the story about Katie's scheme, Emma and Josepha kept adding their two cents' worth, and before long we were all laughing and talking at once. We almost didn't seem to notice at first that it was only the blacks of the Rosewood family who were together right then, with Katie and Papa and Uncle Ward off in town.

Then came a moment when we looked around at one another and all seemed to realize it at the same time. It was a strange feeling. It didn't seem right that Katie wasn't with us. Part of our family-ness was knowing we were white and black . . . together. Yet there was a peculiar bond that I think we all suddenly felt toward each other that we never had before. We didn't just all live at Rosewood together . . . we were all black together.

And we were having such a good time sharing and talking that maybe for one day it was kind of special to be together under Henry's roof, all of us except Micah, who remembered what it was like to be slaves. That was a part of our bond together that Katie and the others couldn't share. Not only were we black—we'd been slaves.

"You remember that rainstorm we had in Tennessee, Jake?" Micah now said. "That was the hardest rain I've ever seen, maybe with the exception of today."

"Man, dat wuz bad, all right!" said Jeremiah. "We had no place ter git out ob it, an' it wuz cold dat day too."

"January, if I recall," added Micah.

"All we cud do wuz keep ridin', even though we wuz soaked all da way ter our toes. I thought my boots had turned ter chunks er ice, an' it jes' kep' blastin' down in our faces an' on our shoulders. Dat wuz some miserable day!"

"Josepha," said Micah, turning toward Josepha, "where are you from—I don't think I ever heard."

"You know all you need to know about me," Josepha replied.

"But you said you were educated," I said, hoping maybe she would tell us something about her past.

"Maybe I wuz an' maybe I wuzn't," she answered cryptically. When Josepha didn't want to say something, nothing you did could get it out of her.

"Den why you talk like a colored?" asked Emma. "All my life, dat is after I wuz sold ter Master McSimmons, I neber heard you talk but jes' like da rest ob us niggers. You din't soun' like no uppity colored."

"Dat's cuz I learned soon enuff ter keep my mouf shut an' not ter call no attention ter myself. I's learned jes' ter be a fat ol' woman who had memories ter keep ter herself an' dat didn't need ter—"

She stopped, like she'd already said more than she wanted.

"—I learned ter be jes' an' ol' slave woman who wuz nuthin' more den who she wuz," she added. "An' dat's dat."

"But tell us about it, Josepha," I said.

"I don't want ter talk no more 'bout it."

She got strangely quiet and remained that way for most of the rest of the time. But by then we were all curious about each other's lives and places we'd all been and how we'd ended up there together like we were.

So even Josepha clamming up like she did couldn't stop the flow of stories. There's something about being inside during a rainstorm that makes you feel cozy and happy. And somehow it felt good to be there together, knowing that we were all colored and that most likely, besides sharing black skin, we shared hardship and pain too. In those days, you didn't have colored skin without pain to go along with it.

"What 'bout you, Emma?" asked Jeremiah. "You all knows how I got here an' met Duff after my mama died an' den foun' my daddy an' met the rest ob y'all. But where'd you come from?"

"Yonder at Oakwood, wiff Mayme an' Josepha," replied Emma. "You knows dat."

"I mean afore dat. Where wuz you born an' how'd you git here?"

"I don't know none er dat," said Emma. "I wuz sol' so many times afore I cud even remember anythin' dat I growed up always movin' from one place ter da nex'. I neber knowed who my mama wuz, or my daddy neither. I wuz jes' a little kid dat kep' gittin' sold wiff a few other niggers dey wanted ter git rid ob."

"Why did dey want ter do dat, Emma?" asked Jeremiah.

"I reckon dey wuz always tryin' ter git rid ob da worthless ones," said Emma. "I recollect once I wuz sol' wiff a little boy wiff a lame leg dat got whupped too hard an' cud neber walk right after dat. An' I heard da mistress talkin' in da nex' room, an' she says, 'Y'all git rid ob dat little lame fool ob a boy—I don' want ter see his whinin' face no more, limpin' an' whimperin' roun' like a little puppy dog dat ain't fit but ter put in a sack wiff rocks an' toss in da *ribber. I don' care what you git for him . . . gib him away effen you's got to—I jes' can't stand da sight er him. An' while you's at it, git rid ob dat fool scrawny Tolan girl too. She's an idiot—doesn't hab a brain in her head. She ain't neber gwine be good fo nuthin'. Jes' git rid ob her. She's as worthless a piece ob nigger flesh as I eber seen. I know dey's all dumb, but she's da dumbest creature I eber did see.'*

"I din't even know she wuz talkin' 'bout me," Emma continued, "cuz I'd neber heard dat name afore dat. But den when da next day I foun' myself standin' der wiff da lame boy wiff people lookin' at us ter buy us, dat's when I knew maybe my mama's name wuz Tolan er somethin'. Dat's when I knew I wuz dumber eben den mos' other niggers, cuz after dat day, dey'd always call me dat, dey called me Dumb Nigger Girl, an' I kep' gettin' sol' on account er being a dummy an' not understandin' things too well, an' den da master or da mistress'd yell at me an' den pretty soon dey'd sell me agin, an' I knew I'd neber be any good at nuthin', an' wuz jes' a worthless nigger. I knew I wuzn't worf nuthin' cuz other nigger girls wud sell fo good money, but no one eber wanted ter pay nuthin' fo me, not till I got older an' den dey figgered I might turn out prettier den some ob da others. An' den one day I walked inter a new place an' dey wuz talkin' bout what ter do wiff me, an' a big colored lady walked in an' dat was Josepha, an' she said she'd put me ter work an' take care er me. An' she did."

Emma glanced over at Josepha with a smile that

was obviously full of gratitude, and it succeeded in bringing a smile to Josepha's lips too.

"I reckon Josepha's jes' 'bout da first person dat wuz eber nice ter me," said Emma. "An' den a little while later I come here an' foun' out what love really wuz, din't I, Mayme? You an' Miz Katie taught me what love atween friends wuz, din't you?"

"I think it was something we all discovered together, Emma," I said with a smile.

Katie and Templeton and Ward Daniels went into the bank in Greens Crossing.

"Mr. Taylor," Templeton said to the manager, "we recently had a new deed drawn up for Rosewood, and we want to be certain our financial arrangements and bank accounts are consistent with the change."

"What change, Mr. Daniels?" asked Mr. Taylor.

"That there are now four equal owners of Rosewood. We want to make sure all four names are on our bank account in case something should happen to either Ward or me."

Mr. Taylor glanced up from his desk at the two men, then at Katie.

"There are only three of you," he said.

"Miss Daniels, my daughter, is also included," said Templeton. "She could not make it into town with us."

Mr. Taylor nodded but kept his thoughts to himself.

"Do you have the new deed?" he asked.

"Yes, sir—it's right here."

Templeton pulled out the paper they had received from the lawyer in Charlotte and handed it to Mr. Taylor. The bank manager looked it over, then pulled out some forms for them to sign. Fifteen minutes later they were on their way to the general store.

Mrs. Hammond heard the bell from the door tinkle and looked up to see the three walk in. She greeted them with uncharacteristic friendliness and was pleasant during their entire visit. Katie was mystified at first. It wasn't until later that she realized it was probably because all three of them were white, and that, for once, none of Rosewood's blacks were with them.

"Hello, Mr. Daniels, and you too, Mr. Daniels," she said. "And, Kathleen, goodness—you look more like your mother every day. My, but you are nearly a lady!"

"I just turned nineteen," said Katie.

"And a beautiful nineteen at that," returned the shopkeeper. "I'm sure your mother would be very proud."

"Thank you, Mrs. Hammond."

"And that reminds me—there is a letter for you."

"For me?" asked Katie.

"Yes, from Philadelphia, I believe."

Katie looked at her two uncles with question. They glanced at each other and shrugged their shoulders.

Mrs. Hammond bent down behind her counter a moment.

"Here it is," she said as she stood, handing Katie the envelope. "And here is the rest of your mail," she added, handing a small stack of envelopes to Templeton.

"It's from Aunt Nelda," said Katie, scanning the envelope. "Why would she be writing me?"

"We wrote a while back and told her everything," said Ward. "Maybe she's decided her two wayward brothers aren't so bad after all."

"She didn't write to us, Brother Ward," grinned Templeton, "only to Katie. It may be she thinks we're not suitable guardians for Rosalind's poor daughter, eh, Katie?"

"If she thinks that, then I shall set her straight!" laughed Katie. "You two are the best uncles a girl could have!"

"What do you think, Mrs. Hammond?" said Templeton, throwing Katie a brief wink. "Are we suitable guardians for the refined daughter of Rosalind Clairborne?"

"I, uh . . . really couldn't say," stammered Mrs. Hammond, so caught off guard that for once she didn't have a reply ready. "It wouldn't be my place to interfere in . . . uh, family matters."

Templeton laughed good-naturedly. "Well then, Mrs. Hammond," he said, "here's a list of some things we need. I'm sure you will be able to handle that. And a newspaper too, if you please."

"Of course, Mr. Daniels."

As we continued to laugh and tell about our lives, even laughing about things that had happened when we were slaves, the rain kept coming down in sheets and we didn't even think about going back outside. Gradually an hour slipped by, then another.

"It could rain on dat ol' Mississippi, I kin tell you dat," said Henry. "Dere were times when I wuz a boy

dat I looked out an' cudn't tell where dat brown ol' ribber ended an' da sky began."

"Tell us about it," I said.

"Dere wuz one time," chuckled Henry with a far-off smile on his face, *"when three or four ob us colored boys wuz playin' at da ribber. Dere wuz a storm brewin', but we didn't mind cuz we wuz full er mischief.*

"We foun' a white man's boat tied wiff rope ter da side ob da ribber an' dere wuz nobody around. It wuzn't big but wuz enuff ter hold four boys lookin' fo adventure. We untied dat rope an' hauled dat boat upribber fo an' hour er two. We wuz plumb tuckered out, but we had ter git it far enuff up ribber so's we cud float down. So we got up what we figgered wuz two er three miles. We wuz so excited ter git in dat little thing an' float down we cudn't wait fo nuthin'. We wuz jes' young scamps an' we didn't know one end ob a boat from da other.

"So we got ter a spot we figgered wuz far enuff, an' two er da tykes jumped in an' somebody yelled, 'Shove us out!' an' da third jumped in, an' I gave da boat a big push away from da shore an' jumped over the edge an' plopped down inside. An' we wuz off down da mighty Mississippi.

"We floated along an' it wuz jes' as quiet an' nice as it cud be, an' we wuz feelin' right proud ob ourselves watchin' da shore git gradually further an' further away as we drifted out into da current. It wuzn't fast or dangerous, but it wuz carryin' us along.

"Den afore long da rain started ter fall. An' den

a great blast er lightnin' lit up dat dark sky an' da thunder sounded like it wuz right on top er us. An' dat's when we began ter git a little skeered cuz suddenly dat ol' Mississippi seemed like a fearsome place ter be all alone. An' dat rain it started ter come down an' dat thunder an' lightnin' it kept explodin' above us an' we looked ober an' dat shore wuz further away den before.

"An' somebody said, 'Let's git back—dis be far enuff.' An' dat's when we realized we wuz nuthin' but a pack er cracked coons—we hadn't brung us no oar er pole or nuthin'. Dere wuzn't nuthin' in dat boat but four skeered little nigger boys dat couldn't steer dat tub no how. Dat ribber wuz jes' gonna take us where it wanted an' dere wuzn't nuthin' any ob us cud do 'bout it."

By then we were all laughing to hear Henry chuckle as he told about it.

"But it weren't funny den," he went on. "It wuz mighty fearsome, I kin tell you. We wuz gwine drown on dat ribber jes' like all our mamas had warned us 'bout all our lives. An' we wuz shakin' an' yellin' out fo help. But dat rain wuz poundin' down an' dere wuzn't nobody gwine hear us an' da rain wuz startin' ter pile up in da bottom er da boat an' our feet wuz sittin' in water, an' ef dat rain kept comin' we'd sink too. An' den I looked ober, an' it wuz rainin' so hard you cud hardly see in front ob you, an' da shore had disappeared from sight. By den I wuz mighty skeered. For all we cud see we might er been out in da middle er da ocean! We wuz jes' floatin', an' we

wuz goin' faster by now cuz we wuz in da current, though still I reckon we wuzn't nowhere close ter da middle on account er dat Mississippi's a mile wide here an' dere."

"What did you do?" asked Emma, her face looking terrified.

"We jes' floated an' floated," chuckled Henry. "Pretty soon we got so skeered we all jes' quieted down an' sat dere still in dat boat, wet ter da bone an' shakin' from fear an' cold, an' jes' waitin' ter sink an' drown cuz we knew dere wuzn't nuthin' we cud do ter save ourselves. An' I wuz thinkin' 'bout dem ribber pirates an' white men an' what dey'd do ter us ef we got caught by da likes er dem."

"How did you get rescued?" I asked.

"We din't exactly git rescued," chuckled Henry. "But dat ol' Mississippi—it kin be yo frien' or yo enemy. It can take a life—an' it's taken plenty er lives!—or it kin give life back too, an' on dat day I reckon it gave back da lives ob dose four fool nigger boys instead ob drownin' dem fo stealing dat boat."

"What happened?" asked Josepha.

"Well, when we'd gone maybe four miles, dat ol' ribber takes one ob dose giant bends like it does. Sometimes it goes all da way aroun' like a big horseshoe. An' though we cudn't see too far an' cudn't see da shore, we wuzn't really so far out in da ribber—only maybe a hundert or hundert fifty yards. So when dat ribber swung roun' in dat big arc, dat boat it jes' kep' goin' straight an' din't git turned quite as fast as da current, an' by'n by we looked up an' dere wuz da

shore comin' close agin.

"An' it din't take long fo us ter figger out what wuz ter be done. We scrambled up an' jumped outer dat boat lickety-split an' we wuz all swimmin' fo our lives dat nex' minute, an' when we walked up out er dat mud onto da bank, we wuz 'bout da happiest four young scamps in all Louisiana. Den we jes' had ter git home wiffout any white boys seein' us. We knew we wuz likely ter git whupped fo bein' gone so long, but we still lit out runnin' up dat ribber till we got ter where we knowed where we wuz. An' dat rain, it didn't stop till we got all da way home."

Henry stopped, but we were all still staring at him.

"What happened then?" I asked.

"We got our behinds whupped somethin' fierce," chuckled Henry. "It still hurts when I think 'bout it. My papa wuz a good man, an' he din't put up wiff no foolishness from me."

⁂

When Katie and her two uncles walked out of Mrs. Hammond's store lugging several bags and parcels of supplies, Ward glanced up at the threatening black clouds approaching from the direction of Rosewood.

"That looks like a nasty storm," he said. "I say we get on our way home . . . and fast."

"It's coming this way, Ward," said Templeton. "Maybe we should stay in town and wait it out."

"We don't know when it's going to unload."

"Looks like it's already raining back home. I say we make a run and hope it stops or swings around us. We don't want to be stuck in town several hours."

"Yeah, you're right—let's go."

They put their parcels in back, along with the sacks of feed and some garden seed from Mr. Watson's, then jumped up onto the wagon and headed out of town as fast as they dared push the two horses and still manage to keep their seats.

"What's Sister Nelda have to say?" asked Templeton.

"I don't know, Uncle Templeton," replied Katie. "I haven't opened the letter yet."

"Why not? Open it up, girl."

"I don't think I could read it bouncing around like this."

"I'll slow down, then," he said, easing the horses back to a gentle walk.

Katie tore the edge of the envelope, took out the single sheet of white paper, and began to read. Her two uncles waited, not exactly patiently but glancing over at her every so often, obviously curious.

Finally she set the letter down in her lap and sighed thoughtfully.

"Well . . ." said Ward impatiently.

"She, uh . . ." Katie began, "she invited me to Philadelphia for a visit."

Ward and Templeton glanced at each other in surprise.

"She apologized for not keeping in touch," Katie went on. "She said they have had some difficult times in the last few years, but that after reading your letter, Uncle Templeton, she realized how important it was to keep in touch with family and, with me not having a mother now, wondered if I would come to Philadelphia for a while. She mentioned a finishing school for young ladies."

"There, you see—she doesn't think we're suitable," said Ward, obviously perturbed.

"Don't jump to conclusions, Ward," said Templeton. "Just because she invited Katie for a visit doesn't mean—"

"Why didn't she write us, then?" asked Ward. "She never answered your letter. She only wrote to Katie."

"She did say at the end to give my uncles her best," said Katie.

"There, you see, Ward—nothing so sinister at all."

"Yeah, I suppose not," mumbled Ward. "But . . . I don't know—it still seems a mite peculiar, her saying nothing to us about Katie visiting. But Nelda was like that—she never had much use for me. She was different than Rosalind."

It was silent a minute or two.

"I suppose in a way you're right, Ward," said Templeton at length. "It was always Rosalind who was looking out for her two brothers. I guess that's why we both stayed closer to her over the years. She's the one we went to see, not Nelda."

"Yeah, Rosalind was good to us, all right. Richard never had much use for us, for me anyway—meaning no disrespect to your pa, Katie—but Rosalind, though she might grouse at us, she'd never turn us away."

"In a way, you know, Katie," said Templeton, "Mrs. Hammond back there is right—you are a lot like your mother. And you're looking more like her all the time too, just like the lady said."

"I will take that as a compliment," smiled Katie.

"And, you know, maybe Nelda's right too—it wouldn't hurt you to go to a finishing school. Maybe you ought to go for that visit."

"Uncle Templeton . . . a finishing school!"

"You're getting older, Katie. We've got to think about your future—yours and Mayme's too. Some education would be good for you both. I want my daughter and niece to have the best."

"Why don't we send them *both* to Nelda's finishing school?" suggested Ward with a twinkle in his eye that looked strangely like his brother's.

"Somehow I do not have the feeling Nelda would be altogether receptive to that idea," said Templeton. "And I doubt, even in the North, that they mix their races quite like we do at Rosewood."

"Did you tell her about Mayme, Uncle Templeton?" asked Katie.

"Well, in a roundabout way," replied Templeton. "But I didn't *actually* tell her about her mama and me in so many words. I figured getting her used to the three of us together here was enough for one letter."

"We have to tell her," said Katie. "Do you mind if I write back and tell her about Mayme? I won't say anything you don't want me to. I could never even think of going to Philadelphia without Mayme."

"So you think you might go for a visit?"

"I don't know. I'm not interested in finishing school. But she is kin. It seems like, now that I am nearly grown, that maybe I ought to get to know her."

"Oh-oh!" exclaimed Ward.

"What?"

"Didn't you feel that? I think I felt a drop of rain."

They glanced up. The storm clouds were blacker than ever and nearly directly overhead.

"We'd better get these horses moving!"

*

We all became quiet and reflective. Henry's story, I think, reminded us all of our former years as slaves.

"Micah," said Jeremiah, "when we were together in da army, I recall you tellin' me dat you had a hard life. But you wuzn't no slave, wuz you?"

"No, Jake, I never was."

"You ever picked cotton, Mister Duff?" asked Emma.

"No, Emma," smiled Micah. "There's not much cotton in Chicago."

"Well den, son, you's got somethin' ter look forward to!" chuckled Henry. "You can't be black in da Souf wiffout pickin' cotton. Jes' consider yo'self lucky, son."

At the words, Micah grew pensive. These people around him had all had a much harder life than he had. Nothing of what he had had to endure compared with how dreadful and demeaning slavery must have been. It was part of the cruel heritage of his race that he had not experienced.

Maybe his life hadn't been so hard after all. Being a Negro in the North was nothing like being a slave in the South.

Jeremiah's voice interrupted Micah's reverie.

"Den what made yers a hard life, Duff?" he asked.

A strange and far-off look came into Micah's eyes. He drew in a deep breath, then sighed with the hint of a smile, though a sad one.

"Do you really want to hear about it?" he asked.

"Oh, yes, Mister Duff—please tell us," said Emma. "I likes hearin' stories 'bout everybody."

Micah smiled again.

"All right, then, Emma," he said. "How can I resist a request like that?"

As Micah began, his voice got quiet. It almost didn't seem like the same voice at all, like it was coming from far away. It almost sounded like he was telling about someone else altogether.

And in a way, I guess he was. The boy he told us about might have once been him . . . but it wasn't him any more.

We all got quiet too as we listened to the boy's story.

Boy in Chicago

15

A BOY OF ELEVEN DUCKED OUT OF SIGHT IN A DARK alleyway of Chicago's dreary waterfront district, where respectable people did not venture out at this hour. His skin was as black as the shadows where he hid.

All the local flatfoots knew the youngster, and none would have given him worse than a box on the head or a surly warning or two, even if they had caught him red-handed. That he had to steal a loaf of bread, or a piece of fruit or meat if he was lucky, to keep himself alive was well known to the neighborhood the boy haunted. So was the fact that his mother would probably not be alive without what he shared with her. The meager earnings from her disreputable trade selling her body mostly disappeared down her throat in the form of whiskey, rum, or gin.

By the time her unwanted son was of an age to beg, she sent him out with a forlorn expression and tin cup. By the time he could run fast enough to keep from getting caught by unwary shopkeepers, she taught him to steal. He had been doing both ever since and had grown proficient at both trades. He begged by day in those sections of the city bordering on respectability. He stole by night wherever food was to be had, and wherever shadows and alleyways offered refuge and escape.

Over the years he had learned every nook and cranny of the bustling metropolis for two miles in every direction from what he called home, though a more disgusting environment could scarcely be imagined for human habitation. Many nights he curled up in his own little corner on a dirty thin pad on the floor, wrapping a single blanket around him, with words and sounds coming from his mother's bed no child should have to hear.

But he was too young to understand, had no idea why sailors of all races, skin colors, and origins came and went every night, and thus was not badly damaged by it. Like most children of adverse circumstance, he possessed a remarkable capacity to adapt and to make the best of the sordid condition fate had thrown at him. He had probably slept cuddled to the warmth of his mother's side—certainly as an infant, surely as a young child, but he did not remember it. No human affection within his memory had touched his cheek, no kiss graced his lips. Out in the city, he saw men and women kissing, he saw parents and children hugging and walking hand in hand, but he did not know what any of it meant.

His life could not in any way be called pleasant. But it was filled with variety and interest, which for a child are as important as food for the mind and heart as is bread for the body. What he lacked in companionship from his mother he made up for in the infinite sights and sounds of the city. From the smile of a stranger, the pat on the back to accompany a penny tossed in the cup from a passing businessman, from the affection of a hundred dogs of the city who knew him as a roamer like they, the tough words of the beat cops who secretly watched out for him, even from the angry scolding of the shopkeepers and their wives as he passed . . . from all these, life somehow reached out and smiled at him. Even strangers were his friends. The human creature is a social animal and will derive companionship of soul from the unlikeliest sources. It will be fed by even the hint of a smile or twinkle of the eye from a passerby where no more vital companionship-food is to be had.

He turned at the end of an alley into a flight of rickety outside stairs, where he bounded up two at a time in near total blackness. It was after ten o'clock. About halfway up he heard a door close above him. A dark figure loomed on the landing, nearly indistinguishable from the blackness of the sky. Heavy footsteps began tromping down the stairs.

"Get out of the way, kid!" said a deep, surly voice as he stood with his head against the railing to let the man by. As soon as he was gone, the boy raced the rest of the way to the top and inside the filthy hovel lit dimly by a lone candle.

"Hi, Mama," he said. "I brung you a roll an' a couple er sausages—dey's fresh too, Mama, from jes' dis mornin'. I stold 'em from da man wiff da meat cart fo you, Mama."

A few mumbled words were all the thanks he received for his evening's labors. He expected nothing more. A few minutes later he was curled up in his corner, silently munching on the day-old crust he had kept for himself. He had pulled his blanket up over his head and was sound asleep twenty minutes later when the door opened again and the next customer walked in.

Day followed night, night followed day, in the endless succession of moments from which destiny is written and character fashioned.

The boy did not know his life was miserable because he did not consider it miserable. It was simply his life and he lived it . . . and went on. Misery is only misery to those who pity themselves in the midst of it. For those who seek to make the best of it, the same circumstances are pregnant with opportunity waiting to be born.

His mother rarely went out, for the fact was—she was not well. Though they shared the same hovel, in truth he rarely saw her. She still lay snoring and half drunk in her bed when he rose and left each morning to begin his daily round of activities as a street urchin, beggar, and budding thief. He usually returned once or twice a day to leave what few coppers he had inveigled in the streets, and then went out again.

But more and more she was in bed at these times too. The cough, which had been growing ever since the previous winter and now seemed constant, he hardly noticed. He heard such things all day from people in the city and thought nothing of it. He was unaware that it was a deep cough and wracked her lungs with increasing pain. The gradual failing of her liver from years of hard drinking and poor nutrition did nothing to help her condition. Whether it was pneumonia or consumption that eventually killed her was never looked into—she was not the sort whose passing the city mourned. Nor did she have friends who would have known the difference, or even cared. In the end, if tuberculosis was the cause, her lack of intimacy with him no doubt saved her son's life. For as severe as her cough became during her final weeks, mercifully the infection never reached him.

It was merciful too that he himself did not have to bear the burden of the discovery of the body at such an impressionable age. The landlord arrived early one afternoon to take out his wages for rent in flesh, as was his weekly custom, and found a corpse awaiting him rather than a warm body. The woman whose earthly life left no mark of eternal value on this world as she had passed so fleetingly through it, had now gone to see what the next world could make of her. Behind her she left but a child—the most precious and lasting legacy of humanity. Perhaps he might, in time, if not redeem the squalid existence she had led, at least bring redemption to her memory through his own life.

He arrived late that same afternoon, a few pennies and the huge wealth of a shiny nickel clutched in his excited little palm, to see a policeman standing at the bottom of the stairs talking with the landlord. A premonition swept over him—he had never before seen a white policeman this close to the building he called home.

"Dere he be, Officer," said the black man, nodding the boy's direction.

Almost the same instant he glanced up at the landing above. Two men were coming out of the topmost door carrying a stretcher with a blanket over it—a blanket bulging with an indistinct but recognizable form beneath it—the shape of a human body. He glanced again at the two men.

"Your mother's dead, boy," said the policeman.

He might not know human affection, but he knew what

dead meant. The depths of its mystery did not occur to him at that moment, only the stark fact that his mother's voice had been silenced, that he would never see her again, and that he was now alone in the world.

Only a moment more he stood, unable to comprehend the totality of what this change meant.

The two men continued talking. Only fragments of their conversation reached the ears of his spinning brain.

". . . have a father?" asked the policeman.

". . . you kiddin', Officer . . . half da men in Chicago . . ."

Suddenly the boy turned and darted away.

"Hey . . . hey, boy!" called the policeman. "Come back . . . we'll try to—"

But he was gone.

He ran and ran and ran. Whether he cried he could never remember. To run himself to exhaustion was the sole remedy for his confusion and anguish. When he came to himself a few hours later, his fingers were still clutched around the eight cents, and he was aware that he was beginning to feel the pangs of hunger.

Old habits returned. He pilfered half a loaf of bread and an apple or two and gradually, sometime after nightfall, returned to the only home he had ever known.

He crept up the stairs, somehow knowing that it would be best for the landlord not to be aware of his presence. The door opened to his touch, for it did not even have a lock. He crept inside and to his familiar corner.

Now at last he cried . . . cried himself into a sound and

dreamlessly forgetful sleep . . . and slept until morning.

He rose as usual, took one last forlorn look about the place, cried briefly again to see the vacant bed of his mother, empty and lifeless, and then left, never to return.

Streets for a Home

16

EVEN THE STREETS OF A CITY, WHEN ONE HAS someone *else* to live for, can give life and energy and even smiles. But when mere survival is the only objective, the streets of a city become cold and hard. And such they now became for the young black orphan.

The faces from which he had always derived the camaraderie of shared humanity now became adversarial. His own contentment, which had reflected twinkling eyes and teeth ready to glisten in a bright smile toward friend or stranger, now took on a calculating expression of suspicion, greed, and wariness. The innocence of childhood vanished, replaced by the cunning of avarice. The pickpocket replaced the boyish opportunist.

How one lives without a home in a city will always be a mystery to those unacquainted with the invisible subterranean workings of life for those who call the streets themselves home. He met others of his kind—old men, tramps, crooks, con men, hobos. Among them were men of honor, and others who would slit a man's throat for a few dollars.

Life among them all taught him to read character, taught him to keep on his toes, taught him to sleep—whether under bridge or in vacant alley—with an ear always cocked for danger. It also subtly revealed, though he did not yet recognize this most valuable of life's lessons, the truth that every man is on his way through life in one direction or another, eternally bound for one of two very different and opposite destinations.

As the months became a year, then two years, he grew and took on the gradual shape and form of teenage masculinity. His features hardened, his eyes narrowed. He became an angry black youth whose very gait drew the looks of the police, whom he now avoided.

He could no longer flit about the city unnoticed. No longer a cute little boy, he began to appear dangerous, which the look on his face did nothing to contradict. Stealing became more difficult because wherever he went, eyes were upon him. He looked suspicious and thus drew unfriendly stares.

A day came. A day of crisis, a day of destiny, a day of decision.

The boy, thirteen now, though he looked older, had fallen in with a rowdy group of half a dozen young thugs who prowled the streets with no good on their minds. Two or three had already been in jail for petty crimes. Remarkably, for youth is not only blind but also a little stupid, the younger ones looked up to these and sought to curry their favor with impressive deeds of ever more serious mischief.

They were out late one afternoon, roaming the streets looking for what might provide an easy target, venturing a little closer than was their custom to the white part of the city in hopes of slipping into some shop as a group and distracting the store owner with pretended shoplifting while one of their number sneaked behind the counter and pilfered the till. But there were crowds and occasional police about, and thus far their plans had come to naught.

A white man approached along the boardwalk. The first of their number slowed and looked him over, muttering a few threatening words as if sizing him up and wondering how much money he might have on his person. One by one they slowly passed him, until the last of their number, the youngest, came face to face with the tall commanding stranger. Something about the man's face drew him and he glanced up. The eyes of the white man and black youth met.

A sudden look of shock and astonishment spread over the man's face. The boy saw it and it startled him. His steps slowed. The two stared at each other a brief moment before a voice interrupted the silence.

"Duff . . . hey, Duff, whatchu doin', man? Come on . . . quit starin' at dat ol' white man an' let's go."

The boy pulled his gaze away and hurried to catch up with the others. Their running steps echoing along the boards were soon gone. Still the man stood in amazement, watching as they disappeared from sight.

Later that same night, the group of street toughs had still not had their thirst satisfied for excitement and conquest. They had been watching the shop of a certain jeweler for several days and this was the night their leader had chosen to raise the stakes of his deadly cat-and-mouse game with the police. Being the seventeen-year-old street thug he was, the fact that he planned to use his younger accomplices as decoys was not something he divulged to them.

He waited until after midnight when the streets were deserted. He signaled to his small gang to follow him to the vicinity of the store. There he would place them in position—two as sentries watching the street in both directions, two others to break in with him, and the last to make himself seen and run off in the wrong direction if anyone came.

They were some two hundred yards from the store when the youngest, feeling a growing anxiety in his stomach, begun to lag a few steps behind. Duff was afraid and he knew it. But he could not dare admit it to the others. Yet as they neared the store he slowed still more and fell all the farther behind, first only a step or two, then four, then—

Suddenly a bright light shone in his face. Trembling from head to foot, he stared into the blinding whiteness.

He froze in terror.

He became vaguely aware of the figure of a large man in the midst of the light.

"Don't go with them," said a commanding voice.

His comrades heard it too. They stopped to see a figure step from out of the shadows of a building into their path.

"Hit's dat crazy ol' man we seen earlier," shouted one. "Git him!"

The ringleader turned and ran back, angered at this interruption of his plans. He went straight for the white man. As he approached, the glint of a knife blade flickered in the light of a distant street lantern.

But the man was shrewder than the young troublemakers gave him credit for, and twice as strong as any two or three of them together. He waited for the attack, then with invisibly deft speed grabbed the older boy's wrist as he advanced and twisted it viciously.

A sharp cry of pain sounded in the night. The steel blade clattered to the boardwalk. Still holding the boy's wrist as if he would break his arm, the man forced him to his knees. The boy yelled in helpless fury.

"You young fool—what did you take me for!" the man said. "Now you get away from me and don't come back. If I see you again, next time I will break both your arms and personally walk you straight to the police station."

He let go his grip.

Swearing violently, the ringleader retrieved his knife and ran off, followed by his young admirers.

In the fifteen or twenty seconds that the skirmish had taken, the bright light faded from the vision of the young black boy who had been following. The exchange of words had sounded distant and muffled to his ears. He was still in a trance, watching and listening to events from which he had suddenly become detached. He saw . . . he heard . . . yet within his own brain time seemed to stand still.

He now saw the man, whom he too recognized from earlier in the day, though he was still enveloped in a glow of fading brightness no earthly source could account for. He could also see the shadowy forms of what he had thought were his friends. In truth they were no friends at all, for they failed utterly in the first and primary test of friendship—they did not seek for his best, only what would gratify themselves. But the forms of his companions were dark, distant, and shadowy. Though they were but fifteen or twenty feet away, he could barely make out their voices, as if they came from far away through a tunnel of darkness.

Gradually the sound of their retreating footsteps came to his ears as the gang of boys disappeared into the night. He took several steps toward them, trying to follow. But his feet were leaden.

"Come on, Duff," called a voice after him. He stepped toward the sound in a living dream. But slowly the voices and running footsteps faded into the blackness of night.

Fearfully he turned back. There stood the strange man of the light only a few feet away. He stood bathed in the glow of an eerie brightness coming from behind him.

A chill swept through him. What was this! Had he fallen and whacked his head? Was he dreaming? Had he fallen asleep somewhere and would wake up any instant? Or was he going crazy! What was this light in the middle of the city in the dead of night?

He turned again. The dark tunnel was still spread out in the opposite direction. One faint final, *Come . . . on . . . Duff!* came from it. He spun around yet again. There still lay a path of brightness. Back and forth he looked two or three more times in bewilderment. He knew he must follow one path or the other.

Still the strange man stood silently waiting between the two.

"Your life is in front of you, boy," now said the man. "Your whole life—right here, right now. Every choice makes you who you are. This is where it begins—with this choice, this moment. You've made some bad ones. But they can be put behind you in an instant. Don't be a fool, like those others. They are no friends. But I will be your friend. They will lead you nowhere but to trouble. Turn to the light and let them go. I want you to come with me."

One more fleeting look to the right and then to the left, then gradually the vision of light and the dark tunnel faded. He was alone on a deserted street in the middle of the night.

All around was silence. A white man, a complete stranger, stood in front of him, waiting.

He felt his eyes begin to fill with the hot tears of loneliness. A hand clasped his shoulder. He looked up. The man was staring deeply into his eyes.

"What will it be, son?" he said. "I will force you to do nothing you do not choose to do. Will you go with me?"

A moment more the boy waited, then slowly nodded his head.

Without another word, the man led him away. He remembered nothing more of how the rest of the night passed.

MENTOR 17

THE BOY WOKE UP WITH DAYLIGHT STREAMING through two windows above a warm bed in which he slept. He had never slept in a bed with actual sheets and blankets and a mattress in his life. He had no idea where he was.

Gradually the events of the strange night returned to his consciousness.

His natural instinct was to flee. But almost as quickly, he realized the folly of the idea. He had never lain in anything so soft and clean and comfortable in his life. It felt good! Why would he run from this?

Now he realized that he was wearing some kind of strange clothing. It was clean and soft like the bed. And he didn't smell anymore—his body was clean too.

A door opened. The man from yesterday walked in. He was carrying a tray.

"Good morning, son!" he said. "How did you sleep?"

"Uh . . . okay, I reckon."

"Would you like some fresh orange juice?"

"Uh, sure," he replied. The man handed him the glass on the tray. He sat up, took it, tasted it, and then drank it down in a single long gulp.

He handed the man the glass and looked up at him. "Uh . . . thanks," he said. "I ain't neber had dat before." His forehead wrinkled in question. "Why'd you bring me here, mister? Who is you, anyway?"

"My name is Trumbull," the man answered. "And I didn't bring you here, you chose to come."

"How you mean dat?"

"I put a choice before you, then you made your own decision. You may leave anytime you like. There are always two roads before us. They are before us every minute of our lives."

"What does you mean . . . two roads?"

"The two roads between light and darkness. They are the two roads of character that determine what kind of people we become."

"What kin' er nonsense you talkin' 'bout, mister? I ain't neber heard nuffin' like dat. What wuz dat light I seen las' night?"

"I don't know. I saw no light."

"When you come out from dat buildin', dere wuz light all roun' you."

The man called Trumbull smiled. "Well, that is amazing," he said. "He must have wanted to save you even more than I did."

"Who you talkin' 'bout? Whatchu mean He must hab wanted ter save me?"

"I'm talking about God, son."

"What! Now I knows you's crazy! I's gettin' out er

here. Where you put my clothes?''

''I was planning to have them washed this morning. But if you want them back now, I will get them for you.''

He turned to walk away.

''Hey, mister—how'd you know where ter fin' us las' night?''

''I followed you,'' answered Trumbull, turning back into the room.

''Why—why you doin' all dis? Why you foller us?''

''I followed *you*, son—only you.''

''Why me?''

''I have my reasons.''

''Well, I want ter know why.''

''What's your name, son?''

''Duff . . . Micah Duff.''

''Well then, young Micah Duff,'' said Trumbull, pulling a chair to the bedside. ''If you want to know why, I will tell you.—Why don't you have some breakfast from this tray while I tell you about it.''

Trumbull drew in a deep breath and thought a minute. ''I have a brother,'' he began. ''He is older than me. From as long ago as I can remember he was full of anger and hostility. Though we had a gentle and soft-spoken father, my brother became angrier and more rebellious and violent as he grew. He finally left home, got into trouble constantly, and eventually killed a man. He is now in jail and I have not seen him in many years.''

The man paused and stared again deeply at the boy.

''Do you know what all that taught me, young Duff?'' he asked.

''What?''

"It taught me that everybody has choices in life. It taught me that the way people make those choices determines the kind of people they become. I realized I did not want to become like my brother—angry, hard, self-centered. Look where it led him. I didn't want that. So I set out to take a different road in my life, a road leading in another direction. It took me a while, but I eventually set out to try to figure out the kind of person God wanted me to be. And that's what I've been trying to learn to be ever since."

"What's all dat got ter do wiff me?" asked Micah.

"You've got that same choice before you, just like my brother did, just like I did—the choice of what kind of person you want to be."

"But I want ter know why you followed me."

Trumbull smiled. "Because of something I saw in your eyes when I ran into you and your gang of street thugs yesterday."

At the words the boy bristled.

"Dey ain't no gang er thugs, dey's—" he began.

"Come, come, young Duff," interrupted Trumbull. "You and I will never get anywhere if we're not honest with each other. Those boys you were with were no-good thugs who are going down the road of darkness. The sooner you admit that, the sooner you can understand the difference between that and the road of light and truth. Now do you want to know what I saw in your eyes?"

"Yeah," he answered.

"I saw a look I remember in my own brother's eyes when he was still young enough to have gone either way. The instant I saw you and looked into your face, it was like seeing my brother again. There was nothing I could do for him—he made his own choices in life. Those choices took him down the path of darkness. But in that moment, I thought that maybe I could help *you*."

"Help me . . . how?"

"Not to become like my brother, or like those toughs you were with."

"Yeah, well, maybe I don' need any er yo help, mister. Who ax'd you, anyway! What business is it of yers what I's like?"

"Just the business of every human being to his brother."

"Yeah, well, you ain't my brother and I don' need yo help. I's doin' jes' fine afore you come along."

"Were you, young Duff? Were you doing just fine? What kind of life were you living, Micah?"

"It wuz all right."

"Was it? Tell me, Micah, can you read?"

"No, I can't read."

"You want to learn?"

"Neber thought much 'bout dat."

Trumbull left the room. He returned half a minute later holding a newspaper. He opened it and held the front page toward where Micah Duff still sat upright in bed.

"Do you know what this says?" he asked, pointing to a caption at the bottom of the page.

Micah shook his head.

"I'll read it for you," said Trumbull. "It says, '*One Negro youth stabbed, one shot, three jailed, in midnight robbery attempt thwarted by police*'."

He went on to read the names listed in the brief article.

Young Micah Duff's throat went dry.

"Now, young Duff," said Trumbull, "are you ready to listen to the difference between light and darkness, between good choices and bad, and between becoming a person of dignity and worth and character or a person of selfishness and anger?"

It was quiet a long time.

When the boy spoke again, his voice was soft and sober.

"Yes, sir," he said. "I reckon I's ready."

REFLECTIONS

18

The cabin fell silent as Micah paused.

The look on his face showed how deep were the memories he had relived in telling us his story. The rain had let up some but was still falling steadily on the roof. The fire in Henry's stove was toasting us, and we were so engrossed that none of us even thought of moving from where we sat listening.

"So that was the beginning of three years spent with the man called Hawk Trumbull," Micah went on with a smile. "I stayed with him till I was sixteen. After that I joined the army."

"Dat's da man you tol' me about," said Jeremiah.

"Yes it is, Jake," smiled Micah. "Hawk's story is why I said some of the things I did to you back then. I know it wasn't too pleasant, but I felt I had to."

"How you mean, Duff?"

"Well, you see," Micah replied, "Hawk's brother's name was Jake too. And so the moment I met you, I

thought of Hawk, and I knew that maybe you'd been sent to me just like I'd been sent to Hawk—to help you face your choices just like Hawk helped me face mine."

"An' dat you did—though I didn't care much fo it at da time, I's mighty thankful now dat you had da courage ter make me face my anger."

"Me too," added Henry.

"I am glad to hear that, Jake," smiled Micah. "I was the same way too at first. I was thirteen when I met Hawk. You were twelve or thirteen when you and I first met. So we were a lot alike, Jake. Maybe that's one of the reasons I was so hard on you—I saw myself in you. Mine was a terrible life, though at the time I was too young to know anything different. But God will use anything He can to find a way to get His love into us. So He used the dreadful circumstances of my life to accomplish that. When Hawk took me under his wing, I squawked and complained too. But on that first day, after he showed me the newspaper, I realized that he had saved my life."

"Just like you did mine," said Jeremiah.

"I reckon so," nodded Micah. "And knowing that, I realized I could trust him. And once you learn to trust someone, everything changes. When I realized that he wanted only good for me and was willing to do anything, even make sacrifices for me, for my good—that turned my whole life around. I realized that he cared about me, even loved me. He treated me like a son, even though he was white

and I was black. He became like a father to me. Since I never knew my own father and since my mother was dead, I had no one else. I suppose I became a little like him. Even as I talked to you, Jake, I found myself saying some of the very things he had told me.

"He taught me about God, about how God works in our lives, about who God is. He taught me to understand myself and to understand people. He taught me to speak intelligently, taught me to read, to write, even to read whole books, something I would never have dreamed of doing as long as I was stuck in that life I was in. He gave me not only an education about God and reading and writing, but mostly about life and choices and deciding what kind of man I wanted to be. He always put choice in front of me. For Hawk, everything is always reduced to the two *Cs*—choice and character. He always said that light and darkness are before us at every moment—the two paths of life, he called them, and how we allow God to make better people of us.

"And after that, ever since, I have been intrigued by the character and growth of the people I've met. Hawk taught me to look beneath the surface for a person's true character. I saw that people weren't always what they seemed. It made me think a lot about what kind of person I wanted to be myself. If you're observing people for the wrong reasons, it will only lead to judgment. But for the right reasons it helps you grow yourself. That's what Hawk helped me to see . . . both in others and in myself. He helped me decide what kind of person I wanted to be, just like I told you when we first met, Jake."

"What waz dat light you seen when dat man come out an' stood dere when you wuz runnin'?" asked Emma.

Micah smiled. "I don't know, Emma. I've often wondered if I had a momentary vision. For a time I wondered if Hawk was an angel. I don't know. Sometimes God does things we do not understand to get our attention and to tell us it's time to look to the light and find out who and what He wants us to be. That was such a moment for me. I can't explain it. God wanted to speak to me. He used Hawk to say what He had to say."

"Does you think God will eber speak ter me, Mr. Duff?"

"God speaks to everybody, Emma. But He uses different ways to speak to us all. We have to be listening when His voice comes, even though we might not know what it's going to be like. God's voice came to me through Hawk. For you it will be different."

"Will I see me a vishun, Mr. Duff?"

"Probably not, Emma. Most people don't. But God always speaks, if we're listening."

"Where is Hawk now?" I asked.

"I don't know," answered Micah with a sad smile. "I've wanted for years to see him again so that I could thank him for all he did for me. He always *talked about going west, about living off the land. He was fascinated with the high desert. I never quite understood why. He never really seemed like a city man. If anyone could live off the land, it was Hawk. He was remarkable in more ways than just knowing things about God that most folks never discover. But I joined the army and traveled around a lot. Then the war came. I wanted to get back to Chicago to see if I could track him down. But I doubt he's still there. Besides that, he would be getting to be an old man by now. I don't know . . . something tells me he made it out west, and may still be there, for all I know."*

It grew quiet and suddenly we were all aware that the rain had stopped. Almost immediately the whole cabin brightened as sunlight streamed in through the window.

Micah's story had been so interesting and moving. But it left me feeling strangely melancholy. I didn't know why.

Maybe it wasn't his story at all but all of us being here together like we were, listening to everyone else talk about their lives. But I hadn't shared much at all about mine the whole time. All of a sudden it struck me why.

I was different from the rest of them—different from Micah and Henry and Josepha and Emma and Jeremiah. Even though I had been a slave too, my father was white. That set me apart from them.

And the realization made me feel very, very strange.

But I hardly had the chance to think about what it meant. All at once the door opened and there stood Katie.

"So this is where you all disappeared to," she said. "We got home and there was nobody to be found!"

I smiled as Katie came in. She was smiling and exuberant as she looked around at us seated in chairs and on the floor, her hair wet looking as if she'd been caught in the rainstorm too. But I was still feeling funny.

"What have you all been doing?" asked Katie.

"Sleepin'!" William announced.

We all looked over at the bed, not realizing the little boy had woken up. The others laughed and Emma scooped William from the bed and held him in her arms.

"We been tellin' stories, Miz Katie," Emma said.

We continued to talk and tell Katie everything we'd been talking about. But even the sound of their happy voices couldn't shake off the peculiar mood that had come over me.

Strange as it is to say it, even though I was surrounded by so many people, a wave of loneliness swept over me.

I got up. The voices and everyone's talk and laughter faded behind me, and I walked out the door

Katie had left open. Slowly I wandered away from the cabin.

Confusing Thoughts
19

It was so wet the water was running in tiny little streams through the grooves of every path and road and at the edges of the fields. There were puddles everywhere and every inch of the ground and every blade and leaf of the crops and the trees was glistening in the sunlight from millions of raindrops everywhere.

I walked away from the cabins, still hearing the voices of those I loved so much behind me but feeling, for some strange reason, very alone. I wasn't even sure what exactly I was feeling. I walked slowly, and it was so muddy that I had to pick my way so I wouldn't step in any puddles. I suppose I was feeling sorry for myself. Not only was I not totally colored like the others, I think for the first time I was realizing that I couldn't take Katie all the way into my world, and that I would always be separated, too, from Katie's world. None of the others back in Jeremiah's cabin could fully understand how I felt either, because I was half white. I was caught between the two worlds of white and black but not fully a part of either.

I hadn't gone that far from the cabin when I heard steps behind me. I assumed it was probably Katie. I turned and there was Micah Duff walking after me.

I tried to force a smile, but I don't think it was very convincing.

"You look like someone carrying the weight of the world on your shoulders," he said. "Would you like to talk about it?"

"How did you know?" I said as we began walking slowly together.

"I suppose another thing Hawk taught me was how to read what people are feeling. Well . . . not know what they are feeling exactly, but perhaps know when they need to talk . . . or need a friend."

"I guess I'm not very good at hiding it, am I?" I said, smiling again.

"Let's just say I could tell something was on your mind. I hope nothing I said in there—"

"Oh no, it's not that at all," I said. "It's just that I—"

I looked away. My eyes were suddenly filled with tears. Micah waited patiently.

"Oh, I don't know," I said, sniffling and wiping at my eyes, "I just . . . in there—all of us, only us coloreds like we were talking—all of a sudden I realized that I wasn't like the rest of you at all. I am half black, half white. I have a white father. I don't know

why, it made me feel like . . . I don't know—where do I fit? Am I colored . . . or white? I'm neither."

My eyes filled again. I looked over and Micah gave me the most tender smile I think I'd ever seen.

"You are who God made you," he said. "You are His beautiful child. You are exactly the young lady He wants you to be. Do you think the color of your skin matters to God?"

"No," I said, hardly able to keep from weeping at his words.

"Your mother loved you," Micah went on. "It is obvious your father loves you—God loves you, all these people here, Mayme—they adore you. None of that is because of the color of your skin. It is because of the person you are."

"Thank you," I said, wiping at my eyes again.

Micah nodded with one last smile, then turned and walked back to the cabin. Even as he went I saw Katie coming toward me. She and Micah passed, slowed, exchanged some words I couldn't hear, then Katie joined me and we continued on toward the house together.

Neither of us said a word for a minute or two. When Katie finally spoke, her words were not what I had expected.

"Jeremiah and Emma were watching the two of you through the window," she said.

I turned toward her. "Did Jeremiah say anything?" I asked.

"No, they were just watching. We've all been watching, Mayme."

"Watching what?"

"What do you think . . . you and Micah."

"But, Katie," I said, "it's nothing."

"Is it, Mayme? Are you sure?"

I didn't answer. I wasn't sure I knew the answer.

"What were you and he talking about?" Katie asked.

"He saw that I was sad and asked me about it, that's all."

"I'm sorry, Mayme—why are you sad?"

"I don't know . . . I was just feeling funny about being half white and half black. Sometimes I feel strange around the others calling Papa *Papa*, with him white and them black. I'm not like them, I'm not like you. It made me wonder who I am at all. I don't fit in anywhere."

Again I felt myself starting to cry.

Katie took my hand and squeezed it. "We may be different, Mayme," she said. "But we are sisters, remember . . . cousins. Nothing can ever take that away from us."

I nodded.

"What did Micah say?" asked Katie.

"He said some nice things . . . mostly that God loves me exactly as I am. He always seems to know just the right thing to say. He is the most amazing person. I can't imagine him as an angry street thief."

"What!" said Katie.

"He was telling us about it when you were in town. That's what he used to be. Can you imagine it? It hardly seems possible."

Katie looked at me with the oddest expression.

"Mayme . . . you're not in love with him . . . are you?" she asked.

I looked at her in astonishment.

"My papa asked me the same thing," I said. "No—of course not."

⁂

While Katie and Mayme were talking and continuing toward the house, Micah made his way back where the others all slowly emerged from Henry and Jeremiah's cabin. He reached Emma and William, then paused and stooped down.

"William," he said, "I want to have a little talk with your mother. You don't mind, do you? Why don't you run up to the house and she will join you in a minute."

"Okay, Mister Duff," said William and scampered off with Josepha hurrying after him, though not with his energy or speed.

"That's quite a boy you have," said Micah as they walked slowly away from the others. Emma did not reply and her nervousness at finding herself suddenly alone with Micah Duff was obvious.

"I am going to have to have a talk with you one of these days, Emma," Micah said, "about some of those things you said about yourself in there."

"What about dem?" said Emma.

"About how you think of yourself, Emma," replied Micah. "Sometimes it takes someone else to help us see the good in ourselves."

"Dere ain't no good in me."

"That's where you're wrong, Emma. There is good in everyone."

"Maybe in people like Mayme and Miz Katie but—"

"Emma," interrupted Micah; then he turned and stared straight into her eyes. "God wouldn't have created you just as you are if He didn't think you were worth creating. He looks at you with even more love in His heart than you feel when you look at William. I've seen how you look at your child and the love that is in your eyes."

"When you see dat?"

"I've seen it since the day I arrived here. You love him, don't you?"

"Yes, Mister Duff. But . . . you been watching me?"

"I have, Emma. And I see a lovely child of God that He cares for very much."

"You sure you mean me, Mister Duff?"

"I am telling you what I see when I look inside you, Emma. And I am going to pray that you begin to see it too."

Micah turned and walked away, leaving Emma more speechless than she had ever been in her life.

Later that night, Katie came over and sat on my bed. We didn't have as many times to share alone like we once had. I smiled and took her hand.

"I love it with everyone else here," I said, "but you and I don't have so many special times as we once did."

Katie was quiet a minute. Was she thinking some of the same things I had been earlier, realizing that as much as we loved each other, we couldn't help the fact that we were different.

"But we wouldn't go back, would we?" said Katie.

I shook my head.

"What's going to become of us, Mayme? The world doesn't see whites and blacks the same."

"I don't know," I said. "But at least here, in the midst of our differences, we all love and accept each other."

"Maybe that's more important than anything," smiled Katie.

Stories, Dances, and Memories

20

Something about the rainstorm and everybody sharing about their lives seemed to fill us all with good feelings and happiness from realizing how good our lives were at Rosewood. A few nights later, we gathered in the living room after supper like we usually did.

"You gwine read ter us, Miz Katie?" asked Emma.

"If you'd like," Katie replied.

"I wish you wud. I likes it when you reads."

"I've been waiting to hear something from that book we got in Charlotte that you've had your nose in ever since," said my papa.

"The Grimm's Fairy Tales*?" said Katie.*

"Read us something from it, Katie," I said.

Katie got up, went to the bookshelf and got the book. She sat back down and thumbed through it a minute.

"Here's one," she said, "that I just read last night.

It's called 'The Town Musicians of Bremen.' It's about a donkey, a dog, a cat, and a rooster."

"What's Bremen?" asked Micah.

"It's a town in Europe," said Katie. "It was known for its freedom, so the four animals left their masters and went to Bremen to live together without having any owners. They came to a house with thieves inside and they drove them out of the house at first by making a terrible racket. That's why they were called musicians. Then they frightened them so much that the thieves fled, and the animals took their house for themselves."

"Just like us, ain't it?" said Jeremiah. "We ain't slaves no more either."

Laughter broke out over the room. Gradually it quieted and Katie began to read.

"Once upon a time," she began, *"a man had a donkey which for many years carried sacks to the mill without tiring. At last, however, its strength was worn out. It was no longer of any use for work. Accordingly its master began to ponder as to how best to cut down its keep. But the donkey, seeing there was mischief in the air, ran away and started on the road to Bremen. . . ."*

All around the room the rest of us listened. Even William was caught up in the story and he sat on Emma's lap, eyes wide open, without making so much as a peep.

"Finding all quiet, the thief went into the kitchen to kindle a light, and taking the cat's glowing, fiery eyes for live coals, he held a match close to them so

as to light it. But the cat would stand no nonsense. It flew at his face, spat and scratched. He was terribly frightened and ran away.

"He tried to get out by the back door, but the dog, who was lying there, jumped up and bit his leg. As he ran across the manure heap in front of the house, the donkey gave him a good sound kick with his hind legs, while the rooster, who had awoken at the uproar quite fresh and gay, cried out from his perch: 'Cock-a-doodle-doo.' Thereupon the robber ran back as fast as he could to his chief, and said: 'There is a gruesome witch in the house, who breathed on me and scratched me with her long fingers. Behind the door there stands a man with a knife who stabbed me, while in the yard lies a black monster, who hit me with a club, and upon the roof the judge is seated, and he called out, "Bring the rogue here," so I hurried away as fast as I could.'

"Thenceforward the robbers did not venture again to the house, which, however, pleased the four Bremen musicians so much that they never wished to leave it again."

Katie stopped and we all sat a few seconds.

"Dat's jes' like you done wif dem bad men, ain't it?" said Emma after a minute. "You an' Mayme fooled dem an' chased dem away, din't you, an' dey neber knowed who you really wuz."

Katie and I looked at each other and began to smile.

"You're right, Emma," said Katie.

"That was some pumpkins!" I laughed. "I'd

almost forgotten. How did we ever get away with it!"

"But we did fool them," said Katie.

"What is all this?" now said Micah, looking back and forth between us with an expression of humorous bewilderment on his face. "This sounds better than the fairy tale."

"Oh, it is, Mister Duff!" said Emma excitedly. "Mayme an' Miz Katie wuz so smart an' so brave. Dey shot guns an' everythin'."

"Hardly brave, Emma!" laughed Katie. "I was scared out of my wits. I'm afraid Mayme was the only brave one."

"I wasn't brave either," I said. "It all happened so fast, we just did what we had to."

"So what happened?" asked Micah.

"There were some bad men who came to Rosewood," said Katie. "They were looking for Uncle Ward's gold."

"Gold!" said Micah, looking at Uncle Ward. "There really was gold?"

"But we didn't know it at first," said Katie. "It was down in the cellar. We didn't find it till later. So when the men first came, we had to chase them off, just like the four animals."

"But Mayme and Miz Katie, dey did it wiff guns!" said Emma. "Dey shot at doze men!"

By now Micah's curiosity had spread to everyone else, and they wouldn't stop their questions until we told the whole story.

"It was before Emma came," said Katie, "though we told her about it afterward. And it was before our *idea of pretending that the plantation was still operating normally so that no one would know we were just two girls by ourselves. Chasing off those men helped put the idea into my head. The bad men had already come by once asking questions, and then Mayme got the idea of trying to pretend there were more of us.*

"Mayme was out in the barn cleaning up when I saw them coming. I hurried out to tell her, but I was shaking so bad I could hardly get the words out.

"Mayme snuck to the door of the barn and peeked out. There were three men on horseback coming up to the house. We kept out of sight as they dismounted and looked around. A minute or two later we heard the barn door creak open and the sound of boots coming across the wood floor. I was sitting huddled up close to Mayme. Suddenly a man called out, 'Anybody there?'"

"He stood looking around for five or ten seconds. Then he walked back outside. We heard another man call out, 'Ain't nobody inside.'"

"The one who'd been in the barn asked, 'Where are they? From the looks of it, there's folks about.'"

"'We'll just wait and kill 'em when they come back,' said the other man."

As Josepha listened, she shook her head in disbelief.

"That was all we needed to hear!" Katie added. "Mayme whispered for me to follow her, and we crept out of the barn on the opposite side where they wouldn't see us, made a dash for the woods, then

made a great big wide circle back toward the house from the opposite side where the men couldn't see us. As soon as we were back to the house and crouching low, Mayme asked me about the guns. I asked her what she wanted with my daddy's guns and she said, 'We're gonna try to scare those men away.'"

"'But how?' I asked. Back then I was pretty dense. Mayme had to tell me what to do. She told me to sneak around the side of the house and when I got to the corner, to get some rocks and throw them at their horses."

"What wuz da rocks fo?" Emma asked.

"To startle their horses," I answered. "I figured when the men ran outside to see what was wrong, I'd dash in and grab the guns."

"But I was so scared," Katie went on, picking up where she'd left off. "I didn't want those men coming after me. I asked Mayme what I should do after I threw the rocks. She told me to stay hidden, then get back out to the woods. She'd meet me there with the guns."

By then everyone was listening as attentively as they had when Katie had read the story from the book of fairy tales.

"Well, we did it," Katie went on. "I threw some rocks to distract them, and Mayme snuck in and got the guns, and we ran back to the woods. I don't know how we did it, especially with Mayme lugging two heavy rifles, but we did. I asked Mayme, 'What are we going to do now?'"

Katie looked over at me expectantly. "You'll never guess what she said."

All eyes in the room turned in my direction. I bit back a smile and answered, "I told her, 'We're gonna shoot 'em.'"

"Yeah!" Little William cheered, forming his hand into a "gun" and making explosion noises with his mouth. Emma quickly shushed him up.

"I had never held a gun in my life," Katie said. "Mayme told me there was nothing to it and showed me how to hold it against my shoulder and aim. I was terrified. I said, 'Mayme, you don't mean . . . we're not going to try to shoot those men!' 'No, silly,' she said, 'just scare them away.'"

"So that's what we did. Mayme showed me how to load the rifle, gave me a box of bullets, and told me what to do. Then Mayme took the shotgun and went back to the barn. I was so scared. . . ."

"I was too!" I chimed in. "But I knew we had to get rid of those men."

"You were so brave, Mayme," said Katie, smiling at me. She turned back to the others. "First Mayme snuck back and swiped the men's rifles off their horses," she went on. "Then she disappeared into the barn. She had told me to count three minutes and then start shooting—up in the air or over the fields someplace. But I was so nervous that I counted way too fast. When I thought it was time, I picked up the gun and pointed it off toward the fields and held on real tight. Then I closed my eyes and pulled the trigger. The sound scared me more than anything, but it

didn't knock me over like I was afraid it would. When the sound died away I shot again, and then again.

"By this time there was yelling from the house because the men didn't know who was shooting at them. And it's a good thing they didn't! I fired the six shots and started fumbling to reload like Mayme had shown me.

"The men ran for their guns, but Mayme had taken them and now she was shooting at them too from the barn. I managed to get the rifle loaded and started shooting again. I accidentally shot one of the windows in the house!"

Papa and Uncle Ward burst out laughing.

"The men were yelling and swearing," Katie went on. "But their guns were gone and they were getting shot at from two directions at once. So they mounted their horses and rode away, with Mayme still shooting after them."

By the time Katie was finished telling what had happened, everyone was laughing.

"That is unbelievable!" said Micah. "I can hardly imagine it."

"An' den right after dat is when I came," said Emma. "An' den Mayme an' Miz Katie an' Miz Aleta, we done jes' like dem animals, din't we, Miz Katie? Wheneber folks'd come, we'd make noises an' fool dem so dey'd neber know who we really wuz."

Again Micah laughed and asked what it was all about.

"That was Katie's scheme," I said. "We lit fires in

the empty cabins and had Aleta pound on the anvil with a hammer in the blacksmith's shop and did whatever we could to make Rosewood look normal."

"I've got to admit," laughed my papa. "They almost fooled me!"

"Did the men ever come back?" asked Micah.

Gradually the room got quiet.

"Actually . . . yes, they did," said Katie.

"What happened?"

Katie glanced at the three older men. But none of them said a word.

"By then Uncle Templeton was here," Katie said. "He was shot saving my life and almost died. The leader of the gang of men was killed. His name was Bilsby. He's the one who killed our families."

Katie stopped. I saw Jeremiah glance at Henry, who was looking down at the floor. But neither of them said anything. Even Emma seemed to sense that Henry's role in what had happened was not for any of the rest of us to tell about.

Katie got up and put the book back in the bookcase.

We sat in silence for a few minutes. Finally Josepha got up.

"I's gwine put on a pot er tea," she said. "Who wants a cup?"

"That sounds fine, Josepha," said my papa. "Count me in."

"Me too," said Katie, walking slowly about the room.

"You got any of those oatmeal cookies left?" asked Uncle Ward.

"I may at dat, Mister Ward," replied Josepha, disappearing into the kitchen.

Now Katie sat down at the piano and started playing absently. Then she got out some of her music, and pretty soon she was playing a lively jig.

Uncle Ward jumped up and started dancing in time to the music. We all laughed and started clapping to the rhythm. That made him dance all the harder until his feet sounded like drums on the floor.

"Come on, Emma!" said Uncle Ward, going over to where Emma was sitting.

He took her hand and pulled her to her feet. A minute later Uncle Ward's and Emma's feet were bouncing and jumping and echoing on the floor in perfect time as if they'd been dancing together for years. The rest of us kept clapping and laughing to Katie's music.

Suddenly I looked up, and there was Micah standing in front of me with his hand outstretched.

"Come on, Mayme," he said. "Let's join them!"

I took his hand and stood up. We didn't put on quite the show Emma and Uncle Ward did, but it was so much fun! I hadn't danced like that, with a black man, since I was a little girl dancing with my grandfather to the music of a fiddle. I could tell Micah had danced the jig before. He was real good on his feet.

"Whew!" said Uncle Ward a minute or two later. "That's enough to tucker an old man out!—Jeremiah,

get up here and take over for me."

Jeremiah's feet had already been itching and he didn't need to be asked twice. He was out of his chair in an instant and the next had Emma's hand, and they danced all around the room.

Josepha came in with the tea a few minutes later and, after serving the men, sat down beside Henry to watch. Finally Katie's fingers began to slow, and she gradually brought the lively dance to an end. Jeremiah and Emma and Micah and I all stopped and let go of each other's hands and just stood laughing, panting, and grinning. We were tired but hadn't had such a time in ages!

"That was downright fun!" said Papa. "Almost makes me wish I was a kid again. Remember when Mama taught us to dance, Ward?"

Uncle Ward chuckled.

"Did she really, Uncle Templeton?" asked Katie from where she still sat at the piano.

"That she did, Kathleen," he replied. "Your grandmother was quite the lady for making sure her sons and daughters—me and Ward and your mama and your aunt Nelda—all had culture and refinement, at least as much as she could give us herself. I think she would have liked to send us to expensive schools if she could have, but they didn't have that kind of money. So she made us read books and study—yes, and dance too. Why, Ward and I even took our turns there at the keyboard with her trying to teach us the piano."

"Uncle Templeton!" exclaimed Katie. "Come . . . show us!"

Papa laughed. "She tried to teach us, I said. I'm afraid she wasn't too successful in my case. What about you, Ward?"

"Not me!" laughed Uncle Ward. "I was always a stubborn cuss when it came to practicing like she wanted me to. Listening to Kathleen play, I regret that now. That's mighty fine playing, Kathleen. It sure takes me back. Your mama could play just like that. She was the musical one of the family."

"She taught me," said Katie. "I used to have a violin too. But it was ruined when the marauders came."

"Well, she taught you real well." Uncle Ward paused a moment. "You know who else was musical," he added, "—that was Lemuela. Everything Rosalind did, she did too. She could play the piano, the violin . . . and sing! Remember how Lemuela could sing, Templeton?"

I looked at Papa. A faraway look had come into his eyes. The faint hint of a smile crossed his lips.

Slowly he nodded.

"I remember . . ." he said softly. "How well I remember."

The sound of Papa's voice as he remembered my mother quieted us all. Especially me. I was reminded again how much he loved her, and of the sadness he always felt at her memory, knowing that he had never seen her again.

Softly Katie again began to play. But the quiet

melancholy of memories had gotten into her soul too. All of us, everyone in the room—except little William, I suppose—would always have sadness in our hearts from the loss of people we had loved. But we had each other, and we were sure grateful for that. Yet even then, sometimes the melancholy swept through our hearts for a while when we remembered the others who were gone.

It was a while before I recognized what Katie was softly playing. Then I remembered. It was the minuet, like she'd taught me on her fifteenth birthday just after I'd first come to Rosewood. That had been a special day that had done a lot toward making two heartbroken girls into friends.

Katie played and we all sat absorbed in our thoughts. The music of the minuet, though happy, couldn't help but put us in a nostalgic mood. I suppose we were all thinking about the ones we loved who weren't there.

Josepha was sitting next to Papa. I noticed her swaying a bit and her feet moving ever so slightly to the music. Papa must have noticed too.

"Josepha, how about you dancing with me?" he said. "Looks to me like your feet know the minuet."

Josepha looked over at him with a look of sadness and longing. "I don't think so, Mister Templeton," she said. "Dat's jes' too long ago."

"What's too long ago?" he asked.

Then her expression changed and the familiar Josepha was back.

"You jes' neber mind," she said. "Dat's my business,

and you jes' mind yer own."

A minute later, as I sat there, a shadow slowly appeared in front of me. I glanced up.

There stood Papa.

He reached out his hand. I took it. He pulled me to my feet. I wouldn't have thought I could remember it so well, but suddenly I found myself dancing in perfect rhythm to the music as Papa led me through the graceful steps. Katie's and my grandmother had taught him well! His feet were so light on the floor he hardly made a sound. I could almost imagine him dressed all fancy in a palace court at a ball in honor of a king! He held my hand so lightly, turning and slowly spinning me around in all the right places. Somehow I knew just what to do from his touch.

Everyone else watched as we danced, in awe that we both simply stood up and started dancing a perfect minuet. I even saw tears in Josepha's eyes.

Katie played and we danced, and it was almost like the whole world had stopped for those few minutes. Suddenly I was inside my own fairy tale, dancing like a princess in a story. But I wasn't dancing with a prince. I was dancing with my very own father, which was even better.

Gradually the minuet came to an end.

Our steps slowed and finally stopped. We stood facing each other a moment more. I gazed up into Papa's face. His eyes were wet.

"If I didn't know better, Mary Ann," he said softly, "I would think that you were your mama. You *are the most beautiful young lady in the world."*

I went to him, stretched my arms around his waist, and leaned my head against his chest as he wrapped my shoulders in his embrace.

Baptism

21

How exactly word began to spread was never clear. I think Henry picked up word of it from people coming into town. But wherever it came from, there was a report that a black preacher was heading our way, baptizing and preaching and holding revival services as he went.

Then one day came when his wagon rumbled into town with the words painted in bright red against yellow sides that looked like a traveling medicine show: *Dr. Giles Smithers Colored Camp Meeting Revival Service.* And underneath, it said, *Jesus is the way to salvation, turn from sin.*

The man talked to Henry at the livery and asked about a good place on the river to hold a baptism. Before we knew it, the man had set up his revival tent beside the river on the border of Rosewood—with Papa's and Uncle Ward's permission, of course—and flyers were being circulated everywhere.

Reverend Smithers was an old-fashioned hellfire

revival preacher, and when he got wound up, you could hear his voice for half a mile. Katie, Papa, and Uncle Ward were the only whites at the first meeting, along with about twenty or so blacks. But the second night there was double that number, and on the last day, a Sunday afternoon when Reverend Smithers announced that there would be a river baptism, there must have been a hundred colored folks from fifty miles around. They were all people we hadn't seen before. We never knew how they all heard about it, but they did.

There was singing like I hadn't heard since I was a girl on the McSimmons plantation when the twenty-five or thirty slaves would get together in the evenings and break out in old spirituals.

I'd never seen Josepha so keyed up and excited as on that Sunday afternoon at the river, clapping and swaying her big body and singing louder than anyone. Henry entered into the spirit of it too. It was as if being around all the other former slaves had opened a part of them that had been quiet a long time. Jeremiah and Emma and I sat on the ground together. William was with Katie at the house because Katie said she had felt funny being the only white person the day before. Papa and Uncle Ward hadn't been back since the first day either.

Jeremiah and I were singing and clapping along, but Emma was strangely quiet. I didn't understand why because I knew she loved to sing, and she had such a beautiful voice. After the preacher started preaching, she got quieter and more somber yet.

From the look on her face I almost thought she was about to start crying.

"My brothers and sisters," Reverend Smithers was saying in a loud voice, "for years our people prayed ter know that life er freedom in dat ol' Promised Land. So now we's free, all right, but have we really entered dat Promised Land in our hearts? Have we crossed dat River Jordan in baptism for sin? Have we risen out of dose waters, jes' like this water behind me here, into dat new life of salvation? Have you felt da fire, my brothers and sisters? Which fire is calling with your name—da fire of hell or da fire of da spirit of the living God!"

His voice had risen to such a pitch that all through the listening crowd, murmurs and shouts and comments rose to join him.

"Amen!" now shouted several voices, followed by a chorus of more Amens.

"Don't wait, brother . . . delay not, sisters," the preacher went on, nearly shouting every word. "Now is dat day of salvation! Another day may be too late. Da fires of hell burn bright and are eternal and unquenched. But da fire of da spirit blows where it will. Salvation is offered on that appointed day, and he who turns away will find da spirit fires waxing cold. Come to Jesus, brothers and sisters, and confess your sin in your hearts dat His salvation may burn bright."

"Yes, brother," cried half a dozen voices. "Yes. Amen! Amen!" came more shouts.

"Now come, brothers and sisters, and come up

beside me and confess your sin, and let da fire of da spirit fall on you. Then step into da waters of da Jordan to wash away da evil stain of sin."

All around there were shouts and movement and more shouts—"Praise Jesus! Amen!"

People made their way to the river's edge, while others went up and fell on their knees and raised their hands in the air, shouting and praising God and some praying in shouts—"Forgive us, Lawd . . . yes, Lawd, forgive our sin. Redeem us, Lawd . . . save us from dose fires er hell!"

I glanced beside me. Emma was trembling. She didn't have a look of happiness on her face but one of fear.

All of a sudden she stood up. But instead of going down to the river to join the preacher like I expected, she turned in the opposite direction and walked back to the house. I glanced at Jeremiah and he shrugged—knowing no more of what was going on with Emma than I did.

After another minute or two, Jeremiah stood up. I looked up at him.

"I wants ter be baptized," he said.

He walked down toward the river. By now Reverend Smithers was standing out in the water up to his waist, and there was a line of people waiting to reach him. On the shore everyone was singing and praising and praying, and great shouts of praise sounded every time he raised the next man or woman out of the water with shouts of "Praise Jesus!" and "Amen!"

Suddenly it dawned on me that I had never been baptized either. It didn't take me long to decide that I wanted to be too.

I got up and followed Jeremiah to the river. He was several people in front of me in line and never looked back once. But after Reverend Smithers lowered him down in the water, and he came up dripping—I heard Henry and Josepha both shouting, "Praise da Lawd!" from the shore.

Jeremiah saw me behind him and smiled at me. I took his hand as he walked by and gave it a big squeeze. Then a couple minutes later it was my turn.

When Reverend Smithers raised me up out of the water—and this time I heard Jeremiah's voice shouting praises along with Henry's and Josepha's—Jeremiah's wasn't the first face I saw. It was Emma's. She was marching down toward the river with a look of determination on her face. At her side holding her hand was four-year-old William. They stopped long enough to take off their shoes, then walked into the river and toward the preacher at the end of a line of three or four others.

"I want you ter baptize my son," said Emma when she reached him. "Dis is William."

"Well, William," said Reverend Smithers. "Does you believe in Jesus for da salvation er your sins?"

"Yes, sir!" said William, though I'm not sure he realized what was coming.

The next instant the preacher took hold of him by the shoulders, put his hand over his nose and mouth, and two seconds later, William was sputter-

ing and struggling out of the water, shouting for Emma. She scooped him up and turned and walked out of the river where she joined the rest of us.

"I din't want dose ol' fires er hell ter be lickin' dere lips at my William!" she said as they sat down.

By that evening, everyone was gone. Reverend Smither's salvation wagon was rumbling away toward some other harvest field of salvation. Rosewood was returning to normal—except for the fact that for an hour that evening we all excitedly told Katie and Papa and Uncle Ward all about the day's events.

One thing puzzled me, though. For as wholeheartedly committed to God as he was in his life, I couldn't understand why Micah Duff hadn't gone to the baptism, or why he said almost nothing that entire evening.

A Conversation to Remember

22

THE MAY SUN HAD RISEN HOT, AND THE GROUND was soft and moist and perfect for planting. The three Rosewood young women had been in the vegetable garden most of the morning hoeing and raking the warm earth into furrows. Half the garden had already sprouted hundreds of green shoots that would become potatoes, turnips, carrots, beans, and peas. Tomorrow they would plant beans, peas, pumpkin, and seasonal varieties of squash.

Katie had gone in to help Josepha with lunch. Mayme had gone with her to the house to take down the morning's laundry from the line. For the last fifteen or twenty minutes Emma had been working alone. The others had noticed how quiet she had been for several days. And now, alone with her own thoughts as she methodically hoed the ground, Emma's eyes slowly filled with tears.

Many new feelings had been swirling around in her brain and heart in recent days and weeks. She didn't know what to do with them. Why did they make her cry?

Why was she happy and sad and afraid all at once? She never remembered crying much before in her life. She had not been whipped much like other slaves. She had had a relatively easy existence as a slave. But last night she had cried herself to sleep . . . and for no reason.

And now here were the hot, unsought tears overwhelming her again.

All at once something made her glance toward the house.

Twenty yards away sat Micah Duff on the ground watching her.

Emma drew in a surprised breath and wiped unconsciously at her eyes with the back of a dirty hand.

"I'm sorry, Emma," he said, smiling and getting up from the ground where he sat. "I didn't mean to startle you." He walked toward her.

"How long you been dere, Mister Duff?" said Emma.

"Only a few minutes. I was trying to decide whether to disturb you or not. You looked lost in thought."

Emma glanced away, strangely embarrassed. There came the tears again!

"What is it, Emma?" asked Micah softly as he came forward and stood in front of her. She continued to stare down at the ground. The hoe in her hand was still.

"I don't know," she said with a mournful tone. "I's jes' feelin' all mixed up, dat's all."

"Mixed up about what?" Micah probed gently.

"I don't know . . . God an' hell an' everythin', I reckon."

"What about them?"

"I don't know . . . I reckon I wuz jes' thinkin' dat I oughter been baptized mysel' when dat preacher wuz baptizin' my William."

"Why didn't you ask to be baptized, then?"

"I don' know," wailed Emma, "I knows I shoulda. Jes' like my William. I ain't neber been baptized neither, but I wuz . . . embarrassed an' afraid. . . ."

"Why do you think you should have been baptized?"

"Cuz I felt dat fire er da spirit in my heart dat da preacher wuz talkin' 'bout. I felt da urge, but I didn't do it, an' now I's feared even more."

"Afraid of what, Emma?"

"Dat I ain't been baptized, an' dat I's go ter hell an' burn in dem fires forever effen somefin' happens ter me."

Micah smiled, but it was a smile mingling sadness with obvious tenderness.

"You will not go to hell, Emma," he said.

"How kin you be sure, Mister Duff? I ain't neber been baptized an' I's a terrible sinner, I knows dat, an' dat preacher, he say dat wiffout bein' baptized, dose fires er hell, dey'll burn yer soul fo eber an' eber."

Hearing such words hit almost like a visible pain as Micah heard them.

"Come, Emma," he said, taking the hoe from her hand and setting it on the ground. "Let's you and I go for a walk."

He led her away. Like a compliant and hungry child, Emma followed.

Micah Duff and Emma Tolan walked for several minutes toward the woods in silence.

Emma's countenance was quiet, but her heart was pounding. What was this most unusual man walking alone with her about to say? Unconsciously, she glanced back at the house, wondering if anyone was watching them go off together.

What would Mayme think!

"Emma," said Micah after a few minutes, "do you mind if I ask you a very important and very personal question?"

"I don't reckon so, Mister Duff," replied Emma, suddenly more nervous than ever. What kind of a question was he going to ask!

"All right, Emma," Micah went on, "here it is. Why do you think you're such a terrible person?"

"Oh, dat ain't a hard one ter answer," said Emma, almost relieved. "Everybody always told me I wuz a bad girl—ain't dat what a sinner is, Mister Duff?"

"I am not so sure it is, Emma," smiled Micah. "What other people think and what God thinks may be very different things."

"But I ain't never knowed anythin' 'bout God, so I figger other folks knows more den me."

"Well, maybe it is time you learned about God for yourself, Emma . . . and learned what *He* thinks of you, not what other people say about Him, or what *they* say about you."

They walked on.

All of a sudden the words that came from Emma's mouth, more unexpectedly to her ears even than to Micah's, revealed that she had slowly been absorbing more than either of them realized.

"Mister Duff," she said, "does you really mean what you tol' me before, dat dere's good in everyone?"

Micah turned and looked at her deeply as they walked. Emma felt as though he was looking all the way inside her.

"It isn't only that I *think* so, Emma," he said. "There *is* good in everyone because we're made in God's image. God himself said so."

"Even in a lame-brain dat can't read an' dat folks say ain't too bright an' who's a bad sinner like me?"

"Oh, Emma—you are not a lame-brain. It grieves me to hear you say such a thing. Yes—there is wonderful good in you."

"You really think so, Mister Duff?"

"Yes, Emma . . . yes! If I can see good in you, imagine how much more God sees."

"But He ain't lookin' fer good, is He? Ain't God only lookin' fer sin?"

"Where did you hear a lie like that, Emma?"

"Ain't dat what dey all say—dat preacher an' folk like him. Ain't dat what hell's for, ter punish our sins?"

"Even though God might have to deal with our sins to help us get rid of them, He isn't *looking* for our sins. He is mostly looking for the good in us that He put inside us when He created us as His children. It's the good in us that helps Jesus get rid of the sin in us. Without that good, Jesus couldn't help us become more like Him."

"But I's a terrible sinner, Mister Duff. I's sure ter go ter hell. God couldn't love me da way He does you er Mayme er Miz Katie."

"We're all sinners, Emma. You heard me tell what I was like when I was young. But God saw good in me, just like Hawk did. And realizing that Hawk valued me and that God valued me as a person also helped me recognize my sin and then begin to overcome it. We can't properly deal with sin in our lives until we realize that God is our Father and that He created us with good in us too. It won't do you any good to be baptized just because you are afraid of hell. Baptism won't save you from hell, Emma."

"What will, den?"

"Recognizing that God loves you, that you are His precious child, and then living as His child just as Jesus did. That's why Jesus is called our Savior, because He saves us and shows us how to live as God's children, and then helps us."

Again it was quiet.

"I don't know, Mister Duff," said Emma. "Dat's all a mite hard fo me ter understand. I din't neber hab a real father, so I neber heard dat God wuz dat. I thought God wuz a big fearsome giant like a white man dat sent sinners ter hell."

"Do you think God *wants* sinners to go to hell, Emma?"

"I figgered He must."

"What if He doesn't? What if God is doing everything He possibly can to *prevent* people from having to go there?"

"Dat don't soun' like folks say, Mister Duff. Dat ain't nuthin' like dat preacher said."

"No . . . it surely isn't," said Micah. "But what if it is true?"

"You mean dat God's tryin' ter keep folks *out* er hell?"

Micah nodded.

"I don't know, Mister Duff—den God, He'd be different den I thought. I don't know what ter think 'bout dat. Den . . . den who *is* God anyway, Mister Duff?"

"He is your Father, Emma. He wants to help you because He created you and loves you and because you are special to Him. That's who He is, Emma."

"Den ef . . . ef He ain't wantin' ter sen' me ter hell, an' ef He ain't fearsome an' mean like I thought, den . . . what does . . . what does He . . . what is I supposed ter do? Ef He's different den all dat, Mister Duff . . . den who is I? Dat must mean I's different too."

Micah smiled again.

"You are His child, Emma—His very own daughter, that's who you are, and that's who He wants you to be."

Learning to Read
23

One morning Katie and I slept in longer than usual. When we got up and dressed we realized that Emma was just getting up too. William had been up earlier, but Emma had gone back to sleep. I didn't know where William was until we went downstairs and heard him in the kitchen chattering away to Josepha.

As we descended the stairs together, we were surprised to see Micah Duff sitting there on the couch in the parlor, reading the Bible from Katie's bookshelf.

"Good morning, ladies," he said, glancing up.

"What you be doin' here, Mister Duff?" said Emma.

"I came up for a cup of Josepha's coffee," he said. "The men were out on the porch enjoying theirs. So I decided to sit down here and read awhile."

"You really reading dat big book, Mister Duff?" said Emma, walking over and looking with amaze-

ment at the thick book in his hands.

"I am, Emma."

"What's it about?"

"It's about Jesus and the things He taught and did."

"Oh, da Bible. I knows 'bout da Bible. I wish I cud read."

"You could."

"But I can't," said Emma, looking at him as if he was speaking nonsense.

"But you could," repeated Micah.

"How?"

"Reading is like anything else. It's something you have to learn."

"Just like I did, Emma," I said.

"But how does you learn ter read an' talk better?" she asked, looking back and forth between Micah and me.

"If you want to learn anything bad enough, you can," said Micah. "There's no secret to learning anything. Anyone who wants to read bad enough can learn to read. It might be hard work. Learning anything new is usually hard work."

"But I could neber learn ter read somefin' like dat," said Emma, pointing to the big Bible in Micah's lap.

"Sure you could. Sit down here, Emma."

Interested ourselves, Katie and I sat down opposite while Emma took a seat on the couch at Micah's side. I was curious what he was going to say because I was still practicing to learn to read better myself.

❧ ✻ ☙

"Here," Micah said when Emma was seated. Micah pointed with his finger. "This is what I was reading when you came in. Look at this word."

"What it mean?" asked Emma.

"That word says 'house.'"

"How does you know?"

"I learned it. See—that letter is an *h,* that's an *o,* that's a *u,* that's an *s,* and that's an *e*. Put them all together and those letters spell the word 'house.'"

"Dat's mighty complicated!"

"But it isn't really, Emma. Stare at that word 'house' a minute. Memorize what it looks like."

Micah waited, keeping his finger in place as Emma looked at the word for several seconds.

"Now I'll show you another word," said Micah. He moved his finger a little way up the page. "See this word?"

Emma nodded.

"It's pretty small but is a very important word. That's the word 'the.' See, it's got an *h* and an *e* in it, just like 'house,' with a *t* in front. Put them together and it spells 'the.' So now look at that 'the' and memorize what it looks like."

Emma did.

"What do you think, Emma?" said Micah after a few seconds. "Do you think you could read something I wrote down on a piece of paper?"

"I cudn't do dat, Mister Duff. I done told you—I can't read."

"I think you're wrong, Emma. I think that if I wrote

something down and gave it to you—I think you could read it."

"Dat'd be a rip-staver, all right, but I cudn't!"

"Katie," said Micah, looking over at her. "Would you mind fetching me a pencil and piece of paper?"

Katie jumped up and ran upstairs. By now everyone was eager to see what was going to happen. When Katie bounded back downstairs and gave the pencil and paper to Micah, he turned again to Emma.

"All right, Emma," he said, "now close your eyes."

He took the paper and wrote on it. "I am writing something down, Emma," he said. "Now . . . open your eyes . . . and I want you to read back to me what I wrote."

He handed her the sheet. Emma looked at it, and a big smile spread over her face.

"It says 'da house'!" she said excitedly.

"You see, I thought you could do it. You just read something."

"Dat's da first thing I eber read in my life! So how does you read a big book like dat Bible dere?"

"You have to learn many, many words. Hundreds of words . . . thousands of words. But it isn't so hard as you might think. And after a while, when you know all the letters of the alphabet and what they look like and sound like, you can even read words that you haven't memorized."

"Kin you show me how you wud read in dis?" she said, pointing to the Bible, which still lay open on Micah's lap.

"All right. I'll point with my finger to the words as I read them. You can look at the words as I say them. I'll show you what I was reading."

"I's do dat!" said Emma eagerly.

"All right, I'll start right here," said Micah. " '*And he called them unto him,*' " he read, saying each word slowly, " '*and said unto them in parables, How can Satan cast out Satan? And if a . . .*' "

He paused.

"Do you see that word, Emma?—you read it for me"

"It says 'house.' "

"That's right. Now you've read something in the Bible. '*And if a house be divided against itself, that . . .*' "

Again he waited, his finger pointed to the next word.

"House," said Emma.

"Good—'*that house cannot stand. And if Satan rise up against himself, and be divided, he cannot stand, but hath an end. No man can enter into a strong man's . . .*' "

"House," Emma said again.

" '*. . . and spoil his goods, except he will first bind . . .*' "

This time Emma hesitated.

"Do you remember this word?" asked Micah, pointing to the page.

"Oh, I forgot a minute. It says 'da.' "

"That's right—'*he will first bind the strong man; and then he will spoil his . . .*' "

"House," said Emma once more.

Micah set the Bible down. Emma had a great look of pride on her face.

"You just read five words out of the Bible," said Micah. "So you see, it isn't so hard."

"Show me another word, Mister Duff!" said Emma excitedly.

"Don't you think those are enough for one day? I don't want you to forget those two."

"I won't forgit. I'll learn dem. I promise. Please, Mister Duff, show me two more words. I kin do it!"

Micah laughed. "All right, Emma," he said.

He glanced over the passage.

"Okay, look at this word," he said, pointing down at the page. "This is a name. It's the word 'Satan.'"

"Oh, I knows about him!" said Emma. "Dat da debil—dat ol' rattlesnake!"

Micah laughed again. "That's him, all right! Do you see that first letter, the squiggly one? That's an *s*. That letter is in 'house' too. All the letters get used over and over in different words. They combine differently to make different sounds. It's like putting foods together in different combinations to make different things. Josepha uses the same flour to make bread one day, flapjacks the next, biscuits the next, and a cake the next. Reading is a lot like cooking. You have to know how to mix the ingredients. There are twenty-six letters—that's all. There are a lot more foods than that. So you see, Emma, reading is even easier than cooking!"

"Dat can't hardly be, Mister Duff!" laughed Emma.

"But do you understand what I am saying?"

"I reckon I does."

"You have to learn how the combination of letters makes different words. That squiggly *s* at the front of the word 'Satan,' for instance, is the same *s* that is in the word 'house.'—Look, do you see?"

He pointed to the two words.

"They even sound the same—Satan . . . and house. Do you hear that *ssss* sound? That's the *s* in both words."

"It looks an' soun's like a snake!" said Emma.

"You're right, it does," said Micah. "It's squiggly and it hisses, just like a snake! I never thought of that before."

"An' da word 'snake' soun's dat same way. Does it got dat same letter, dat *s*?"

"Indeed it does. Very good, Emma. You see, you are catching on to this very quickly. You are a good learner. They all have that same hisssss sound, because they all have an *s* in them—sssssatan . . . sssssnake . . . housssse," he said, drawing out the sound of each.

"Show me another word," said Emma.

"All right . . . uh, let me see—how about this one here," said Micah, pointing again. "This is the word 'man.'"

Emma stared down at the page.

"So there are four words for you, Emma—'house,' 'the,' 'Satan,' and 'man.' Do you think you know them?"

"I think so, Mister Duff, but dey's startin' ter run together in my brain. But kin we read it agin? Kin I try ter read dem words?"

"I'll read along slowly," nodded Micah, "and when I come to a word you know, you read it."

"I kin do dat!"

"All right," said Micah, then returned his gaze to Katie's Bible. " '*And he called them unto him,*' " he read, saying each word slowly, " '*and said unto them in parables, How can . . .*' "

He paused.

"Satan," said Emma proudly, then added, almost muttering softly to herself, "—dat ol' rattlesnake!"

Micah smiled to himself, then continued to read, " '*. . . cast out . . .*' "

"Satan," said Emma again.

" *'And if a . . .'* "

"House!"

" *'. . . be divided against itself, that . . .'* "

"House!"

" *'. . . cannot stand. And if . . .'* "

"Satan!"

" *'. . . rise up against himself, and be divided, he cannot stand, but hath an end. No . . .'* "

"Uh . . . man!" said Emma after a moment's hesitation.

" *'. . . can enter into a strong . . .'* "

"Uh . . . dat looks kind er like dat man," said Emma, "but den der's da squiggles on it. Dat's a mite confusin'."

"That's right—it is the word 'man' with an *s*. What is an *s* supposed to sound like?"

"Da hiss ob a snake," said Emma.

"So say it like that," said Micah. "Say 'man' and add that sound."

"Uh . . . manssss," said Emma, exaggerating the sound.

"That's right—it's the word 'man's.' And when you say it quickly, it is, *'can enter into a strong man's . . .'* "

"House!" added Emma.

" *'. . . and spoil his goods,'* " Micah now went on, " *'except he will first bind . . .'* "

"Da!"

" *'. . . strong . . .'* "

"Man!"

" *'. . . and then he will spoil his . . .'* "

"House!" said Emma triumphantly.

"You did it, Emma! You are a fast and excellent student. You will be reading in no time!"

"Does you really think so, Mister Duff?"

"Of course. Just look how quickly you learned those words. And you know several letters already, especially the *s*."

"I knows dat one, all right," smiled Emma, "—dat ol' rattlesnake!"

Josepha walked in from the kitchen, unable to contain her curiosity any longer at what she had been hearing.

"What's going on in here?" she asked.

"Emma's learning to read the Bible!" said Katie enthusiastically. The look on Josepha's face said that she would need more convincing than Katie's enthusiasm.

"Watch this, Josepha," said Micah.

Again he picked up the paper and pencil and wrote something down on it. He held it up to Emma.

"Can you read this, Emma?" he asked.

She looked at it and her eyes got wide in amazement. She was more astonished than Josepha was about to be.

"Yes!" she said excitedly. "I kin read it! It says, 'Satan's house' an' den it says, 'da man's house'!"

She glanced over at Katie and Mayme with a look of pride and accomplishment on her face.

Even Josepha was impressed.

"Will you teach me more words, Mister Duff?" asked Emma eagerly, turning again to Micah.

"I would be happy to," he replied. "And so would Katie, or Mayme. And unless I miss my guess, there is a book on that shelf over there that you could be reading in no time."

"What book?"

"It's called a *McGuffey Reader*."

"That's the one Katie taught me to read with, Emma," Mayme said.

"Teach me too, will you, Miz Katie!"

⁂

It was only two or three days later when I came upon Emma and Katie in the kitchen with the McGuffey Reader on the table in front of them. Emma was trying to sound out a few words, with Katie helping her along.

"Isn't she doing wonderfully, Mayme?" said Katie.

"She is. Micah was right, Emma—you are a fast learner."

⁂

ALTERCATION

24

JEREMIAH HAD TOLD MR. WATSON ABOUT MICAH, and Micah had now gone into town several times when Mr. Watson had extra work for a day or two or when there was an especially big delivery to make to one of the nearby plantations. It wasn't regular work but was enough to make him a little extra money so that he didn't have to depend on Ward and Templeton, or occasionally a few dollars from Jeremiah on his payday, for everything.

After his own first payment from Mr. Watson, Micah tried to give the money to Templeton for room and board. But Templeton would hear nothing of it.

"Son, I told you at the beginning," he said, "that I would put you to work. You've earned every penny I've paid you, and if you can earn a little more from Mr. Watson, so much the better."

"I am very appreciative, sir," said Micah. "But it still seems that I ought—"

A wave of Templeton's hand put an end to any further discussion of room and board.

Several days after their discussion, Mr. Watson again asked Jeremiah to bring Micah along with him to work the following day.

Jeremiah and Micah got up early the next morning to ride to the mill. Henry had risen even earlier and was already halfway to town by the time the younger men were ready to go.

The two friends stood at the hitching post together, saddling up their horses. Micah's purebred was broad and black, a good two hands taller than Jeremiah's horse. The young pinto had the typical brown and white markings of a common "paint" horse and was still easily spooked.

"That's a fine horse, Jake."

"Not nearly as fine as yers, and you knows it."

"What do you say we see about that?"

"Whatchu mean, Duff?"

"How about a race?"

"Aw, Duff. Dat horse er yers is a Union war horse, 'bout da best-trained horse I eber seen. Dis paint is still only half broke, and not full grown."

"Come on. From here to the river and back."

"Why—whuppin' me at fishin's not enuff fer you?"

"Just for fun, Jake. It's not about one of us being better. We're equals. Brothers. And this brother wants to race."

"And dis brother wants ter see you eat dust."

Micah grinned. "That's more like it!"

Jeremiah mounted up and could hardly keep his horse from bolting before Micah had untied his horse from the hitching post. Jeremiah pulled back hard on the reins and the paint reared up on its hind legs. Jeremiah muttered soothing words to the horse and stroked its neck, trying to calm the animal down.

"Ready?" Micah asked.

"I's past ready."

"On the count of three. One, two . . ."

But Jeremiah's paint wasn't inclined to wait. Before Micah could shout *Three!*, the pinto bolted. With a cry of surprise, Jeremiah grabbed at the saddle and clenched the horse's sides with his knees, desperate to keep his seat.

"Hey!" laughed Micah, then shouted to his own mount. The big black reared, then tore off after Jeremiah's pinto.

Even over the sound of the galloping hooves beneath him, Jeremiah heard the thunder of the great beast in pursuit. He glanced back, face full of excitement and also a little terror at the sight that met his eyes.

"Git goin', Paint!" he shouted. "He's bigger'n you, but we kin do it. Come on!"

Within seconds, Micah had drawn even. He glanced over at Jeremiah with a grin. The competitive blood in both young men was by now flowing hot. Both lashed and shouted at their horses as they galloped along side by side. Slowly, Jeremiah saw the rump of the black pulling ahead of him, then the great black tail came into view from the corner of his eye, and within another twenty seconds he was looking up at the tail in front of him. An occasional clump of grass or dirt flew up from beneath the black's hooves into his face.

"Come on, Paint!" he shouted again. "Don't gib up . . . we's git him at da turn!"

Micah reached the river two or three seconds in the

lead. But the size of his horse, and the speed he was moving, caused the big black to swing in a wide arc as he turned. But Jeremiah reined up just as they reached the river, spun his pinto quickly around, and dug in his heels again. And now his paint, whether catching the spirit of the race, or eager to return to the barn in front of him, burst forward with more speed than Jeremiah had ever seen. By the time Micah completed his turn, suddenly he looked up to see Jeremiah now a length and a half—judging by the size of the pinto—in the lead.

"Hey, how'd you do that!" he shouted.

But now the pinto's legs were flying so fast over the ground that they were just a blur of speed, and nothing Micah did could make up the distance between them.

Inexplicably, the paint knew the finish line as well as he had known to turn on the speed at the river. The instant he passed the hitching post, he slammed his hooves to the ground, stopping so unexpectantly and abruptly that Jeremiah lost his balance. He flew straight over the horse's head and landed in the mire of the barnyard, still mucky from the recent rains.

"Jake! You all right?" Micah called, reining in. He jumped to the ground in one smooth motion.

"Yeah. Jes' great," he said, looking up from where he lay.

"You should be. You won." Micah held his hand down to Jeremiah.

Jeremiah grasped his friend's hand and let Micah haul him up. "Din't know winnin' wud feel so *good,*" he groaned. Gingerly he got to his feet and rubbed his backside.

Micah again grasped Jeremiah's hand, this time giving it a congratulatory shake. "What that horse of yours lacks in training it more than makes up for in youth and spirit and determination. Just like you, Jake. Just like you."

When their day's work at the mill was done about four o'clock that same afternoon, they walked up to the livery to see when Henry would be ready to ride back out to Rosewood. Since Henry had been living at the plantation, Mr. Guiness had hired another man for the evening hours at the livery.

The three left together, then stopped at the general store on the way out of town.

"Mister Templeton asked me to check for mail," said Jeremiah.

They dismounted, tied their horses to the hitching rail, and stepped up onto the boardwalk just as the door of the store opened. They glanced up to see Deke Steeves and his father walk out and head toward them. Henry and Jeremiah stepped off the boardwalk back onto the street to let them pass. But Micah continued on by them at the edge of the walkway, brushing arms slightly with Dwight Steeves as they walked by each other. The two whites stopped, although Micah did not realize it immediately as he continued on toward the store.

"Hey, boy!" called Steeves behind him.

Now Micah became aware that he was alone. He paused to glance back to see what had become of Jeremiah and Henry. Instead he saw the two white men glaring at him from two or three feet away. Henry and Jeremiah had stopped and were standing in the street. And now Micah also realized that the words had been addressed to him.

"You deaf, boy!" now said the younger of the two. "My pa's talking to you. Ain't you got no respect for your betters?"

"I'm sorry," said Micah calmly. "I didn't realize you were speaking to me. Is there something I can do for you?"

Deke glanced at his father in astonishment, wondering what he would do, then back at Micah.

"You must be a stranger in these parts, boy," said the elder of the two.

"That's right. I only arrived recently."

"Why you tryin' to talk like a white man? You funnin' with me, boy?"

"No, sir. This is how I talk."

"So you're an uppity one, huh?"

"I hope not, sir. I simply try to be myself."

"Well, you be yourself and get out of our way."

"I'm sorry. I don't understand what you mean."

"When a white man comes along the walk, you get yourself off it to let him pass like a good little nigger boy—that's what I mean."

"Ah, I see . . . there seemed to me to be plenty of room on the walk."

"Plenty of room or not, you stand aside when you see a white man, boy. That's how we do things here."

"I did not realize that. My sincere apologies."

"But you see, boy," said Steeves, "it's too late for that. Apologies are no good now. You didn't stand aside, and you touched my arm. So you see, we gotta teach you a lesson so you won't forget what I told you."

"Look, mister," said Micah, still not intimidated. "I

offered you my apology. I am truly sorry. There is no need to make more of this than is necessary."

"You're telling me what's necessary? You're nothing but a stupid, filthy nigger!"

He took a menacing step toward Micah. The rage in his eyes was more from Micah's calm demeanor and refined speech than from anything that had happened. It grated on his own ignorance and arrogance that a black man sounded more educated—and with a Northern accent besides!—than he.

But now Henry stepped up from the street and between them.

"He din't mean no harm, Mister Steeves," he said. "Like he said, he din't know no better. I'll hab a talk wiff him an' he'll show more respeck in da future."

But by now both Steeves were itching for a fight. Dwight shoved Henry rudely.

"Get out of my way, Patterson!" he shouted. "You mind your own affairs."

Henry stumbled a step or two back but recovered his balance. Angered himself by now, Jeremiah took a step forward and Deke Steeves appeared eager to meet him with his fists clenched.

"We's jes' be on our way," said Henry. "Come on, boys. An' we be wishin' you a good day, Mister Steeves. Come on, son," he said to Jeremiah.

But Dwight Steeves stepped forward and roughly grabbed Henry by the shoulder and restrained him.

"You hold on, Patterson!" he said. "I ain't through with you. You'll go when I tell you to go."

He lifted his other arm to strike Henry with the back of

his hand. But Micah leapt forward, grabbed his wrist in midair and held it fast. With almost the same motion he took hold of Steeves' other hand and pulled it from Henry's shoulder. Henry stepped back. Slowly Micah released his grip of Steeves' wrist, and Steeves found himself standing eye to eye with a young black man who was stronger than he had thought and who refused to be bullied.

"You will *not* lay another hand on that man," said Micah, his eyes boring straight into those of Dwight Steeves. His voice was soft, calm, and full of a confidence Steeves had never before heard from a black man. It was the voice of command.

For several seconds they stood a foot apart, eye to eye. What Micah silently said with his eyes was even more powerful than the words he had spoken with his lips. For once in his life, though his whole body was quivering in white wrath, the wind had been taken out of Dwight Steeves' bluster. His mouth hung open, yet he found himself speechless. The venom in his own heart had been countered by neither hatred nor fear, but by some strange power he had never encountered before. It rendered him, for the moment, powerless.

Micah turned, nodded to Henry and Jeremiah, then led them along the boardwalk and into Mrs. Hammond's store. When they came out a minute or two later, the two Steeves were nowhere to be seen.

Weed Jenkins

25

About a week after the incident in town, Weed Jenkins approached Rosewood. As he had intended, Jeremiah and Henry were both in town. He had no intention of being seen, but if someone should accidentally spot him, he hoped he would not be recognized. It was not easy for a six-foot, two-inch young man of lanky and somewhat ungainly build to creep without being seen into the precincts of a plantation like Rosewood with so many people about. But young Jenkins managed to accomplish it. His first responsibility was simply to figure out how many people were there and who they were. All he knew for sure was that his father was looking for a baby or some kid. He didn't know which. He didn't know what for, either.

He heard a mixture of voices as he crept, crouching as low as his height would permit, within the rows of corn between the barn and the woods. The stalks were only about three or three-and-a-half feet high, and it was no easy task to keep from being seen. But slowly he inched closer. By the time he reached the end of the field, the back of the barn was only fifty or seventy-five yards away. He heard the voices clearly now, but they were on the opposite side, between the barn and the house. The coast looked clear.

Weed stood up amid the corn stalks that only came up to his waist, looked around one final time, then made a dash for it. Twenty seconds later he was standing against the back wall of the barn, catching his breath. Other than the grunting of a few pigs nearby, no alarm sounded. It didn't appear that he'd been seen. He crept along the wall to the open end of the horse stables, turned the corner into the cool overhang of the barn's roof, climbed a couple of stall fences, and within another minute was safely inside the barn. He waited until his eyes were accustomed to the dim light, then tried to get his bearings.

It was wash day at Rosewood, and on this day everyone was helping. Josepha and Katie were at the great washtub, pounding and stirring the contents with two great wooden paddles, and Emma and I were taking the shirts and dresses and trousers and blankets out of the pot one at a time, rinsing them in a tub of clean water, then ringing them out and hanging them on the line. Uncle Ward and my papa were sitting on the porch talking, without even pretending to help. Even if they had tried, Josepha would have run them off, saying that washing clothes was woman's work. But the mood between us all was lighthearted. The day was warm, and it seemed like wash day always brought out mischief of some kind. But the mischief this day brought was not what we could have imagined.

William was scampering around playfully between all of us, running up onto the porch with something to tell one of the men, then back toward the rest of us, time and again. There was never any lack of energy around Rosewood with William at the age he was! I paused at the clothesline, stretched my body a few seconds, and glanced around. I hadn't seen Micah for several minutes.

"Emma, have you seen Micah?" I asked. But before she could reply, William came running toward us.

"What dat, Mama?" cried William, running up to Emma at the end of the line.

"Dat's yer uncle Templeton's trousers."

"Why's you hangin' dem up like dat, Mama?"

"Cuz dey's all wet, and dey's gotter dry in da sun."

But already William had turned on his heels and was running off toward the house.

"William," Emma called after him. "Don't be pesterin' Uncle Templeton an' Uncle Ward."

But her words fell on his back as he ran toward the porch to tell Papa that his trousers were all wet!

From the darkness of the barn, Weed Jenkins' eyes had opened wide at the word "William" from Emma's lips. He stood against the near wall, one eye peering through a half-inch crack of light between the boards, looking out at the commotion and trying to make sense of wash day at Rosewood. He recognized everyone but Josepha, Emma, and Uncle Ward. The white Clairborne girl and the black girl had been involved in the ruckus in town last year with Deke Steeves and Jesse Earl and the fool Patterson nigger kid.

One of the men on the porch was the one who had broken the thing up. He had heard his father talking about the Daniels brothers, and that must be them. He hadn't been able to see too much through the hood on his head that night he was out here with the men. But he had seen the same three that night too, before he had hauled Patterson out of this same barn where he stood now. But the fat colored lady and the scrawny, good-looking nigger girl—he'd never seen them before.

And a colored kid! Just what his father had sent him to find!

A colored kid called William whose mother's name was Emma.

Suddenly Weed Jenkins' eyes shot open even wider.

William!

When he'd asked why he needed to know who was at Rosewood, all his pa had said was that somebody important needed the information for personal reasons.

There was only one important man around here who everybody had been talking about for a month—William McSimmons . . . *William* McSimmons!

He now remembered that he had seen William McSimmons walking into his father's office several days ago!

Weed Jenkins was nobody's dummy. The pieces suddenly began to fit together as to why his father had sent him here. But almost the same instant as his brain began to try to piece together what this information might mean, he felt a hand clamp down suddenly on the blade of his shoulder and a voice sounded at his ear.

"I'd like to know what you're up to, son," it said.

*

When Micah walked out of the barn toward us, half dragging, half leading a lanky young white man two or three inches taller than himself, all of us stopped what we were doing in an instant and stared at them. But it was only for a second or two. We hadn't had any danger around Rosewood for so long we'd become maybe a little too careless. Suddenly the sight of a stranger in our midst, being pulled out of the barn by Micah with a serious look on his face, reminded us very quickly that we still had to do our best to keep Emma and William from being found out. But it looked like it might be too late for that!

"William!" cried Emma. "Git yo'self into da house!"

"Why, Mama?"

"Git, William!" said Emma sternly, dropping the shirt in her hands and running for the house herself, chasing William in front of her like she was trying to herd a chicken back into its pen.

Papa and Uncle Ward slowly stood as the kitchen door banged shut behind Emma.

"Any of you know why this young man would be

standing inside the barn staring at you all?" asked Micah, coming toward us with his prisoner in tow.

Papa and Uncle Ward glanced at each other with a look of question, then slowly came down the stairs off the porch. Josepha and Katie set down their wash paddles, and I draped a dress over the line. We all three made our way toward the house too. Whatever was going on, it would probably be best for us not to be around.

Katie paused as she passed my papa. "That's Weed Jenkins, Uncle Templeton," she said softly. "He's Sheriff Jenkins' son . . . you know, from Oakwood."

Papa nodded as he took in the information with a serious expression. He'd vaguely recognized the boy immediately but didn't know who he was. Then Katie and I continued on inside.

Micah came forward and stopped before Papa and Uncle Ward.

"What are you doing in our barn, young man?" asked my papa.

"None of your business, nigger-lover," said Weed rudely.

A sharp pinch of Micah's grip on his shoulder muscle made him wince in pain.

"I want to know what you were doing."

"I ain't gonna tell you nothin'! What are them niggers doin' inside a white man's house? You're all just a bunch of nigger-lovers."

Another pinch, harder than the first caused Weed to cry out in pain.

"Hey you," said Micah, "show a little more

respect for your elders, son!"

"I ain't got no respect for the likes of them!" spat Weed.

Micah glanced at the two men, silently asking what they wanted him to do.

"We could take him in to the sheriff," suggested Uncle Ward, who hadn't heard Katie's words to my papa.

"Somehow I don't think that would do any good," said Papa. He paused and rubbed his chin a minute, thinking.

"You might as well let him go, Micah," he said. "He's not going to tell us anything.—You get out of here, son," he said to Weed. "And if you have occasion to come back, you come to the door and knock. Don't go sneaking around like this. You hear me?"

He nodded to Micah, who released him. Weed swore at all three of them, gave Micah a look of hatred, then walked off down the road toward town and, after three or four minutes, disappeared from sight.

Emma Hears a Voice

26

We were all more guarded and cautious after that, reminded again of the ill will there was in the community against Rosewood. It seemed that in the last year people had reacted in two different ways. Some people were more friendly to us and seemed to respect us all for what we had done. But on the other side, there was growing resentment too.

But even after this incident, Emma wasn't thinking too much of the danger. She had been thinking the whole time about her conversation with Micah Duff.

Several days passed. How deeply all of Micah Duff's spiritual arguments had penetrated Emma's intellect was not nearly so important as the fact that the spirit of his convictions had penetrated her heart. And it was doing that more than she realized.

Something was slowly changing within her, though she did not know what. Still less did she know how to respond to it. She could not quite believe herself worthy of God's attention. The ancient wind that blows where it will was sending fresh new breezes of life through recently opened windows in Emma's heart and soul. They were windows that had been opened by the affirming kindness of these people around her. And now especially by the compassionate, gentle, ministering presence of Micah Duff.

But the new outlook was so stupendous, and so intermingled in her mind with the remarkable character of Micah Duff—like no black man she had ever imagined!—that Emma was distracted, confused, and hardly seemed to know what to do with herself. She said scarcely a word for two days.

On the third day she went out alone after breakfast. No one saw her for several hours. She walked through fields and into the woods and along the river. She had so rarely cried in her life, yet now the tears were flowing as if they had themselves become a river inside her.

All her life her own worthlessness had been the single consistency she had clung to, the one unchanging fact in a life without any other foundation or anchor. To have someone now tell her that the only thing she had known as *true* was really an *untruth,* and that she was *not* the person she had always thought . . . it had undone her at the very root of her being.

Yet we will often believe what another says of us more than we will believe it when left to ourselves. And Emma was now heroically, almost desperately, struggling to find some way to believe what Micah Duff had told her, and to cast away the garment of inadequacy that clung so close to her. But it was a hard struggle. To believe good about ourselves is sometimes the hardest mental struggle in all of life.

She could not quite believe it yet. But that she was wrestling with her own worth as a person showed that the birth-struggle of the true child of God had begun in her.

Her voice was murmuring softly as she went. She was not praying exactly, but carrying on the ongoing debate and questioning, both with herself and with God, that had been going on for days.

I don't see how dere kin be dat good in me dat Mister Duff is talkin' bout. I's a sinner an' I sinned terrible wiff dat William McSimmons, an' I wuz too lame-brained jes' ter kick him away an' scream my head off. His papa wuz a good man an' he'd hab helped me. I sinned, all right, but I cudn't tell Mister Duff 'bout dat. What wud he think ob me ter know dat I slep' wiff such a no-good man! But God knows . . . a body can't hide nuthin' from Him, dat's fo sho'! He knows what I done, an' He knows what a fool an' dummy I's always been. Dere ain't nuthin' in me dat's any good, an' God must know dat better'n anybody. Miz Katie an' Mayme, dey's different . . . dey treat me good, anyway. An' dat Mister Duff an' Jeremiah, dey's as nice ter me as any man cud be. Dey's all real good ter me, but nobody kin fool God 'bout what's down inside, an' He—

Suddenly Emma heard a voice. She stopped and listened intently. Had someone followed her? Was someone spying on her?

Everything was still and quiet around her. She began to think she had imagined it.

Now the words of Micah Duff came back to her. She remembered what he had said—*God speaks to everyone, but not everyone hears His voice.*

Would God ever speak to *her*, Emma wondered. Micah Duff was different. He was a fine man. He had seen a vision!

But God would never—

Suddenly the voice spoke again. A chill went through her as Emma's eyes opened wide at the astonishing words she had heard.

I love you, Emma.

"Dat be you speakin' ter me, Lawd?" she said aloud. "I don't know ef I heard you right, or ef I heard dat at all, or jes' made it up. Where is you, Lawd? Is you tryin' ter say somethin' ter me?"

Yet a third time came the voice—whether audible or inaudible, Emma never knew.

I love you, Emma, the words gently whispered in her spirit. *You are precious in my sight. You are my child.*

She could no longer keep back the flood of tears. They burst like a dam and Emma fell on her knees where she was, weeping at the very idea of what she now knew she had heard.

"How can you, Lawd?" she said through her tears. "Does you really . . . can you really love me, Jesus?"

A mighty *Yes!* flooded into Emma's heart.

She broke down and sobbed.

Several minutes went by. Gradually Emma began to calm and the flow stilled.

"I don't know why, or how you wud eber care 'bout one like me, God," Emma said quietly. "But ef you does, den

I want ter be like Mister Duff says an' be yer daughter. Help me, Jesus, cuz I don't hardly even know what dat means. Ef everythin's different den I thought wiff you an' wiff me, den I reckon I oughter know it."

⁂

When Emma walked into the house some time later, her eyes were aglow. We all knew immediately that something had happened.

She went straight to Micah Duff.

"Mister Duff," she said, "I wants you ter tell me everythin' dat man Hawk tol' you 'bout God."

Micah smiled and nodded. They went outside together a little while later and were gone most of the afternoon.

That night Emma came to see Katie and me in our room.

She had the most different look on her face. I recognized it from how Katie had changed too during our first year together. It was the change of deciding what was to be done rather than just taking things as they happened to come. Emma had always just gone along with what we said about everything. Now there was a look of determination on her face.

"I wants ter be baptized," she said.

"Do you want me to talk to Reverend Hall?" asked Katie.

"I don't know, Miz Katie," she said. "I doesn't know him too well."

"What about Micah Duff?" I suggested. "I'm sure

he would baptize you, Emma."

"Dat be right nice," she said. "He be da one I want. He cud say some nice words an' a prayer. Dat's what I want."

"Do you want me to ask him, Emma?" I said.

"Yes'm, I wud."

Another Baptism

27

When we all walked from the house down to the river on the following Sunday, the mood was so different than before. It was quiet and peaceful. The conversation between us was serious and subdued, though happy. There was none of the festive atmosphere the revival had had. It was quiet happy, not boisterous happy.

The entire Rosewood family walked along together—Henry and Jeremiah and Micah, Papa and Uncle Ward, Katie and me and Josepha, and of course Emma and William. Emma was dressed in one of Katie's dresses of pure white and walked in front between Ward and Templeton. Their three faces were something to see. The two men loved Emma as much as the rest of us, as was easy to see from their expressions.

We were all smiling. We couldn't help it! We were so happy for Emma. We knew that this was probably the most special day in her life.

Emma was the most radiant of all. The glow in her eyes and the look of her whole face was one I can't even begin to describe. Something had obviously begun to get inside her . . . and change her.

We reached the river—the same place where Reverend Smithers had baptized Jeremiah and me and William. We all sat down on the shore. Then Micah went and stood at the water's edge and faced us.

"When Mayme asked me if I would baptize Emma," Micah said, smiling down first toward me and then toward Emma, "I couldn't think of any greater honor I'd ever had in my life. I've never done this before, so it will be as new to me as being baptized will be to Emma. But baptism isn't a ritual or rite that gets you into heaven and must therefore be carried out exactly the same every time. It is a symbol of something else, a symbol of something that has already taken place in a person's heart. And I think all of us here know very well just from watching her that something new has come alive in Emma's heart recently, don't we?"

We all nodded and smiled and glanced over at Emma. She looked down shyly, though she was smiling too.

"No, it's not baptism that changes anything by itself," Micah went on, "but what happens inside us when we tell God we want to be His, that we want to begin living like He wants us to. That's what baptism symbolizes, a new way of life . . . that we have decided to follow a new master.

"That master is Jesus. He says, 'Follow me.' He was baptized, and so we too are baptized, not as a ritual but as a symbol of a life dedicated to following Him. Jesus was not baptized by a priest but by his own cousin. There is no one that must stand between us and God. We can come directly into God's presence ourselves. Emma does not need me or anyone else—she met God herself.

"And so I stand here today, not as a middleman between Emma and God but as Emma's friend, to help her say to all the world that God's life is alive inside her."

He paused and glanced down at Emma with a smile. "Would you come up here with me, Emma?" he said.

Emma stood up and walked to his side, the most beautiful look of quiet joy on her face.

"Do you have anything you would like to say, Emma?" asked Micah.

"Jes' dat I love you all," she said softly. "You's all been so good ter me, an' I's more grateful den I kin say."

I wiped at my eyes. I couldn't help it. To see Emma like this was like seeing a princess emerge out of inside her, like coming out of a cocoon—the real Emma that had always been there but that none of us had seen clearly before, not even Emma herself.

It was almost like Micah knew what I was thinking, because at that moment he glanced toward me with a knowing smile.

"As Emma and I talked at length a few days ago

about God and what life with Him means," Micah said, Emma still at his side, "she asked me what it meant to be God's son or daughter. I told her that I thought one of the most important things it meant was learning to see ourselves in the same way God sees us—learning to recognize both the good that is in us as well as the sin that is in us that God wants us to conquer and grow out of. It doesn't seem to me that we can be fully God's children without both. Some people are so proud that they can't see their own sin. Others are so defeated and discouraged in themselves they can't see the good that God put inside them when He created them in His own image. Neither kind of person can be fully God's child because they are not seeing with God's eyes. They can't love their neighbor as themselves because they don't know themselves the way they really are.

"We have to learn to see people with God's eyes. To do that we need to learn to see ourselves with God's eyes too. And that is what Emma is now learning to do."

Micah paused and glanced at Emma. Now they both stooped down to take off their shoes, then walked out into the river. Micah took Emma's hand to steady her until they were about halfway across and waist deep, then they turned back to face the rest of us on the bank.

Micah turned toward Emma with a smile.

"Are you ready, Emma?" he asked.

"Dat I is," said Emma. "An' wiff Jesus' help, I's gwine do my best ter see both myself an' other folk *like He sees dem, an' den ter live like He wants me ter live."*

"It gives us all great joy to hear you say that, Emma," said Micah.

He faced her, put one hand behind her shoulder and the other over her nose and mouth.

"Then be baptized, Emma Tolan," said Micah, "in the name of your Father, who loves you, and His Son Jesus, who will now help you live as God's daughter."

Slowly he lowered her down into the water, then gently lifted her up.

Emma opened her eyes, sputtered a little, wiped her face with a wet hand, and then, smiling radiantly, said so softly that we could just make out the words, "Praise Jesus."

Then slowly they made their way out of the water as Josepha began to sing, "Were you there when they crucified my Lord?"

Josepha's voice was so low and rich and pure that no one thought of joining in with her. We were all content to listen as she completed the old song we knew so well.

"Were you there when they crucified my Lord?
O—o—o—oh . . . sometimes it causes me to tremble . . . tremble.
Were you there when they crucified my Lord?
Were you there when they laid Him in the tomb?
Were you there when they laid Him in the tomb?
O—o—o—oh . . . sometimes it causes me to tremble . . . tremble.

Were you there when they laid Him in the tomb?
Were you there when He rose up from the dead?
Were you there when He rose up from the dead?
O—o—o—oh . . . sometimes it causes me to tremble . . . tremble.
Were you there when they crucified my Lord?"

SHAKEDOWN

28

WEED JENKINS DID NOT GO TO HIS FATHER IMMEdiately after leaving Rosewood. All the way home on the day of his eventful visit to Rosewood he had revolved the thing over in his mind, recalling rumors he had heard over the years. The result was a visit to the McSimmons plantation several days later, but not by the elder Jenkins that William McSimmons had expected.

"I'm here to see Mister McSimmons," said Weed when a white housemaid opened the door. The lady disappeared inside. A minute later the tall form of Charlotte McSimmons appeared.

"I understand you want to speak to my husband."

"Yes, ma'am."

"What about?"

"It's personal, ma'am."

"Then you can tell me."

"Sorry, ma'am. I got information that's just for Mr. McSimmons."

Muttering a few words of frustration, the lady disappeared.

When William McSimmons himself appeared, the expression on his face was neither warm nor welcoming.

"You're young Jenkins, aren't you," he said, "Sam's boy?"

"That's right, sir."

"What do you want, then?"

"I got some information that might be valuable to you."

"I'll be the judge of what's valuable to me and what isn't. All right, then—out with it. What is this information?"

"I was thinking that maybe you'd make it worth my while, Mr. McSimmons."

An expletive burst from William McSimmons' lips.

"How dare you come to my house and try to blackmail me!" he shouted.

"I wasn't trying to blackmail you, sir," said Weed nervously. "I just thought maybe if I could be a help to you with what I found out, that maybe you might find me a job on your plantation. Work's hard to find these days, sir."

"Not as hard as decent help," rejoined McSimmons. "You tell me what's on your mind and I'll decide what it's worth to me. It'll have to be mighty valuable information to be worth a job."

"It's about something I learned out at that plantation of the Daniels brothers, Mr. McSimmons. My pa said you wanted to know what was going on there."

McSimmons eyed Weed carefully. "What your father and I discussed is between us," he said after a few seconds. "All right . . . tell me what you learned."

"I saw who was there," said Weed, "—there were three whites, the Clairborne girl and the two Daniels brothers, and a bunch of coloreds—a fat old lady, a man maybe twenty-five or twenty-six, and a girl, maybe twenty, scrawny but mighty pretty for a nigger girl. They called her Emma, and she had a kid she called William—"

William McSimmons' eyes shot open at the two names, but he did his best not to show it.

"How old was the boy?" he asked.

"I don't know, sir. I reckon maybe three or four . . . somewhere in there."

"All right, Jenkins, you've given me the information."

"What about the job, Mr. McSimmons?"

"I told you I would have to wait and see."

Obviously disappointed, Weed Jenkins turned to go. When he was gone, Charlotte McSimmons walked into her husband's study, her face red, her nostrils flared, her eyes burning with fire.

"So the creature has turned up at last," she seethed, angered anew at her husband. "You had *relations* with that idiot house slave and now your bastard black child has come back to haunt us."

"Look, Charlotte," rejoined McSimmons testily, "these things happen. Don't make more of it than it is."

"These things don't just happen, William," she shot back. "Babies don't just turn up accidentally. So I want to know what you're going to do about it. I will not be made to look the fool in public. If this thing is not dealt with, and I mean *permanently*, William, you can count me out of your Washington plans. I would rather not go at all than have a little black child turn up later calling you *Daddy* and having all eyes turn to me in silent question. How do you think that would make me look! Can you imagine the humiliation? Well, I won't put up with it. You end this sordid mess once and for all, or count me out."

She turned and left the room, leaving William McSimmons feeling like a scolded child. If he did not even have the guts to stand up to his wife, how would he fare in Washington when going up against the nation's politicians?

He would have to worry about that later. Right now there were more pressing concerns on his mind. And those politicians were no match for his wife!

McSimmons left the house.

Across the yard he saw Weed Jenkins mounting his horse to go. Angered anew at the boy's bold-faced presumption, his forehead clouded over with dark thought. If the kid blabbed about his interest in the Daniels' place, it could cause unpleasant talk. Maybe he had been a little hasty.

He called out and signaled him to wait.

"Hold up there a minute, young Jenkins!" he said, walking toward him. "About that job . . . you just keep quiet about our conversation today and I'll see what I can do. Can you do that?"

"Yes, sir, Mr. McSimmons!"

"If I find I can trust you . . . then I'll take care of you."

"Gee, thanks, Mr. McSimmons."

"But it will be just between the two of us."

"Yes, sir."

McSimmons watched him ride off a minute later, then went in search of one of his men he knew he could trust.

"Bert," he said, "there's something I'd like you to do for me. Ride over to the McNally place—you know, east about twelve miles. There's a hand there, white fellow by the name of Griggs. Tell him to come see me."

Bert nodded.

"Tell him to come at night," McSimmons added. "No one can see him."

Three nights later, William McSimmons and his old associate, a man who was resourceful and who could keep his mouth shut, were seated in the former's office with the dim light of a lantern on the desk between them.

"I have a job for you," said McSimmons. "It's a little out of the ordinary, but if you come through for me, I won't forget it."

The other man nodded. He was not opposed to getting his hands dirty once in a while.

"There's a plantation between here and Greens Crossing somewhere—west, I think, though I'm not sure. It's those two Daniels' place, the brothers with the niggers."

"I heard of them."

"Get a couple of boys, but make sure they know nothing about me. Your arrangements with them are up to you."

"Whatever you say."

"There's a nigger girl there," McSimmons went on. "Nineteen, twenty, twenty-one, tall, thin, good-looking for a colored. She's got a brat of a kid. I need you to get over there, keep out of sight, and figure out some way of snatching her and the kid without being seen. We've got to get rid of the two of them if you get my meaning."

Griggs nodded.

"But it can't be traced to me. So you've got to nab her without being seen, when she's away from the others, or . . . well, I don't know—that's what you've got to find out. See if she's ever away from the place. We've got to have the kid too. It does me no good to get rid of her without the kid. Then get rid of them."

"How do I know which one's her?"

"I just told you, you—" McSimmons retorted angrily, then stopped.

He needed the man's help . . . there was no use losing his temper.

"I suppose you're right," he said irritably. "The place is crawling with coloreds and I don't want you making off with the wrong one."

He grabbed a sheet of paper from the desk where he sat and picked up a pen. He scribbled quickly on it and handed it to the other man. Griggs looked it over.

"Emma Tolan—twenty, tall, black, thin, pretty, dumb as a post," he read aloud. *"Brat called William—four years old."*

"Think you can memorize that?" said McSimmons.

"Shouldn't be too hard," grinned the other man, folding the paper and stuffing it into his pocket. "I'll study the descriptions real good."

"You do that. Then you just take care of them, that's all."

"You can count on me, Mr. McSimmons."

UNEXPECTED FEELINGS

29

MICAH DUFF WAS DIFFERENT AFTER EMMA'S BAPtism. No one noticed immediately because they were so caught up in the day's events. The walk to the river had been quiet and peaceful and serene. But the walk back to the house was joyous, with Emma still the center of attention. Everyone was talking and excited.

Everyone, that is, but Micah Duff.

They returned to the house, Emma dripping and glowing, to change her clothes and get ready for the special dinner they had planned for that afternoon. Micah lagged behind the others. Sudden new thoughts and feelings were spinning through his brain. He went straight to his cabin, also to change clothes. Then he sat down on his bed, staring ahead, wondering what was to be done.

His heart was pounding.

Where had this sudden revelation come from? The expression . . . the eyes . . . the smile—why had he not seen them in the same way before that moment back at the river?

Suddenly a whole new world of meaning had exploded into his brain. Everything had changed in an instant.

He had been moving about on his own for so long, and in the army before that, he had encountered but a handful of young women near his age. And then only in passing. He had never given the idea of love much thought. He had certainly not expected his heart suddenly to be turned upside down.

Micah was the last to arrive at the festive dinner two hours later. He found it difficult to enter into the exuberance of the celebration in such close proximity to one who suddenly dominated his every thought. He excused himself at the first opportunity. He left the house and sought the fields. He needed air. He needed to breathe. His heart was beating too fast.

It had been too close in there! It had been all he could do to keep his eyes from betraying him.

Up till now, since the day he had arrived at Rosewood, he had not been attending closely to his own feelings. True, there had been that first day and the unmistakable pull the first time he'd seen her. It hadn't really begun today, he knew that. He had felt it from the first moment. But he had tried to dismiss it from his mind—tried to tell himself it was just a fleeting fancy. He thought he had done so. Apparently he hadn't. It had crept upon him, growing without him realizing it, swelling inside him . . . and now the feeling had suddenly sprouted stronger than ever.

What was he to do?

It was obvious he could no longer ignore what he felt. He had come here to mend and get his health back. Instead he had apparently fallen in love.

He shook his head and tried to dismiss the thought from his mind. How could *he* be in love with *her*? They were so different in so many ways, as different as night and day, from such different backgrounds.

But he could not dismiss it. He knew it was true.

Should he tell her?

How could he? He was still a relative outsider. The last thing he wanted to do was upset the Rosewood family. This unique blend of individuals was too wonderful a thing. He could do nothing, say nothing, to alter the delicate balance of relationship. To declare himself openly might change things in ways he could not foresee. He could not risk it. The Rosewood family must not be disrupted. He cared about them all too much to be responsible for that.

And yet everything within him cried out to tell her. Was it possible they might have a future together? How could love such as he felt remain silent? Was love meant to exist in a lonely vacuum of silence, or to be shouted from the rooftops?

Love or no love, he could never take her away from all this. This was her home. This was her family. He was the stranger, the wandering soldier. She had a family. She had begun to put down roots here. He had nothing to offer her.

And what of his own future? He could not just stay indefinitely. He was still but a guest presuming on their hospitality.

Perhaps, he thought, the best solution would be to leave the way he had come. He was back on his feet. He and his horse were both healthy. He was restored in body and spirit. Perhaps Rosewood had done its work in his life and it was time to move on . . . as he had always planned to do.

Perhaps, rather than declaring his love, with all the confusion and unsettling it was likely to cause, he merely needed to seek an opportunity to say good-bye.

Micah remained quiet most of the rest of the day, pondering his dilemma, and retired early. He slept, however, but fitfully. He was too preoccupied—alone at night more than ever with the expression, the eyes, the smile . . . so familiar and yet suddenly so new.

The following day, he hoped, would bring clarification, and perhaps decision. He would be on his way the day after that. Templeton had helped him think through his own goals. It was time to follow them . . . time to go west as he had long dreamed of. But he could not go without speaking to her—if not of his love, at least of his decision to leave Rosewood. He needed to for himself. He had to try to make her understand, even if he could not tell her . . . *everything*.

Lunch came. The entire family was together. When the meal was over, one by one the men excused themselves—Henry and Jeremiah first, to go into town for the afternoon.

Then Ward stood.

"I think I need a short nap before we get on with that field," he said. "What about you, Templeton?"

Templeton also stood.

"I think I'll just go out and work a little more on the plough," he said.

Both men left the kitchen.

"Well, I might jes' lay myself down too as soon as dese dishes is done," said Josepha.

"Don't worry about that, Josepha," said Katie. "We'll

take care of them. You go have a rest."

"Dat right nice ob you, chil'. I think I jes' might at dat."

She stood up and walked out of the kitchen. Still Micah sat at the table with the three girls. Now at last Emma stood also.

"Come on, William," she said. "It be time fo yer nap."

Mother and son left the room and followed Josepha upstairs.

Katie and Mayme stood up and began clearing away the lunch things from the table.

"More coffee, Micah?" asked Mayme.

He glanced up into her face from where he sat and smiled. "Thank you, Mayme," he said. "Yes . . . I believe I will have another cup."

Mayme poured most of what remained in the pot into Micah's cup. His eyes now glanced up toward Katie as she pumped water into the tub. Mayme began carrying the dishes from the table to the counter. The conversation lagged. Micah seemed distracted.

Emma returned.

"Get William down?" asked Katie.

"He's almost asleep already," replied Emma, taking up a dish towel.

"Anyone gather the eggs this morning?" asked Mayme.

"Not me," said Emma.

"I'm about done with these plates," said Katie. "I'll go look." She wiped her hands on her apron and walked outside.

Still Micah sat, sipping slowly at what was now a cold cup of coffee. Neither of the two remaining girls could have possibly guessed what was going through his mind.

When is she going to leave, he thought to himself, *so I can talk to her alone?*

Perhaps, he thought, he ought to just go back to his cabin himself and find some other time. This did not seem to be working out.

Micah began to rise. But the words from Mayme's mouth as Katie walked back inside with a handful of eggs stopped him.

"I think I'm going to go upstairs and have a rest too," she said.

"I'll join you," said Katie.

The two left the kitchen.

Micah remained at the table. It was silent a minute or two. He watched Emma as she continued to dry the last of the dishes and put them away. Gradually she felt his eyes on her back. Her neck grew warm.

"You know, Emma," said Micah at length, "you are truly beautiful."

The words did not seem to surprise or embarrass her.

"I knows dat, Mister Duff," she replied with matter-of-fact simplicity. "People been tellin' me dat all my life. Dumb but fetchin', dat's what dey say. But bein' pretty ain't worth nuthin' ef you ain't got da brains ter go wiff it."

"You are thinking differently about all that now, aren't you?"

"Dat I is, Mister Duff, thanks ter you. I ain't worried effen I's smart er dumb cuz I knows God loves me. I's special in His sight, ain't dat right, an' dat's all dat matters."

"I am so happy to hear you say it, Emma—more happy than I can possibly tell you," said Micah. "But what I meant a moment ago was that you were beautiful *inside,* not merely on the outside. It's that inside part of you that is changing and growing every day. That's the *you* I meant. The person you are deep down inside is a beautiful, wonderful young lady."

Emma turned toward him.

"You's callin' me . . . a *lady,* Mister Duff," she said in a confused expression. "How kin you say dat? I ain't neber been called such a thing."

"I believe you *are* a lady, Emma."

Emma stared back in disbelief.

"You's always sayin' da mos' out er da way things, Mister Duff!" she said with a smile. "How's a body ter keep up wiff all da strange things you say? I knows I been baptized, an' I knows God loves me, an' I'm right grateful, but . . . me, a *lady*!"

She set the dish towel down. Now Emma was embarrassed. She was afraid she might start babbling like she sometimes did, and say something she would regret.

"I's think I'll go upstairs an' hab myself a rest too," she said, then walked from the kitchen.

Micah Duff was left alone at the table. Still he had not said what he had hoped to say.

Give Me Jesus
30

FOR DAYS AFTER HER BAPTISM EMMA HAD BEEN quiet, peaceful, the glow of changed life and self-acceptance radiating from her countenance.

God *loved* her!

The wonderful reality of that truth opened whole new worlds within her heart, as did the realization that all these friends in her Rosewood family loved her too. They did not just put up with her. They truly loved her. She was not an outcast; she was as much a part of this family as anyone else. They *valued* her. Every time the startling truth came back to her, a smile spread over her face.

Yet none of these changes were equal to the victorious new wonder that salvation brings in its wake of at last loving *herself*.

How can one love one's neighbor as oneself if one despises who he is? Emma was now on the upward path of recognizing her true self as a child of God. For she had begun to recognize His gift to her, the goodness within her own being.

Except for her brief lapse in the kitchen when she had become nervous to find herself alone with Micah Duff and had started to talk too much, she had been almost silent for days. All these new personal revelations were so huge that even the sound of her own voice distracted her from the inner silence needed to absorb them. She needed time to be alone with God, alone with herself . . . to drink it all in.

Two days after the baptism she again went to the river. There she sat down and stared out at the place where Micah had baptized her.

She recalled his words:

"Then be baptized, Emma Tolan, in the name of your Father, who loves you, and His Son Jesus, who will now help you live as God's daughter."

Quietly she began to hum.

It was an old tune . . . where had she learned it? She hardly knew where the words came from.

Give me Jesus . . .

From somewhere deep in her memory, slowly and mysteriously more words rose from within her and she began to sing, faintly at first, then with increasing power. Her heart seemed to rise on the wings of the old spiritual and carry her into lofty regions of praise to God for the new life flowering within her.

Give me Jesus.
Give me Jesus.
You may have all the world.
Give me Jesus.

For an hour her prayers and the soft singing of her voice were intermingled in quiet thankfulness and praise.

For the next several afternoons she went daily . . . to sit, to remember, and to pray.

Micah Duff did not leave Rosewood on the day he had planned. The business of his heart remained unfinished.

How exactly he intended to say good-bye without making the situation intolerable he did not know. But he could not depart this place without trying to find some meeting of minds between them, even if not a meeting of hearts. He would be haunted forever after, and would never be able to live with himself if he did not at least make the effort.

He had seen the changes in Emma and rejoiced in them. He had also observed her daily pilgrimages—for in their own way, her walks to the river truly were, though the distance was less than a mile.

Three days after their aborted talk in the kitchen, twenty or thirty minutes after he saw her disappear across the fields, Micah followed.

Even before he arrived in sight of the river, the soft high tones of Emma's voice, barely discernible yet with a crystal clarity such as he had never before imagined her capable of, floated out on the warm air to meet him.

"Give me Jesus . . ."

A surge went through Micah's heart. The words and haunting melody filled him with feelings as deep as those in Emma's heart prompting them. To see another human soul yield in humble acknowledgment to the loving Fatherhood of the universe was enough to bring the joy of heaven not only to the angels but to all fellow pilgrims who observe it. But there was more to the stirrings of his heart on this day than the new birth of Emma's spiritual being.

And in truth it had been building within him since the very day of his arrival.

Micah sat down on the bank some distance away and listened with growing reverence and awe. Whether Hawk Trumbull had been an angel appearing to him that night in Chicago, he didn't know. But this soft voice ringing out so pure and high was surely that of an angel in humble human form.

"Dark midnight was my cry,
Give me Jesus.
In the morning when I rise,
Give me Jesus.
And when I come to die,
Give me Jesus.
Give me Jesus.
Give me Jesus.
You may have all the world.
Give me Jesus."

How long the two sat, he couldn't say. Time on love's clock runs at a slower pace.

He listened . . . at peace to be near her. She sat gazing out at the river . . . at peace too, but unaware that she was not alone.

After some time she stood, her heart quiet, and turned to walk back in the direction of the house. She had only taken a few steps before her gaze rose to the top of the bank where she saw him seated.

She stopped. She was too contented to be surprised. He was always turning up at the most unusual times. She had almost begun to expect it.

She stood a moment returning his gaze. She sensed instantly that there had been a change, but still did not suspect what it was. Then she smiled and walked up the slope toward him.

He waited. Emma sat down about ten feet away. Neither spoke for a long time. But neither was uncomfortable. At last Emma was at peace even in the presence of this one she judged her superior in every way. She was at peace in his presence, though strangely shy to glance toward him too readily. The secret of her feelings toward him was one she would never dare expose to anyone. Her heart was blossoming in many ways. But the flower of love was one whose fragrance she would conceal within the solitude of her own private world. No remote suggestion entered her mind of what lay as an aching burden on his heart to be so near her.

"That was beautiful, Emma," said Micah at length. "I enjoyed listening to you sing very much. It was like listening to angels' praises. I hope you don't mind."

"I don't mind, Mister Duff," she replied softly, her eyes in her lap.

Again it was quiet.

"Are you happy here, Emma?" asked Micah.

"Oh yes. Dis is da best place I cud imagine, da best place I been in all my life. Especially now. I's happier den eber."

"You would never leave Katie and Mayme?"

"No, I cudn't neber leave dem."

A long silence followed.

"I, uh . . . have something to say to you, Emma," said Micah at length. His voice was soft, different, unlike what she was accustomed to. It possessed none of his characteristic confidence. He sounded almost timid to continue. "I don't . . . know exactly how to say it," he haltingly went on, "but I . . . I want you to know how special this time has been for me . . . getting to know you, the talks we have had . . . sharing with each other about God and life . . . your asking me to baptize you. I want you to know that I will never forget any of it. I am so happy for the life you have here . . . with the others, with Katie and Mayme . . . and for your new walk with God."

He drew in a deep breath, struggling not only to find the right words but also struggling to breathe.

"Dat all makes it soun' like you's fixin' ter go someplace, Mister Duff," said Emma softly. "You almost soun' like you's—"

She stopped abruptly.

"Mister Duff, you's not leavin'!" she added. "Is you sayin' good-bye?"

She glanced up at him, her face full of terrible question. But Micah was looking down and did not see the expression on her face. If he had, it would have melted him on the spot.

"Yes—I, uh . . . I have been thinking," he went on, picking absently at a tuft of grass, "that maybe it might be time for me to—"

"You can't leave, Mister Duff," said Emma, cutting him off in an imploring voice that caught him off guard. "Everybody'd be sadder den dey cud be. Mayme an' Miz Katie, I know dere hearts wud break ef you wuz to leave."

Theirs were not exactly the hearts Micah was thinking about right then!

"I know it seems difficult," he said, "which is the reason I wanted to tell you first . . . why I had to tell you how . . . that you are more special to me, Emma, than—"

Emma again grew quiet. A sense began to steal over her that this was about more than a farewell between friends. The flower hidden in her own heart sent a sudden burst of perfume into her brain!

". . . and that is why I . . . why I had to tell you . . ."

Micah began to falter.

"You know how much God loves you?"

Emma nodded.

"But . . . but it's more than that, Emma . . . and I . . . I . . ."

It was no use! He could not hold back the floodwaters. At last the dam burst.

"It is not only . . . God is not the only one who . . . that is . . . I . . . I love you too, Emma."

Once the words left his lips, Micah knew that he *had* to say them all along.

A gasp escaped Emma's lips. Her hand went to her mouth and her eyes widened in astonishment.

Silent and exquisite thunder exploded within her. What were these unbelievable, terrifying, wonderful, incredible words she had just heard!

Speechless in stunned awe and shock, she did not even try to speak. Such a man . . . love *her*! She could not bring the two opposites together in her brain.

Yet even as she sat silent and still as a statue, her heart opened to receive the stupendous truth that she was loved by the best man she had ever met.

At last she found her voice, but her throat was very dry.

"Me?" she said faintly.

Micah rose and walked the few steps to where Emma was and sat down beside her. Emma heard the movement and felt his presence. She could not dare turn to face him.

Micah took her hand and clasped it in his own.

"I love you, Emma," he whispered softly.

Emma closed her eyes, fighting to still the flood rising in her heart. Finally she opened her eyes and turned her head. Their eyes met, hers swimming in liquid incredulity, his aglow with love that had at last found expression.

"But . . . but how kin dis be?" she said, her voice barely audible. "You can't . . . but . . ." she struggled to continue. "You can't . . . mean dat you . . . you cudn't . . . love *me*, Mister Duff!" she finally managed to say. "*Me* . . . I's nobody . . . I's jes' Emma . . . what 'bout Mayme . . . or eben Miz Katie? I thought you an' Mayme . . ."

"What about her?"

"Isn't you . . ."

"What . . . do I fancy Mayme?" said Micah. "I love her and Jake as dear friends. But I saw how it was between them from the beginning. It is *you* I have loved since the first day I got here . . . from the moment when you and Jake walked in from chasing the cows . . . I saw something in you the first time I laid eyes on you . . . something special. I knew I loved you then. And when I took your hand and led you into the river and saw the radiant look on your face, that's when at last it broke upon me what I'd felt all along. And I knew I either had to tell you, or leave."

Great tears fell from Emma's eyes. Slowly, summoning the courage of her new self-acceptance, she turned all the way toward him, hesitated but once briefly, then let his waiting arms enfold her in their embrace. She leaned her head down and let it rest against his chest, then slowly spread her own arms around him where they sat.

The clock of love slowed yet more, and thus they remained for several long wonderful seconds.

"Oh, Mister Duff . . . you's some man!" said Emma as they gradually fell apart. "How you kin love someone like me, I don't even want ter ax why or how. Wiff Miz Katie an' Mayme jes' 'bout da two bes' girls dere eber wuz, how you cud say you love *me* . . . dat jes' be too much fo me ter understand. But ef dere's one thing you's taught me, it's ter accept da love dat's dere . . . so I reckon ef it's good enuff fo God, it ought ter be good enuff fo da love ob a man too. So I'll try ter believe what you say, though it's too good ter be true."

Micah laughed lightly and stroked her hair. The wonderful quiet contentedness of love settled upon their hearts. There was but one more thing burning on Emma's heart to say.

"Please . . . don't leave, Mister Duff," she whispered. "Not now. I think my heart wud like ter break ef you did!"

"Emma . . . Emma," Micah whispered, "when will you ever be able to stop calling me *Mister* Duff?"

"I's try . . . *Micah*," said Emma softly with an embarrassed smile.

Katie and I were out walking when we saw Micah and Emma coming toward us in the distance. As they drew closer we saw that they were walking hand in hand.

We looked at each other with our mouths hanging open, then we started running forward. Emma saw us and now left Micah and ran toward us. We met laughing and talking excitedly like three little girls!

"Emma, Emma," exclaimed Katie, "what happened?"

"Dis good man," said Emma, beaming as she glanced behind her, "he says he loves me, Miz Katie! How dat kin be, I don' know. Almost like a miracle, ain't it? I thought he had taken a fancy ter you, Mayme," she said to me, "an' now he says he loves me!"

"Oh, Emma, we're so happy for you!" I exclaimed. And I truly was.

Katie's smile was as big as Emma's, and she now gave Emma a big hug. The next instant we were all three in each other's arms laughing and crying all at once.

Emma stood back, giving us each a look and a smile that melted our hearts, a look of such love and gratitude like I'd never seen. Then she turned and ran back to Micah, who opened one arm wide to receive her. They continued toward us, his arm around her shoulder, Emma's head contentedly leaning against him.

I turned and looked back toward the house. Jeremiah was standing there watching.

I gave a little wave and left Katie and went to join him. I walked straight to him, put my arms around him and rested my head against his chest.

He reached around and held me close.

"Isn't that wonderful to see, Jeremiah," I said, "—Micah and Emma like that? Who would have imagined it?"

"I had a feelin' 'bout it," said Jeremiah, "though at first I wuz afraid he might take you away from me."

"What!" I said, laughing and standing back to look in Jeremiah's face to see if he was serious.

"Well, he's a mighty handsome man."

"No more than you, Jeremiah."

"An' you an' he . . . that is, well . . . bein' around Micah made me wonder ef I wuz good enuff fo you."

"Jeremiah Patterson!" I said. "What kind of talk is that? You're not just good enough for me, I love you—so let's have no more talk like that."

"I'll try," he said.

Again I embraced him and we were quiet for a minute.

"Did you really think that?" I asked more seriously.

"For a spell," he said. "I couldn't help comparin' myself ter him."

"I'm sorry, Jeremiah," I said. "I'm sorry I didn't realize you were feeling that way. I suppose I was caught up in . . . I don't know, just enjoying getting to know Micah as a person and talking to him. I didn't realize what it must have looked like to you. Katie even thought I was falling in love with him. But when she asked me if I was, I had to stop and think, and it made me realize that I wasn't, and that

you were still the one I loved. I didn't think that maybe you were seeing the same thing Katie was. I am sorry."

"Dat's all right, Mayme. Everythin's all right now."

⁂

The River's Claim

31

Summer was approaching and it started to get hot.

One particular day came and you could tell from the moment the sun came up that it would be a hot and muggy day. Micah had said nothing more about leaving Rosewood, and we were all glad of that.

By ten in the morning it was ninety degrees. At noon it was over a hundred. Not a breath of wind came from anywhere. What work there was to be done we got finished by lunchtime and no one felt inclined to go out in the hot sun after that if they didn't have to. Everything would take care of itself until milking time came late in the afternoon. Only Uncle Ward had the energy to venture outdoors. He rode into town to make a withdrawal at the bank and pick up our mail.

Emma was still going out to the river a lot. She had been doing so ever since that day she would never forget. Usually she went alone—to pray or sing. It was obvious that her baptism, and now her growing love for Micah, had changed things so deep in her heart that she was still trying to grasp it. I think she went to the river every day or two—to sit as the river flowed slowly past her, to try to figure it all out, but also just to let it sink yet deeper into her heart.

"You want ter go dab dose feet er yers in da ribber, William?" said Emma to her four-year-old son as we sat around the table in the kitchen about noon.

"Dat I do, Mama!" replied the boy eagerly. "Kin we go now?"

"We'll go right after lunch," answered Emma.

Forty minutes later, the tall slender black girl and chubby little boy of tan complexion walked away from the house hand in hand. I went to the door and watched as they crossed two fields of green ripening stalks whose cotton we would all help pick later in the summer.

Back when Emma had first come here she hadn't been much use to anyone and she knew it. Though she had been the oldest of we three girls who were thrown together by the war and had to figure out a way to survive alone, Emma had needed more taking care of than both Katie and me combined.

But she had grown and changed in the four years since she found her way here. And new and even more far-reaching kinds of changes were now stirring in Emma's heart. A look of peace and self-assurance was gradually coming over her face. More often these days, rather than the most talkative, she was the quietest member of the Rosewood family around *the kitchen table, sitting content to listen, watch, observe.*

Emma's soul was coming awake.

❧ ✼ ❧

Emma sat down at the river's edge and eased her bare brown feet into the shallow water as William ran straight into it.

"You be careful, William!" she said. "You stay near me, you hear. I don't want ter be havin' ter haul you outta dat water yonder cuz I can't swim so good."

Whether William was listening was doubtful. But he was in no danger yet, for the site where Emma had been baptized was out in the middle and the sandy bottom sloped away toward it gradually. He ran and splashed about within four feet of the shore, to no more depth than halfway up his fat little calves, laughing and shrieking without a care in the world, until he was wet from head to foot. Emma watched with a smile on her face.

In this season of peace and happiness in her life, Emma was not thinking of the past, nor of dangerous secrets she possessed whose danger even she herself did not fully recognize. She was thinking of the wonderful now and the bright future. She was thinking of Micah Duff.

Emma had just begun to get sleepy under the blazing sun and had lain down on her back, when sudden footsteps sounded behind her from some unknown hiding place in the brush bordering the river. Startled but suspecting nothing, Emma sat up and turned toward the sound. Three white men ran toward her, two bearing big brown burlap bags.

Before she could cry out, one of the men yanked her to her feet. Emma cried out in pain as the second man pulled her arms behind her. The third went for William, threw the open end of one sack over his head, and scooped the boy out of the shallow water.

"Mama!" William howled. But the next instant he was bundled up, then clunked on the head and thrown over the man's shoulder.

Terror unlike she had ever known clenched at Emma's heart. She screamed at the top of her lungs, struggling and kicking frantically.

"You let him go . . . William . . . git yo han's off me . . . help—somebody . . . Miz Katie, help! Mayme!"

"Shut up, you fool!" yelled one of the men. But even two of them were hardly a match for her. Emma writhed and kicked with every ounce of survival instinct she possessed. As one tried to take hold of her shoulders and force her to be still, Emma's teeth clamped down onto his wrist like the vise of a steel trap.

He cried out in pain and swore violently as blood flowed from his arm. He whacked Emma across the side of the head with the back of his hand. But it only made her scream louder.

"Help!" she shrieked in a mad frenzy. "Git away from me . . . William, Mama's here . . . help! Miz Katie . . . dey's got William. Help!"

Two hands took hold of her head from behind, and the next instant a handkerchief was stuffed into her mouth, muffling her cries. She was lifted off the ground, kicking and wildly swinging her arms about. The three men now made clumsily for their waiting horses and struggled to mount with the two unwieldy bags.

*

The river was not so far from the house that we couldn't plainly hear Emma's screams. The frantic cries quickly brought us all running from several directions at once.

"Is that Emma?" called Katie in alarm, hurrying out onto the porch and glancing all about to see what was going on.

"She went to the river," I said, running around from the side of the house.

"Where's Emma and William?" yelled my papa as he ran toward them from the barn where he'd gone to prepare for milking.

"At the river," I answered, my heart pounding in fear.

"William must have fallen in," he said. "Let's go!"

We all sprinted away from the house in the direction of the river.

Micah Duff had also heard Emma's cries for help. At Emma's first scream he had burst out of the cabin that Papa and Uncle Ward had fixed up for him. He now flew across the ground in the direction of the sounds.

He reached the river twenty or thirty seconds ahead of the rest of us. He was just in time to see three horses disappearing around a bend in the river, two lumpy burlap bags slung over two of their saddles. He looked about hastily and saw signs of a scuffle. Seconds later he was sprinting back for the house. He intercepted us about a third of the way there.

"Somebody's taken Emma and William!" he yelled as he ran straight past us for the house. "They're on horseback!"

Dread filled me. We had tried to keep Emma hidden and protected for so long. Had her worst fears finally come to pass? I swallowed hard as Micah continued on as fast as he could run. Just as he reached the barn, Uncle Ward rode in from town. Though his horse was hot and tired, it was already saddled. Micah grabbed the reins from his hands, and in less than five seconds was disappearing at full gallop toward the river. Uncle Ward stared after Micah in bewilderment until we all ran back into the yard a minute later and quickly explained.

Micah lashed and kicked at his horse, making an angle he hoped would intercept the three horses he had seen earlier. He had no idea where they were going, unless it was toward Greens Ford, a narrow section of river that was shallow enough to cross easily and cut a mile off the distance to town by avoiding the bridge downstream.

He reached Greens Ford but there was no sign of them.

Frantically he tried to still Uncle Ward's jittery horse enough to listen. A hint of dust still swirled in the air where the ground had been stirred up beyond the ford but on the same side of the river. He bolted toward it. If they had not crossed the ford, where were they going? Why were they following the river?

Suddenly a chill seized him. The rapids . . . and the treacherously deep pool bordered by a cliff on one side and high boulders on the other!

He lashed the horse to yet greater speed, then swung up the bank.

Three minutes later he dismounted and ran down a steep rocky slope. He heard them now. They were at the place he feared!

Thinking desperately, he crept closer.

Suddenly a scream sounded.

"William . . . somebody help us!" shrieked a girl's voice. "Dey's got William . . . help!"

Micah sprinted down the precarious slope toward the river.

"What the—" a man exclaimed. "How did she get that thing loose?"

"Just shut her up!" shouted another.

"It doesn't matter now. Let's do what we came to do!"

One more wild scream pierced the air, then a great splash. It was followed by another.

"That ought to take care of them . . . let's get out of here!"

Seconds later three horses galloped away as Micah ran frantically out onto an overhanging ledge of rock some twenty feet above a deep black pool of the river. He saw two widening circles rippling across the surface of the water.

He ripped off his boots, stepped back, then took two running strides forward and flew into the air. With a mighty splash he hit the water and dove deep into the river's depths. But he could only see a few feet in the murky flow and could find nothing before he was forced back to the surface for air. He shot up, breathing desperately, sucked in what air he could in a second or two, then dove again. Up and down two or three times he went, struggling for breath, swimming in a frenzy, diving as deep into the river's depths as possible and feeling about wildly with his hands and feet.

Again he burst above the surface, drew in a great gasping breath, and dove again, this time straight for the bottom.

Suddenly his fingers brushed past something! He kicked wildly to get himself deeper. There it was again.

It was burlap!

He grabbed at it and took hold, but the weight was too heavy to lift. His lungs nearly bursting, he flew again to the surface, gulped his lungs full of air, then dove straight down to the same spot.

With both hands he took hold of the bag and pulled with all his might, struggling desperately with its weight up to the surface. He felt the struggle of life inside the bag. It was a body—Emma's body—and still alive!

With all the effort he could summon, he swam toward the river's edge and lugged the bag out of the water and onto the few treacherous rocks of the thin shoreline. The moment his own footing was secure he ripped and yanked at the neck of the bag. A moment later Emma's head burst through it, gasping for air and spitting out water. She threw her arms around Micah, babbling and crying and kissing him, hardly realizing what she was doing. Then suddenly she remembered.

"William . . . where's my William?" she cried in terrified panic.

But already Micah had left Emma and was back into the river. Again he dove straight into its depth, unable to hear behind him Emma's sobbing and frantic shouts.

⁂

Papa and Uncle Ward had jumped on a couple of horses bareback, taking time only to pull bridles over their heads. Papa leaned down to take my hand and pulled me up behind him onto the horse's back. Uncle Ward did the same with Katie, and off we flew in the direction Micah had disappeared. It was all I could do to keep from falling off as I hung on desperately around Papa's waist.

It wasn't hard to follow the sounds—first from Micah's galloping horse, then as we drew closer from Emma's frantic and terrified cries.

We reached the river, hurriedly dismounted, and ran down the steep and treacherous slope as carefully as we could. Ahead of us we heard the splashing and thrashing of water in the midst of Emma's wails.

We reached the edge of the cliff where Micah's boots lay. What we saw did not look good.

Micah was diving again and again into the river, disappearing for thirty or forty seconds at a time, then flying up past the surface, gasping for two or three breaths, then disappearing from sight again.

Uncle Ward quickly threw off his boots. "You

never did learn to swim, did you?" he said to Papa.

Papa shook his head.

"I learned in California," replied Uncle Ward. "The hard way."

"Then I'll ride back and get a length of rope!" said Papa. "We're going to need it to get them up out of there."

Even as Papa began making his way back up the incline to the horses, the splash of Uncle Ward hitting the water sounded behind him.

Suddenly it seemed to get real quiet. Emma's sobs at the water's edge had softened to a quiet whimpering. Katie and I stood and watched in silence. Even though it was the hottest day of the year so far, a chill swept through me.

Micah and Uncle Ward were under the water so long that everything stilled around us. It got so quiet we began to hear the birds in the nearby trees. Then suddenly Micah burst again to the surface with a cry and gasp for air, then swam frantically toward Emma. Behind him he was hauling another burlap bag.

"William!" shrieked Emma, "William . . . you found my William!"

By now Uncle Ward had also resurfaced and swam after him. Exhausted from the effort, Micah struggled onto the rocky edge of the river and fumbled desperately to open the bag. Its weight, it was now clear, was not merely from William but from several large rocks that had been added to it.

Gently he lifted William's limp form out of the

sack. Emma's hands and lips were desperate to grab and fondle and kiss her son, but somehow she knew she must leave him in Micah's care awhile longer. Micah was probing the tiny mouth with his finger. He laid William on his stomach across his legs and whacked on his back two or three times. Still there was no movement. He turned William over and now bent down and placed his own mouth over William's and blew into it. He continued to do so for several minutes.

All of us held our breaths, not realizing how much time had gone by until Papa appeared with the rope.

Finally Micah slumped back and handed William's body to Emma. She clutched him to her breast, weeping frantically and rocking slowly back and forth.

Micah glanced up to where we stood and slowly shook his head.

Katie drew in a sharp breath of shock and disbelief.

"Oh, God . . . please, God—no!" she said under her breath.

My eyes stung. The next moment Katie and I were sobbing in each other's arms.

Papa had already tied off one end of the rope and was dangling the other down to them. Uncle Ward took the rope first, then struggled to climb up the cliff as Papa pulled from above. Stones and dirt showered down as he scrambled to find footing on the rocky surface. When he neared the top, Papa *kneeled down and grasped Uncle Ward's hand, helping him up over the edge. Then he tossed the rope back down to Micah.*

As gently as he was able, Micah took William from Emma's arms, set him down briefly, then eased her to her feet, tied the rope around her waist, told her to grab the rope above her, then nodded to Papa.

"Hang on, Emma," he said down to her. "You just hold on to the rope and we'll pull you up."

She reached us, her eyes glazed over in shock. Katie and I took her in our arms and we all wept another minute. Beyond us I saw my papa nod to me in the direction of the slope. Katie and I began helping Emma away from the river and back up to the level ground, while the two men now brought Micah with William in his arms, up the cliff.

As they turned to go, Papa's eyes spotted something crumpled up on the ground a few yards away. He stooped down, picked it up, and showed it to Uncle Ward with a look of question.

Katie and Emma and I were all crying as we reached the house. We had walked together the whole way. The men had followed some way behind us on the horses, William in Micah's arms.

Josepha was standing outside waiting for us. She knew while we were still some distance away that something was terribly wrong.

When she saw her, Emma burst away from us and ran straight toward her.

"Josepha," she wailed in a sobbing voice, "William's gonna wake up, ain't he? Josepha . . . you kin

help him, Josepha, you gots ter! You an' Miz Katie—you always knows what ter do—you'll help him, won't you Josepha . . . you gots ter help him wake up!"

Josepha looked past Emma at all the rest of us, saw Katie and me crying again, saw the limp form in Micah's arms, and knew the truth.

"Oh, Emma chil'!" she said, giant tears spilling from her eyes. She folded Emma in a huge motherly embrace, her hands gently stroking Emma's wet hair and kissing her forehead and eyes and cheeks. "Emma . . . dear Emma chil'!"

Emma was whimpering and saying William's name over and over as Micah walked up behind them.

Emma turned and saw him carrying William. A great wail burst from her lips.

"You gots ter save my William . . . Josepha ain't dere somefin' you kin do!"

Micah handed him into Josepha's arms. She took the form, suddenly so frail. Josepha knew in an instant that William's body had already begun to cool.

"I's sorry, Emma chil'," she said, her cheeks wet and a forlorn expression on her face. "Dere ain't nothin I kin do. Our William's God's little boy now."

A huge sob burst again from Emma as Micah took her hand and led her away. Katie and I were bawling like babies. Micah took hold of Emma's two shoulders, gazed deep into her eyes, then spoke to her soft words that none of us could hear. Then he opened his arms to her and she fell into them. Micah pulled Emma close.

She leaned her face against his chest and quietly wept.

CONFRONTATION
32

DEEP DOWN, WARD AND TEMPLETON DANIELS probably knew that nothing would be accomplished by talking to Sheriff Sam Jenkins. He had been uncooperative in the past, and with his own son now likely involved in William McSimmons' scheme, he was less likely to be now.

Still, they thought, they should report the matter.

After listening to their account of Emma's abduction and William's death, however, Sam Jenkins showed no signs of reaction at all, least of all sympathy for the fact that a four-year-old black boy was now dead.

"McSimmons was behind it," said Templeton Daniels again, "and I'm asking you for the second time, Sheriff, what are you going to do about it?"

"There's nothing I can do," replied Jenkins. "Sounds to me that you've got no proof."

"We know it was him."

"Look," said Jenkins, eyeing the two brothers skeptically, "you two boys keep coming to me with all your complaints. But like I told you before, you best get them coloreds out from under your roof and back where they belong, or you're going to keep on having trouble. They're living like whites. They ain't got no right to live in a white man's house. The way things stand now, you're just bringing on your troubles yourselves. And there's nothing I can do to stop it."

"The man's a murderer," said Ward.

"You can't prove that."

"Is what you're really saying is that there's nothing you're *going* to do?"

Jenkins looked at the two coldly.

"All I'm saying is that unless you make some changes at that place of yours, your troubles are bound to continue."

When the four horses rode up to the McSimmons plantation house three days later, Charlotte McSimmons saw them coming from an upstairs window and knew these visitors were up to no good.

She went in search of her husband. The two emerged from the door just as the four were dismounting in front of the porch.

McSimmons' eyes moved over the three white faces—two men and one young woman—without expression, though he well knew who they were and more than half suspected the reason for their visit. Then he let his eyes come to rest upon the young black man he had never seen before.

He was surprised when he stepped forward to speak for the small group.

"Mr. McSimmons," said the black man in flawless English, "my name is Micah Duff. I had the dubious honor of coming upon what I assume to be an attempted double murder three days ago. I was in time to save one of the victims, a Miss Tolan, with whom I understand you are acquainted. Unfortunately, I was unable to save her son, who is now dead."

As they listened, the annoyance of the two McSimmons slowly mounted to a white fury at the man's presumption, not merely to talk like a white man but to speak so boldly, and without apparent fear, to the most important white persons for miles around.

"Whether you were personally present, I do not know," the black man continued, "but you are certainly responsible for the murder. So we are here to ask what you intend to do about it."

He stopped and his eyes bored straight into those of William McSimmons. But McSimmons had heard enough.

"How dare you come here, onto my property, and make such an accusation!" he shouted. "You—a colored man . . . accusing me. What right do you have to—"

"I was there, Mr. McSimmons," interrupted Micah. "Do not make light of my words. I know you were involved."

"You cannot possibly—" began McSimmons savagely.

"Look, McSimmons," Templeton Daniels now interrupted from where he stood at the foot of the porch. "One of your men dropped this at the scene."

He walked forward and held up a torn and crumpled piece of paper. Slowly he unfolded it and held it toward McSimmons. "I think you will recognize the McSimmons brand on the letterhead," he said. "I doubt you will deny it came from here."

McSimmons eyed it a moment without expression. "What of it?" he spat. "It means nothing. You could have picked it up anywhere."

"But we didn't pick it up anywhere, we found it at the murder site, linking you to the crime."

"No court would convict me with ridiculous evidence like that!" laughed McSimmons with derision.

"Maybe not. But you never know. And how good for your reputation would the accusation be?"

"You wouldn't dare, Daniels!"

"That's where you're wrong, McSimmons," said Templeton. "I'm not afraid of you. You make a move and this whole state will know what you are. I can't *prove* that this is your handwriting," he added, folding the paper and returning it to his pocket. "But I think you know it is. And I don't think you will want it publicly known that you were involved in one killing and the attempt of a second. It isn't exactly the sort of thing upstanding people like from their politicians."

"Just what is it you expect us to do?" Mrs. McSimmons now asked. "That one black baby somewhere has met with an unfortunate accident . . . I hardly see how that concerns us."

"It was not a *baby,* ma'am," said Micah. "He was four years old. And what makes you think he was black, if you know nothing about it?"

Mrs. McSimmons stuffed down the volley of fury that would have exploded from her lips at a more opportune moment.

"Mr. McSimmons," Micah continued, addressing McSimmons again, "what I have to say now you might prefer for your wife not to hear."

"Get on with it, you fool, before I throw you out!" McSimmons glanced at his wife but she made no move to go.

"I understand it is your intention to run for Congress," Micah went on. "My friends and I—Miss Clairborne and Mr. Ward and Mr. Templeton Daniels—are going to ask you to change those plans and step down. You are not the sort of man who should represent the people of North Carolina in Washington."

"This is the most absurd—" huffed McSimmons, nearly speechless with wrath.

"If you do not, it will be made public that you arranged for the murder of a black child . . . your own son, in fact. Do not underestimate the consequences to you both should the fact be printed in the Charlotte newspapers that you arranged for the killing of your own son. We will take this paper to Charlotte personally and let it be known where it came from. Do not think that we will not do as we say. Good day, sir . . . ma'am."

Micah turned and rejoined the other three. They remounted their horses and walked slowly away from the house, leaving the candidate and his wife in stunned silence.

Grief, Healing, and More Tragedy

33

The next weeks at Rosewood were bittersweet; there's no other way to describe them. The heart-break over William's loss was so deep it affected us all—though no pain could come close to a mother's loss of her own child. Emma's grief was worlds beyond any of the rest of ours.

We buried William beside Katie's family, in the little plot of graves not far from the house. Everyone wept, even Papa and Uncle Ward. The pain we all felt for poor Emma was so deep. We had all come to love her so much. To see her suffer the loss of her son was one of the hardest things any of us had ever gone through. The two men were so tender toward Emma that you'd have thought she was their own daughter. They must have taken her in their arms five times a day for the next week and just held her a few seconds in consolation.

But in the midst of all that, Emma now had

Micah's love to surround her and give her courage and strength to endure the supreme grief that God himself also had to endure—the loss of a son.

We all watched them daily leave the house to walk slowly and quietly through the fields, Emma leaning against him as Micah's arm tenderly held her to his side. The soft words passing between them were ones the rest of us never heard. We were all so grateful for the love she had found. How she could have endured William's loss without Micah, I cannot even imagine.

❦

When word began to spread through the communities of Greens Crossing and Oakwood, and from there to Charlotte, and then throughout all of North Carolina, that William McSimmons had decided to withdraw from the congressional race, speculation ran rampant about the reasons for his decision.

Nobody knew anything for sure, though there were rumors. Some of these involved his wife. Others involved a child of dubious origin. Still others hinted at wider scandal, even murder.

But nothing was ever learned for certain, and the former candidate never disclosed anything more than "personal reasons" as prompting his action.

The rumors, however, were enough to set the community abuzz about what more might have been involved.

❦

The days moved slowly.

They became a week, then two. Everyone went about their work more quietly than usual. With William's happy voice and laughter and running footsteps gone, all the life seemed gone from Rosewood.

Reverend Hall came out a few times to try to comfort us. But what could he say?

Poor Emma! She walked around, or sat on the porch just staring ahead, her red eyes glazed over. She didn't go to the river anymore. No doubt that place where she used to find peace was now flowing with terrible memories. William had been her whole life, everything she had lived for, and now he was gone.

In one way, I suppose, we all knew how she felt, at least Katie and Micah and Jeremiah and I all did. During those days after William's death I thought back often to the days after Katie and I had met. I had seen my whole family killed. The look on Katie's face when I walked into the Rosewood kitchen and saw her standing over her father's body was a look of horror and desolation I'll never forget.

But we'd lived through it. Somehow we'd found strength in each other. As much as we tried to love her, I wondered if Emma would be able to find that same strength from us as we had from each other. And even though we shared knowing what it was like for death to come so close, we hadn't lost a child of our own. I reckon nothing could be quite so bad as that. My heart ached for her!

One day Emma was out walking alone like she

often did these days, just walking and crying. She came to the place where the graves were. She stopped and just stood there looking down at William's grave.

Katie and Papa and I were watching from the house.

"You know," said Papa, "I think I'll go into town and get the undertaker to make a stone for William."

"That would be nice," I said.

Katie smiled. "It would mean a lot to Emma, Uncle Templeton," she said. "That's a good idea."

"What should it say?" he asked.

We thought a minute". " 'William Tolan, 1865–1869 . . .' " said Katie slowly, then paused. "And then . . . 'one of the first Negro sons of South Carolina who was never a slave, but was born free.' "

"That's nice, Katie," I said.

"I'll ride into town this afternoon and get him started on it," said Papa.

We stood a few minutes more, then Katie walked out to where Emma still stood. She approached slowly. Emma heard her and turned. Katie put her arm around her, and they stood side by side for another several minutes.

Then I saw Katie take Emma's hand and lead her away. They walked toward the fields, still hand in hand, toward the woods, and slowly disappeared from sight.

They were gone a long time, probably an hour. Papa had already left for town and I'd gone back inside when I heard the kitchen door open and Katie *walked in. She had a sad, peaceful, quiet look on her face.*

"Where did you go?" I asked.

"I took Emma to my secret place in the woods," said Katie. "I thought she needed to know about it."

"Is she still there?"

Katie nodded.

"What did you say to her?"

"I told her that I'd been going there since I was a little girl and that when I was young I visited with the animals and thought up silly poems—"

"They weren't silly," I said.

"They seem a little silly now," smiled Katie. "Then I told her that as I got older my secret place in the woods became a place where I went to let God speak to me. I told her I thought that maybe He wanted to use it now to speak to her."

"What did she say?" I asked.

"She thanked me and smiled. Then I left."

Katie sighed and smiled.

"She's changing, Mayme," she said. "I don't think she'll ever be the same again."

"Losing someone you love changes you—you and I know that."

"I know," nodded Katie. "But I wonder if Emma will ever recover completely. It might be different for her than it was for us."

We hadn't heard Micah come in behind us. His voice now startled us and we turned around.

"You have nothing to worry about," he said. "Emma will be all right."

"Are you sure?" said Katie, still concerned. "It seems that nothing I say helps right now."

"There are no words to help someone through their grief," he said. "Love is what she needs, and she is getting that from all of you. Her soul is being fed by your love, even though you may not see it. It takes time to heal. Grief is a long, slow, painful process. Time is the only thing that can heal it. Everyone has to come to terms with the change death brings in their own way. You both know—you lost your families. I know—I lost my mama. Jake lost his mama, and he had to deal with guilt along with his grief. But we all grew strong from it too. It takes time. Emma just needs our love."

"You're . . . really sure Emma will come through this?" said Katie, staring deeply into Micah's face for an answer.

Micah smiled. It was a peaceful, knowing, almost contented smile. "Yes," he said slowly. "She will come through it. You're right in what you said before, Katie. She will never be the same. William will always be with her. The pain of his loss will always be there. But pain can be turned to good. Pain carves out deeper caverns within us for the waters of joy to flow through. Sometimes the deeper the pain, the deeper the joy. Emma will grow strong and she will again know joy, even though she will also always know pain. Have no fear, Katie—Emma will laugh again. And she will grow strong . . . even stronger than she was before."

Micah spoke with such confidence I couldn't

help believing what he said. It was not hard to see that he really loved her.

But even more than that . . . Micah believed *in Emma.*

In the days following that, Emma disappeared across the fields toward the woods a lot—sometimes more than once a day. I know she was going to Katie's secret place to talk to God about William.

Every time she came back, she had a peaceful look on her face. The pain and sadness and grief were still there, but I began to see healing too. It was just like Micah said—the slow passage of time gradually did its work.

Emma would heal. And she would grow strong.

⁂

The town of Oakwood was rocked in the middle of June when suddenly word began to spread from door to door of a new tragedy—one that struck much closer to home.

Sheriff Sam Jenkins had been distracted from his duties for two days, ever since his son hadn't come home after leaving the Steeves place late one night.

It was Deke Steeves who, on the third day, made the discovery at the bottom of a gulch about a mile from town. It was Weed Jenkins lying facedown on the rocky ground with a bullet through his head.

Another Conversation at the River
34

Micah Duff was watching Emma more closely than all the rest. For several weeks he kept a respectful distance, allowing the quiet and solitude of grief to do its slow healing work. He knew that right now she needed the love of friends, and a deeper love of God than she had known before, to soothe her aching heart more than the love of a man to distract and perhaps confuse her. He respected the value of time too much to interfere with it, no matter how long it took.

So he watched . . . and waited . . . until the time was right.

"I notice you haven't been going to the river much lately," said Micah one day after several weeks when he and Emma found themselves alone.

"I been goin' ter da woods ter pray instead," said Emma.

"Do you feel like another walk along the river?"

"I reckon dat'd be nice."

Little more was said. Micah led the way past the barn and through fields of growing cotton, until again they stood beside the river looking out at the place where Emma had been baptized and where love had suddenly awakened in Micah's heart for her. Emma sensed a quiet peace in her heart more than at any time since William's death. She drew in a deep breath and let it out slowly. The words of the song she had sung here so many times returned to her again . . . *Give me Jesus . . . Dark midnight was my cry—give me Jesus.*

Her soul had been through its dark midnight of despondency and desolation. But maybe, she thought, someday the sun might rise again. Then Micah's voice intruded into her thoughts.

"Do you remember the day," he asked softly, "when I said I had something to say to you . . . over there on the riverbank?"

"How wud I ever forgit a day like dat, Micah?" smiled Emma. "'Course I remember. You said you loved me."

"Do you think you could stand the shock if I told you that I had something else to say that was almost as important as that?" asked Micah.

"Ain't nuthin' dat could compare wiff *dat,*" replied Emma, looking at him with a puzzled smile.

"But if I told you I did?"

"Den I reckon I'd tell you ter say it," said Emma. "I's feared er nuthin' *you'd* say ter me, Micah. I knows you'd neber hurt me."

"Of course I wouldn't. I am glad you know it."

"So what does you want ter say, Micah?"

"Why don't we go over and sit down on that big rock, Emma?"

Micah led the way, helped Emma climb up one of the boulders at the water's edge, where they sat overlooking the leisurely summer's flow of green water.

"Do you ever think about the future, Emma?" Micah asked.

"I never done much ob dat," Emma replied. "I ain't neber figgered I had much future ter think about . . . specially now."

"I think about it, Emma. I've always been making plans and thinking of things I'd like to do."

"You's different den me."

"Maybe . . . or maybe you just haven't had anyone to think of the future with."

Emma's neck began to get warm.

"That's what makes the future something to think about, Emma—having someone to share it with. And . . . that's what I wanted to say to you, to ask if you would share the future with me."

Emma sat still, saying nothing, but trembling from head to foot.

"I would like," Micah said. "—No," he added, "I would be honored if you would be my wife."

Emma found her voice again.

"You would be . . . *honored*?"

"Yes, Emma—you are a *lady*, remember? And it would honor this penniless wandering soldier to make the lady his wife."

"You hab da most uncommon way ter say things!"

"Then let me say it like this—will you marry me, Emma?"

"Oh, Micah . . . you make me so happy," said Emma quietly. "I don't deserve any ob dis. 'Course I'll marry you!"

Plans
35

I don't suppose the news took any of us altogether by surprise. But we were so overjoyed by it that it might as well have come as a surprise. Nothing would ever make up for William's loss. But knowing that Emma had a man to love her and that she would be the wife of Micah Duff, and likely have more children in time, gave us hope that her life would be filled with joy in spite of her present sorrow.

The minute Papa and Uncle Ward heard that Micah and Emma planned to be married, they immediately began making plans to enlarge Micah's cabin to accommodate the new husband and wife.

"We could run a water line down there, couldn't we, Ward," said my papa excitedly, "and put in a water pump and tub."

"I don't see why not."

"And while we're at that, why not bring water to Henry and Jeremiah's too. We'll modernize both places at the same time."

With a sheepish look, Micah glanced at Emma. A smile passed between them that seemed to say they knew more about their future than did any of the rest of us.

"That's kind and thoughtful of you, Mr. Templeton," said Micah, "and we appreciate it more than we can say. But . . . well, the fact is, Emma and I have been talking, and . . . actually we have some other plans."

Papa and Uncle Ward stared back as if they had never considered any possibility other than that Micah and Emma would stay at Rosewood.

"I'm not sure Emma will ever be completely safe from William McSimmons," said Micah. "The look in that man's eyes when I was speaking to him, and in his wife's, was not an expression that spoke of forgiveness. We thwarted his ambitions, and I have the feeling that revenge will be on his mind as long as the two of us are anywhere nearby."

Micah looked around at the rest of us with obvious love in his eyes. I think we all began in that moment to sense that a farewell was coming to Rosewood.

"It was you, Mr. Daniels," Micah went on, "who told me that I needed to have plans, and have the courage to follow my dreams. You don't know how much I appreciate your speaking to me as you did. I've tried to take your words to heart ever since. I've talked it over with Emma, and we have been thinking about that new railroad out west . . . and the long and the short of it is that we have decided, right

after we can be married—and we wouldn't be married anywhere but at Rosewood!—to take the train west and try to make our way to Oregon. I had been looking forward to the experience of picking cotton with you all this fall," he added with a smile, glancing around at the rest of us. "But after what happened, and what may still be some degree of danger, I think it best that we not wait. Emma will be safe in the West, and we hope that maybe we can have a little place of our own to begin our life and a family together."

He glanced at Emma and again they smiled.

"Well, son," said Papa, "I think that's a fine plan. We'll miss you, of course, and speaking for myself, I'd much rather you stayed right here. But a man's got to follow his dreams, and I'd be the last one to stand in the way of yours."

I looked at Katie and smiled. We both had tears in our eyes, but we were happy for Emma too. It was hard to believe what a part of our lives she had become. I knew we would miss her more than we realized.

❋

Ward Daniels had business in Oakwood the next day. When he returned, he went immediately in search of his brother. When they were alone he pulled a sheet of paper out of his pocket.

"Look at this," he said. "They're up all over at Oakwood."

Templeton took it and looked it over with a serious expression. "*Wanted,*" he read, "*for the murder of Weed Jenkins—tall Negro man, speaks white English, reportedly former Union soldier.*"

He shook his head in disgust.

"Very clever of them," he said. "Without getting their own hands dirty, whoever's behind this can just wait and let someone bring Micah in for them."

"Who do you think's behind it?"

"I have no doubt it's Sheriff Jenkins. I'm sorry about his kid, but he's had it in for us all along."

"Should we tell them?"

"I can't see any point. Let's just get them married and out of here. They don't need this to worry about starting out their life together."

"Still . . . we better stick close, keep a close eye on things, and not let him go into town again."

"Probably best that nobody goes into town except for Henry and Jeremiah going to work. We better *all* stick close to home for a spell."

❋

I came upon Emma a few days later sitting looking out one of the front room windows.

"What are you looking at?" I asked.

"Oh, jes' at Micah an' Jeremiah out dere," she said.

I went to the window. The two were laughing together like the best of friends.

"We's a couple er mighty lucky young . . . young

ladies," she said, "—dat's what Micah'd make me say—ain't we, Mayme? De're a couple er right fine young men."

"Yes they are, Emma," I said. "We are very lucky young ladies to have such good young men to love us."

I turned and walked away. After a few steps I glanced back. Emma was still staring out the window. And now a figure approached from outside. I could tell from the shadow it cast on the wall that it was Micah, and that he had seen Emma sitting there watching him. She wasn't smiling exactly, but the expression on her face as she gazed out at him said more than a hundred smiles.

It was a peaceful look that said she knew she was loved, and that because she knew it, she would never be the same again.

Happy Day

36

The day of Emma's wedding was one of the happiest Rosewood had ever known.

All morning Josepha and Katie and I fussed with her hair and dress to get everything just right. She was just about the most beautiful bride you could imagine! She was again wearing Katie's white dress, the same one she had been baptized in. We added some green and yellow ribbons around her waist and tied them in a bow in back. We braided a little wreath of ferns with tiny yellow roses woven into them for her hair to match the color of the ribbons. Emma was beautiful anyway, but by the time for the wedding, I'd never seen anything like the picture she looked, not even in a book of fairy tales and princesses.

Our young friend Aleta and her father came out about noon and we went downstairs to meet them. Aleta had grown so much since she stayed with us! When she and Emma saw each other and ran to meet and embraced like sisters, I thought I'd never seen anything so wonderful. We excitedly hurried Aleta upstairs with us to continue putting the finishing touches on Emma's hair and dress.

Reverend Hall and his wife came about an hour later. He hadn't seemed to mind that we weren't having the wedding in his church. In fact he had never encouraged us to attend services, knowing, no doubt, that we would all expect to sit together—which might have angered his other parishioners. He talked awhile to Papa and Micah and Katie about the arrangements. Katie had planned everything and was in charge of telling everyone what to do. More and more she was the mistress of Rosewood!

Emma waited upstairs with Josepha and Aleta and Katie and me. She was nervous but beaming!

Finally everything was ready. But then Emma started crying, and I knew why.

"I wish my William cud be here," she said. "I wanted a good life fo William since he wuz born a free baby. He wud hab been so happy ter know dat he wuz finally gwine hab a daddy. He loved Micah so much."

Katie gave Emma a hug. "But remember, Emma," she whispered, "even though William isn't here with us, he is happy in heaven—and happier for you than you can imagine."

Emma smiled and wiped at her eyes. "Dat's nice, Miz Katie," she said. "Dat's real nice. I hope you's right. Dat'll make me real happy ter think of him like dat. You really think he's happy fo me?"

"I know he is, Emma. He loves you." Then Katie hurried downstairs.

We heard the tramp of men's feet walking up the stairs. A few seconds later, Papa and Uncle Ward appeared.

"You ready, little girl?" said Papa.

"I is, Mister Templeton," said Emma, drawing in a breath to steady herself.

"Then we'll take it from here," he said, looking at the three of us. "Time for you ladies to leave us with the bride!"

Josepha and Aleta and I gave Emma one last smile, then went downstairs to join the others. There stood Micah and Jeremiah in their finest clothes, their faces shiny clean. I had to admit—they were both mighty handsome! The whole house was silent. Katie was sitting at the piano. She glanced around making sure everybody was ready, then began to play.

When they were alone upstairs together, the two Daniels men looked seriously at Emma.

"I haven't ever been too good at things like this," said Uncle Ward. "But both of us want you to know that we're honored to walk you down to that fellow who's going to be your husband. You're a mighty fine young lady, Emma Tolan. You've done a lot of growing up, and we're mighty proud to know you."

He looked over at my papa. By now Emma was crying. But Papa had some things to say to her too.

"I know you had to struggle," he said, "alongside Katie and Mayme, to feel like you were as good as them. But let me tell you something, Emma, and I

don't want you ever to forget it as long as you live. You're a fine person, a good person, and wherever you go you can hold your head up high. You were a good mother too. We all miss William, but you'll have more children and you'll be a good mother to them too. But he'll always be your firstborn and he'll always be special to all of us. You can rest assured that we'll never forget him either, any more than we'll forget you. You'll always be part of this family, Emma. We all love you."

How Emma managed to keep from bawling after that, I don't know. But by now Katie was already playing the music, and at last they were all ready. Emma wiped her eyes one last time, drew in a deep breath, then took hold of the two men's arms.

Emma had asked the two brothers to walk her down to Micah. She had never known her own father and they were more like a father than anyone had ever been to her. Papa had only one daughter and she was black—me!—so why shouldn't he have a black adoptive daughter too? And as they now walked slowly down the stairs, Emma between them on both their arms, I'd never seen such a sight. Here were two white men acting as fathers to a motherless, fatherless black girl. Uncle Ward was trying to keep serious, but Papa had a big grin on his face like he often did. You could tell he was enjoying it!

I glanced over at Micah from where I stood. He was staring straight at Emma as they came slowly down, one step at a time, in time to Katie's music.

The expression on his face was filled with such love. But it was more than that too—you could see that he was proud of Emma, proud of the lady she had become.

They reached the bottom of the stairs. The rest of us stepped back a little as they walked across the room to where Micah stood with Reverend Hall. Beside Micah stood Jeremiah, with Henry next to him.

Katie came to the end of the processional she had been playing and stopped. She stood up and came over to join Josepha, Aleta, and me.

"Dearly beloved," said Reverend Hall, "we are gathered here this day to unite this man and this woman in holy matrimony. If any man should show just cause why they should not be so united, let him speak now or forever hold his peace."

He waited briefly, then glanced one at a time to the two men.

"Who gives this woman to be married to this man?" he asked.

"We do," said Papa and Uncle Ward together.

Emma stepped forward, beaming all the more, turned around, slipped her hand through Micah's arm, and stood at his side. Papa and Uncle Ward went over to stand beside Henry and Jeremiah. Katie and Josepha and Aleta and I all walked up and spread out on the other side next to Emma. Across the room on two chairs, the only two spectators for the ceremony were Mr. Butler and Mrs. Hall.

"I would like to say a few words," said Reverend

Hall, "before we continue with the actual ceremony. I have watched as you here at Rosewood have grown as a family. First there was just Kathleen and Mary Ann. Then Emma came, then Aleta, and gradually the rest of you have joined them. Your numbers have not only grown, but so have your bonds as a family. It is a perfect example of what our politicians call peaceful coexistence of the races. But for you it has nothing to do with politics, but with the love you all have for one another. And though you may not realize it, the whole community is watching. Some may hate you for it. But many are also learning to respect you for it.

"You are following the words of Jesus. You have taken in the widow and the orphan and the homeless. Kathleen and Mary Ann, you were orphans yourselves, and yet you have taken in any and all who came and needed your help. And the rest of you too, you have opened your hearts and your home to one and all.

"Therefore, the love we celebrate this day between Micah and Emma is testimony as the fruit of that love that accepts all people no matter what the color of his or her skin. This is how it is to be among men. This is how God intended it to be. That so few live by God's design does not mean we are not to live so ourselves. You have lived so, and I believe that is why God's favor rests on Rosewood.

"Now I realize, as I said, that there is resentment on the part of some in the community, and that this great experiment in which you are engaged will no doubt continue to face opposition. But let that not deter you from continuing in good faith and with fortitude, for God will surely reward and bless your efforts.

"And so, Micah and Emma, never forget as you journey along life's road together, that your love was born out of obedience to the command of Christ to love one another, and thus may you look to that command likewise to perfect your own love as husband and wife."

He stopped and glanced around at all the rest of us, then again to Micah and Emma.

"Do you, Micah Duff," he began, "take this woman to be your wedded wife, to have and to hold from this day forward, for better, for worse, for richer, for poorer, in sickness and in health, to love and to cherish, till death do you part, according to God's holy ordinance?"

"Yes, I do," replied Micah.

"Do you, Emma Tolan," he said, turning to Emma, "take this man to be your wedded husband . . ."

As he said the vow to Emma, I could not help but think back to the first day Katie and I had seen Emma in the barn, frightened and hysterical out of her wits with William on the way.

"Da missus . . . she's gwine scold me again! I'm done fer now!" I could still hear her frightened and scatterbrained voice in my memory like it was yesterday. *"Please, missus . . . don't hurt me! I'm sorry I done took yer bread. I know I ain't got no right ter*

be here, but I din't hab no place ter go, an' dey's after me an' I'm feared. It hurts fearsome bad. Please, missus . . . please help me!"

How could the calm, radiant, peaceful, grown-up young lady beside me possibly be the same person?

". . . to have and to hold from this day forward. . . ." Reverend Hall was saying.

Seeing Emma standing beside me was like watching a flower blossom. *Just look at her!* I thought.

Was this what God wanted to do with us all? Were we all, in God's eyes, like Emma had seemed to us at first? Was God tenderly and patiently trying to draw the real person out of us, like Micah had drawn the real person out of Emma that he saw so clearly but that she couldn't even see herself?

Was God's business in life doing that same thing with us—trying to help us blossom as the human flowers He saw in His mind when He created us?

Was He doing that, even now, with me?

What a wonderful thought, that God saw more wonderful things, and more wonderful potential, in me than I could imagine. And that He was working to make the flower that was me—Mayme Daniels!—blossom in beautiful ways that I couldn't see right now, but that He could see and that He would bring out from inside me one day.

Again, Reverend Hall's voice came back into my hearing as he finished speaking to Emma.

". . . for better, for worse, for richer, for poorer, in sickness and in health, to love and to cherish, till death do you part, according to God's holy ordinance?"

"I do," said Emma.

"Inasmuch as you, Micah, and you, Emma, have declared before God and these witnesses your wish to be united in marriage, and have pledged love and fidelity each to the other, I now pronounce you man and wife.—Ladies and gentlemen, may I have the honor to present to you Mr. and Mrs. Micah Duff!"

Everybody gathered around Micah and Emma with hugs and handshakes and congratulations, and even a few kisses. But by then I was feeling like Emma was a pretty lucky girl, and so I was looking around the room for Jeremiah. I went up to him and our eyes met, and I think we were probably thinking the same thing. He put his arm around me and we stood there together a little off to the side while everyone else bustled around Micah and Emma.

Meanwhile, Josepha hurried to the kitchen to continue preparations for the great wedding feast we had planned.

FAREWELL

37

The trip to Charlotte the day after the wedding was festive and exciting. We had to take two wagons to fit everybody in. Mr. Thurston's boy came over to milk the cows while we were gone.

Just before we left, I saw Emma standing out in front of William's grave with the new headstone on it. This time she didn't stay long. After one final cry and quiet good-bye, she turned and walked to where the rest of us were waiting in the two wagons. She would never forget her son. But she was ready to leave the place where she had given him birth and where his earthly body would stay behind after she was gone. From now on she would carry William in her heart.

Emma was ready to begin her new life as Mrs. Micah Duff.

Fifteen minutes later we were on the road. This time we took blankets because we knew we'd never find a hotel that would put up a mixed group like us for the night! Papa and Uncle Ward paid for Micah and Emma to stay in a colored hotel. All the rest of us slept outside the city. Then we met them again the next morning to take them to the train station. There we saw Micah and Emma off on their life together and their trip west on the new railroad.

Even before we reached the station, it began to get quiet amongst us. The good-byes were getting close and we knew it would be hard.

Micah bought tickets for Atlanta. From there they would make their way over the next several days to Omaha. After that they would be bound for California and Oregon!

We were all gathered around on the platform making small talk and pretending to be happy when we weren't. But pretty soon the station clock showed that the time was getting close.

At last Emma walked up to my papa and looked him straight in the eyes.

"Thank you, Mister Templeton," she said.

I could see that Papa was fighting tears as he smiled back at her. He took her in his arms and gave her a great fatherly embrace.

"You be good, little girl!" he said in a husky voice.

"I will, Mister Templeton. I will."

"You turned out to be a mighty fine girl. You and me, we both had some growing up to do when we first came to Rosewood, didn't we?"

"I reckon you's right, Mister Templeton," smiled Emma.

"I'm proud of you, Emma."

"Thank you," she said in a whisper.

She stepped back as Papa released her, then gave him a quick kiss on the cheek. Then she turned to Uncle Ward.

"Mister Ward," she said, "I'm so glad you come ter Rosewood when you did. We all owe everythin' ter you. An' thank you for what you said ter me before da wedding. I won't neber forgit it."

Uncle Ward mumbled something, wiped at his eyes, and also gave her a hug.

She and Josepha embraced. Even Josepha was choked up, which wasn't like her at all.

At last she turned to Katie and me. There was a great lump in my throat. I glanced away as she and Katie embraced.

"Remember when I thought you wuz da mistress an' kept callin' you Missus, Miz Katie?" said Emma with a smile. "I cudn't hab imagined dat a white girl cud care about someone like me. I'll never forgit you. You opened yer home ter me. But mostly you let me be yer frien'. Thank you, Miz Katie."

Katie was sobbing by now and hugged Emma but could hardly manage to say a word.

At last she turned to me and smiled. My eyes filled with tears.

"Oh, Emma!" I said and rushed toward her. We held each other for a few bittersweet seconds.

"Mayme," she whispered, "you an' Miz Katie saved my life. I owe you everything. You'll always be da best frien' I'll eber have."

"Emma . . . I love you."

"An' I love you, Mayme. Thank you. I'll never forgit you."

She stepped back. We all tried to draw in deep breaths, but it was hard. I went to Jeremiah's side. He took my hand and squeezed it.

Now it was Micah's turn. One by one he said a few words to each of us, hugged us, then turned to Jeremiah. They embraced and spoke for several seconds, but I couldn't hear what passed between them and Jeremiah never told me. When they stepped apart, Jeremiah sniffed and rubbed at his eyes. Micah shook Henry's hand. Henry was weeping like all the rest of the women, and I knew he felt no shame to let his emotions show.

Finally Micah turned to the two Daniels men. He shook their hands with such a look of respect and affection. I knew he had come to think of them, as did Emma, like either of them could have been the father he had never known.

"You get to Oregon, son," said my papa, "and you build a place, and you make this lady happy. And you keep in touch with us, you hear? Maybe one day we'll come out there and visit you!"

Emma and Micah turned to board the train. Papa stepped forward and handed Micah an envelope. Micah took it with an expression of question, then opened it. Inside were six new fifty-dollar bills.

I don't think I'd ever seen Micah Duff speechless until that moment. He looked back and forth between Papa and Uncle Ward in disbelief.

"But . . . but, Mr. Daniels," he said, "there's . . .

this is three hundred dollars!"

"That's right, son. That might not be enough to build you a whole house, but it ought to get you started."

"We want you to have it as our wedding gift to the two of you," said Uncle Ward.

"You're family, don't forget that," said my papa. "Besides, Emma's picked a lot of Rosewood cotton, haven't you, Emma?" he added, throwing Emma a wink.

"Dat I hab, Mister Templeton!"

"So you take that money, Mr. and Mrs. Micah Duff, and you have a good life!"

Swallowing hard, and blinking back his tears, Micah now embraced Papa and then Uncle Ward. "I don't know how to thank you," he said.

"Look, son," said Papa, "the happiness in Emma's eyes is thanks enough."

"All aboard!" called the conductor behind us.

Emma climbed onto the step, cast one last look at us all, and smiled. She was radiant in her new traveling dress and hat. She even looked like the lady she had become!

Then she stepped inside and Micah followed.

They were in the last car of the train, the colored car, and a minute later Emma appeared at one of the windows, waving and talking at us from inside.

A couple minutes later the train started to move. We walked slowly along the platform beside it, and followed as long as we could next to their window, everyone waving and yelling and talking at once. But it began to pick up speed as it left the station, and finally the caboose sped past us.

Still we stood there on the platform waving as the train disappeared from sight.

"Good-bye, Emma . . ." I whispered. "Good-bye!"

And then they were gone.

Epilogue

THE CLANDESTINE MEN'S VIGILANTE CLUB KNOWN as the Ku Klux Klan had spread throughout the South, dedicated to the preservation of white supremacy, Southern tradition, and exacting retribution on whites who embraced the new order . . . and on blacks who did not know their place.

The Klan had begun in 1865, primarily at first to intimidate potential black voters on behalf of Democratic candidates and to keep that party in power. But quickly its rituals and organization throughout all the Southern states turned it into a secretive force of terror and death. It was often led by the most stalwart male citizens of every community—doctors, lawyers, businessmen, farmers, and even politicians. Securing the Democratic vote soon became a lesser objective beside the cruel tactics of intimidation and violence. Everything the Klan did was aimed at keeping blacks in their place.

The Klan was not the only such vigilante group that roved the counties of the South, tormenting and killing "uppity niggers," but it was the most powerful. With its members clad in white sheets and hoods, and the hooves of their horses padded, the very thought of the silent night riders awoke dread and terror.

The Klan's weapons of choice were three: the gun, the torch, and the rope.

In the North Carolina communities of Greens Crossing and Oakwood, some twenty miles north of Charlotte, there were perhaps twenty of the local citizenry, including several of the more prominent among them, who had been initiated into the mysteries of the Klan. Their mischief thus far had produced no deaths, though not for lack of trying. That fact, however, seemed likely about to change.

On this particular day in the fall of the year 1869, they had decided to change their tactics. They would strike in broad daylight, in full view of the entire town, in order to teach a lesson none in the community would soon forget—to the black man they had known for years but who was now walking a little too high and mighty for their tastes, and to the white man who employed him.

The burning torches in their hands as they rode were not for the purpose of illumination as they might have been had this raid been planned, like most, for the middle of the night.

They intended to put the fire to another use.

AUTHOR BIOGRAPHY

CALIFORNIAN MICHAEL PHILLIPS BEGAN HIS DISTINguished writing career in the 1970s. He came to widespread public attention in the early 1980s for his efforts to reacquaint the public with Victorian novelist George MacDonald. Phillips is recognized as the man most responsible for the current worldwide renaissance of interest in the once-forgotten Scotsman. After partnering with Bethany House Publishers in redacting and republishing the works of MacDonald, Phillips embarked on his own career in fiction, and it is primarily as a novelist that he is now known. His critically acclaimed books have been translated into eight foreign languages, have appeared on numerous bestseller lists, and have sold more than six million copies. Phillips is today considered by many as the heir apparent to the very MacDonald legacy he has worked so hard to promote in our time. Phillips is the author of the widely read biography of George MacDonald, *George MacDonald, Scotland's Beloved Storyteller*. Phillips is also the publisher of the magazine *Leben*, a periodical dedicated to bold thinking Christianity and the legacy of George MacDonald. Phillips and his wife, Judy, alternate their time between their home in Eureka, California, and Scotland, where they are attempting to increase awareness of MacDonald's work.

More from Michael Phillips

Be sure to read the companion series to CAROLINA COUSINS—SHENANDOAH SISTERS. You will also enjoy the similar series from Bethany House, THE JOURNALS OF CORRIE BELLE HOLLISTER. And don't miss Michael Phillips' other newest titles—*Is Jesus Coming Back As Soon As We Think, A Perilous Proposal, Dream of Freedom, Dream of Life*, and *Your Life in Christ* by George MacDonald, edited by Michael Phillips.

Some of Hawk Trumbull's story, and what became of him when he went west, can be read about in the book *Grayfox*, from Bethany House Publishers.

For additional resources from Michael Phillips, see:

www.MacDonaldPhillips.com
www.civilwarsisters.com

For contact information and a complete listing of titles by Michael Phillips, write c/o:

P.O. Box 7003
Eureka, CA 95502